QUEEN OF HEARTS
A DARK ROMANCE COLLECTION

SYBIL KNIGHT

SOCIALS:

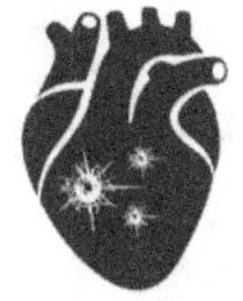

EMAIL: AUTHORSYBILKNIGHT@GMAIL.COM

NEWSLETTER: WWW.SENDFOX.COM/DAHLIAANDSYBIL

FACEBOOK GROUP:
WWW.FACEBOOK.COM/GROUPS/DAHLIAANDSYBILSLITTEDEVILS

INSTAGRAM: WWW.INSTRAGRAM.COM/AUTHOR.SYBIL.KNIGHT

FACEBOOK PAGE: WWW.FACEBOOK.COM/AUTHORSYBILKNIGHT

TIKTOK: WWW.TIKTOK.COM/@QUEENSOFCHAOSBOOKS

AMAZON: HTTPS://WWW.AMAZON.COM/STORES/SYBIL-
KNIGHT/AUTHOR/B09QW5R3MB

II
EYES ON ME

V CARD

A DARK EROTIC ROMANCE

SYBIL KNIGHT

BLURB:

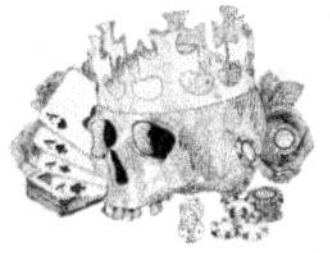

THE STAKES WERE HIGH. HIS BODY COUNT WAS HIGHER.

THE LADIES LOVED ME. BOTH THE ONES I SHOVED OUT MY HOTEL ROOM DOOR EVERY MORNING *AND* THE ONES I WAS CURRENTLY FLICKING BETWEEN MY THUMBS. A PAIR OF QUEENS. MY IDEAL THREESOME.

BUT THESE GALS WERE FICKLE, WHEREAS LADY LUCK WAS THE TYPE TO NEVER LEAVE MY SIDE. IT WAS THE SAME REASON THE GIRL SITTING ACROSS FROM ME NEVER STOOD A CHANCE.

COULDN'T BLAME HER. NOT REALLY. PRETTY LITTLE THING DIDN'T KNOW SHE WAS TREADING IN SHARK-INFESTED WATERS. OR THAT THE ONLY CARD SHE HAD LEFT AT HER DISPOSAL... JUST SO HAPPENED TO BE MY FAVORITE ONE TO TAKE. TAKING WASN'T THE ONLY THING I DID THOUGH. I WAS A GIVER TOO. DEMANDS, DEGRADATION, DIC——

Well, I think you catch my drift. Point was, the moment she decided to go all-in was the exact moment she agreed to let me do the same.

Game on, baby girl.

V Card is a dark standalone novella with a HFN. For a full list of triggers, please check out the original listing.

MALCOLM

PROLOGUE

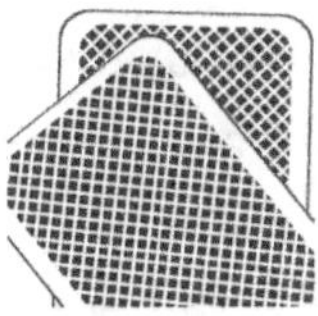

"Your call, sweetheart." I grinned. Watching as a pair of honey-colored eyes peered up at me, then immediately dropped back down to the hand she was clutching a little too tight between a set of manicured fingertips. This particular kitten had pretty pink claws that were two-sizes too big for her.

I shook my head. *And if she wasn't careful, I was gonna have to demand a new deck.* No way in hell was I about to chance someone marking a perfectly good stack of cards. Didn't matter if that shit was intentional or an honest mistake. She hadn't been on this earth long enough to know what was good for her, and I'd been on it too long to let a little girl get the slip on me.

I might not have known her, might not have ever seen her before tonight, but I sure as shit knew her type. I'd clocked her the moment she started rounding the room before deciding I was the chump she was gonna try to distract with one palm on his thigh and another creeping into his wallet. She was used to a bunch of limp dicks letting her win—or at the very least, she was used to throwing them off their game. Because *hers* was shit.

It wouldn't take more than a few rounds for the kid to realize she'd chosen poorly. I wasn't her meal ticket. I wasn't easily distracted either. I might have allowed myself a peek at her tits, but it was the rest of her I was more interested in. It was the rest of her that told me everything I needed to know.

All I had to do was read her facial expressions. Study her mannerisms. Listen for the little sounds she made after each hand was dealt. That's what happened when you were young and your poker face was nonexistent. You were an open book for fuckers like me, the kind of guy who knew better than to drink when he was working a table.

A slurping sound had my glare sweeping over the fruity cocktail the kitten was nursing through one of those straws with the loops in it. Her third since slinking her way into that seat with the confidence of a betta fish that had never seen outside its bowl. And I had to keep from rolling my eyes. Another novice move. You didn't need your senses dulled by alcohol. You needed them sharpened by years of practice.

Unlike the crowds that flocked to the money pits, lured by all that glitter and gold, I had no problem tuning it out. The other players and the environment built brick by brick to distract you. My sole focus glued to the cards in my hand and the chips in front of me. The noise melted away. The lights didn't matter. Even the smoke seemed to clear until all I could think about was the offer that hung between us. Her virginity in exchange for another stack of chips. Unless she happened to be staring at an ace of diamonds.

The sudden droop of those plump, overly-painted lips told me she wasn't, though. Not that it seemed to affect her willingness to bluff. The girl didn't say a word as she tossed her remaining chips into the pot. *All-in.*

It was a bold move for someone whose feet barely touched the floor without the help of those ridiculous heels. She probably thought the shoes and makeup made her look older. They didn't. They made her look like she was trying too hard. A bright-red target for those of us circling the casino room floors as soon as we tasted fresh blood in the water.

I lifted a challenging brow, calling her bluff before the poor kid even realized her mistake as I flipped my hand over on the table. A pair of queens to her jack and king.

Her jaw dropped, her mouth opening and closing a few times like one of those little molly fish with the big bug eyes. She was just as colorful too, in that emerald green evening gown that left little to the imagination when it came to what was underneath it.

I could see the wheels turning in her head, and quickly cut off whatever argument she was planning with a *tsk* of my tongue before gesturing for security to come and collect my winnings. Which tonight included the girl in front of me and whatever she was hiding between those thighs I could see her clenching from all the way over here.

CHAPTER ONE

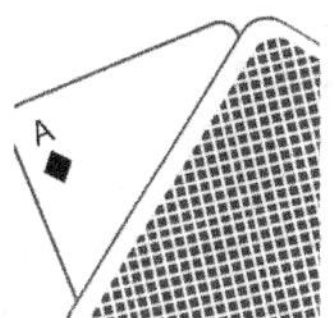

This was just physical. It wasn't about romance or whatever crazy ideas the chicks I brought upstairs got in their minds when I agreed to bury my face in their cunts for a couple of hours. It was one of the very few downsides to fucking around with virgins. They thought going home smelling like my cum was as good as a marriage proposal. When all it really was, was an exchange of bodily fluids. A stress-reliever. Something that helped me relax after a long night sitting in a hard seat when I had no choice but to keep my urges at bay.

But here, in this room, I could let loose as much as I could maintain control. It was my favorite balancing act. Seeing how far I could test my own limits before allowing myself to give in to them.

It didn't really matter what they looked like, the women I allowed the privilege of feeling my dick sinking deep into their cunts. The ones who got the literal plea-sure of having my tongue swirl around their clits until they were screaming a stranger's name. All I cared about was that I was the first one to do it. Because I was an only child, a selfish son of a bitch who never learned to share.

I wasn't about to apologize for that. You didn't have to like me to fuck me. And I sure as shit didn't have to like you either. That was the very definition of hate sex, after all.

It wasn't until we were tucked away in the sanctity of my executive suite, far from the busy Vegas streets below us and all the lurking eyes lingering there, that I was able to fully appreciate tonight's entertainment. And I had to admit without all the flashing lights and noise, without the outside distractions, the girl was more than a bit pleasing to the eye.

She was pretty. With an hourglass silhouette that hinted at the curves she was hiding as she folded in on herself. Her arms crossed over her chest and her weight shifting from foot to foot.

I took a step forward, my hands clasped behind my back as I assessed the little molly who hadn't realized she wasn't the bait. She was the main course. Scanned her from head to fucking toe and memorized everything between. Every freckle, scar, beauty mark. The way her auburn hair had flecks of red in it and curled at the ends. How her pale skin and tight-fitting gown made her eyes pop. Her long lashes framing those same eyes as they stared up at me before dropping back down to her toes. I'd made her remove her heels as well as the several layers of lipstick she had caked on her mouth.

I wanted her natural and... *unencumbered* for everything I had planned for her.

I stepped aside to get a sense of her true height now that she wasn't using those sparkly shoes as a crutch and looked her over once more. From a different angle. She was a petite little thing. Barely five-foot to my six... something. I didn't need to pull out a ruler to get exacts. I was big, much bigger than she was, and that was all that mattered. I intimidated her without having to do a thing but stand upright.

My gaze flicked to her cleavage, and I took notice of how shallow her breaths were, her chest heaving as the air was sucked in and forced out again. How her skin was pebbled even though I hadn't lifted a hand to touch her yet. She was scared. And she should be. She'd offered herself up to a stranger, a man who had the means to ensure she'd never leave this room if I didn't want her to leave it. Had the methods to ensure she was never found again unless I wanted her found.

I could do that, but it wasn't my intention. If she had chosen to sit at someone else's table, she might not have been so lucky though. And she could be going home wrapped up in a body bag, instead of the designer label I had yet to peel back—the same one that she'd be wearing when I shipped her out in a few hours.

That part was coming. Not long after I did. But I had no desire to rush the process.

Despite the fear I could feel radiating off her, the slight sheer of perspiration I could make out on her forehead, I didn't look at this girl like a predator would its prey. No, my appraisal was more refined than animalistic.

She was a delicacy and I was the kind of guy who

enjoyed a good meal. I didn't fuck. I didn't make love either. I indulged in flesh. Consumed it. Worshiped the act like a dying man praying for his salvation. It meant the difference between fingerpainting and swiping the last brushstroke on a masterpiece. Between banging a few keys and conducting a symphony. An apprentice and a master of the arts. *Someone who liked to play Uno and a professional card shark.*

So, yeah, I eyed the girl how an accomplished violinist would examine a commissioned instrument. How taut the strings. How long the neck. How curvaceous the waist. It all fell to my judgmental gaze.

"You can lose the dress now," I instructed as I shifted the material from her shoulders, watching it flutter down her body before pooling at her feet. The satisfaction of my grin meeting the terror of her eyes.

She was clean. Unmarked. No open sores or indications to suggest her claims weren't true. Which meant she would do.

At least for tonight. After that, her spending habits and piss-poor game play were someone else's problem.

CHAPTER TWO

"Your name." It was a command. Not a question. Or a request.

When the girl didn't immediately respond, choosing to stare at her matching pink pedicure instead of doing what she was told, my arm shot forward and my index finger snapped her chin towards the ceiling. Until my narrowed glare met the fluttering of those long, thick lashes she'd spent far too much time dolling up and fanning out just to have them covered in my cum a short few hours later.

I grinned at the thought, quickly shoving my amusement aside before it accidentally slipped free. We had a lot of work to do, only a few hours to do it, and one of us was acting a little bratty at the moment.

It would be a shame if she had to learn the hard way. It meant sacrificing her own enjoyment for mine. Because ticking clock or not, I didn't repeat myself. I wouldn't. The weight of my presence was more than enough to bend someone to my will. Especially this particular someone. Seeing as my little molly fish looked more like a *deer in headlights* now that she was standing in front of me.

"Rose," she stammered out while licking at her dry lips. A sign of her growing distress.

"Your full name." It didn't matter. I wouldn't remember it. But it wasn't about that. It was about dominating the exchange. About absolute compliance. About having her submit to me without physically forcing her to do it.

"R-Rosalind."

Okay, well, that wasn't what I asked. I'd asked for her full name. She was still scared though. Likely not thinking straight with all the blood rushing between her legs and making her lightheaded on her feet. So I'd let that one slide.

I didn't move as I continued to watch her. Didn't show approval or voice dissatisfaction. My expression remained neutral. Unforgiving. This was a dance, and the girl was meant to follow my lead. Not the other way around.

"Age," I tossed out another command as I turned my back to her and began loosening my tie. Fucking thing was strangling me, and not in the way either of us would enjoy.

"Old enough." Her voice was louder this time. It also sounded a little annoyed. *That* wouldn't do.

But once again, I refused to repeat myself. Instead, I spun in her direction and slowly craned my neck, allowing my gaze to travel from the ceiling above her head and drop to her face before searing into a pair of rapidly-widening pupils.

"Twenty-three," she whispered.

I maintained eye contact until all the color was drained from her cheeks and I was staring into two panicked black holes. Each reflecting my silhouette while that honey hue was reduced to a matching set of those flimsy stacking rings the cocktail waitresses liked to wear. Flashy enough to catch the light but missing all the sparkle. I didn't want flashy. I wanted the flames of lust. So overbearing it consumed her.

"Nineteen," the girl quickly corrected herself.

I paused before accepting that answer as truth (or something close to it) and began removing my cuff links. Placing them neatly on the dresser before returning my attention to my tie. By the time I spun back to the girl, my hands were tucked into my pockets and my shirt was hanging open.

I knew I looked good. I also knew my friend here appreciated the view. It was an egotistical thought to have about yourself. But I was the type who relied on facts. Not opinions. And *the fact* was I'd spent more hours than I cared to count focused on perfecting a body that might as well have been a fine wine. Because it only got better and *more defined* with age.

The girl didn't breathe. She didn't dare. She didn't move either, likely too afraid to do much of anything. But it wasn't her fear I sought; it was her obedience. The breaking of her will when she finally understood it was best for both of us.

"The bed." Two words. So many possibilities. But at the moment, I only wanted to position her there.

Seeming to grasp my meaning, the girl stepped away until the underside of her knees clipped the mattress's edge. Then she shuffled back, her eyes locked on mine as she centered herself in the middle of the king-sized comforter. An unwrapped present. Pristine packaging waiting to be enjoyed.

I watched her for another moment, wondering whether she would resign herself to her fate or try to weasel her way out of it.

Fortunately for her, I didn't have to wonder for long. Because no more than a few seconds ticked by before acceptance stared back at me.

Good girl. The praise danced around in my head but I wouldn't give it to her just yet. She hadn't earned it. Baby steps and all that.

CHAPTER THREE

I allowed the silence to stretch on between us. I didn't question her again, and she seemed to pick up on the fact she shouldn't ask anything herself.

It made her uncomfortable, though. It quickened her pulse. Sent surges of anxiety-induced adrenaline coursing through those veins of hers. I could see them throbbing in her throat. Could already imagine my fingertips gripping just under her chin, holding that quivering band of muscle in place while restricting her air supply. She wouldn't know what to make of it. Whether she liked it or feared me. Teetering on the edge of both before succumbing to the pleasure I would give her.

I cracked my neck, anchoring myself to the present instead of all the delicious possibilities the future held. And watched her watching me. The left side of my mouth creased into an almost-smirk. Just barely there. "I won't lie to you, baby girl. This is gonna hurt. But then it won't and you'll hardly remember a time when it did."

She mumbled a response. But I had impeccable hearing and perfect 20/20 vision. Which meant there was no hiding the way her lips parted and twisted on a sneer.

"I didn't catch that... Say it again." I took the two steps that brought me to the edge of the mattress and slid up the bed before she realized I was even moving. "Louder this time."

Defiance. I saw a glimmer of it. It twinkled in her eyes. Youth did that to you. Innocence too. Sparked a sense of invincibility that life sought to extinguish. It never lasted long and I knew it wouldn't last long here either.

"I said... why virgins? Why do you like virgins?" She was trying to understand me. Or perhaps just stall the inevitable...

Didn't matter which it was. This thing between us was only temporary. And then she'd be on her way. Out my door and on her ass. She'd given me her word and I didn't take kindly to those who didn't make good on their promises.

"Why do I like virgins? Why does anyone like anything?" I shrugged a single shoulder, deciding to indulge the girl for a moment. Though I had no idea why I was bothering. Boredom maybe. "It's a preference, an acquired taste. Like the first bite of veal served at the ideal temperature. Tender and expertly seasoned... There's just something about knowing it's both delicious *and* wrong that has your mouth watering..."

I leaned forward and flicked my tongue across her lips.

"Your pants stretching…"

I wrenched her arm away from her side and forced her to grip my cock through the layers of fabric between us. A slight grin tipped up my face as I squeezed once, my palm guiding hers before I quickly dropped her hand back onto the bed. Watching her stare down at her fingertips like I'd somehow burned her. Then I lowered my mouth to her ear again.

"Your pupils dilating." This had my grin widening as her eyes seemed to follow my command without her brain realizing she was doing it. "It's not about the poor innocent calf. It's about your body's instinctual reaction to that pink juice dripping onto a fresh white linen. How that being's sole purpose is to be born, thrive, and wait to bring you pleasure. Before you move on to the next one."

"So, you're saying I'm no better than a piece of meat? Livestock? *A bloated baby cow?*" she huffed, and my nostrils flared as I suppressed my laughter. She was insulted when she should be grateful.

This wasn't a punishment. It was an opportunity. For each of us. Just in a slightly different way.

"Oh no, sweetheart, you're missing the point. You aren't just a meal. You're an *experience*. Something meant to be enjoyed in the moment, over an extended period of time, but never dwelled on. And that's the difference between a drive-through cheeseburger and a gourmet spread."

On the last word, I gripped the girl's ankles. Tugged her forward and yanked her legs apart. Her slight gasp sent a jolt from my fingertips digging into her skin straight to my cock.

I took a deep breath, forcing the pounding in my chest to even out as the thrill of the chase tried to do the opposite. It was hard to maintain your composure when your favorite meal was laid out in front of you, no matter how well-practiced you were at doing it.

I lowered my face to her body, gliding my flattened tongue from the sensitive flesh just above her knee up the seams of her thigh, pausing at the juncture of where her leg met her pelvic bone before pulling back to savor the way her sweat danced across my tastebuds. Once it dissipated, no more than a distant memory, I grasped each of her wrists in one of my hands and wrenched them above her head. My control hanging on by a loose thread as I stretched her out in front of me.

I paused for a moment, appreciating the erotic display like an artist trying to determine if this stroke was his first or his last, before I wrapped her fingers around the fabric of the bedsheet until she clutched a handful in each tiny, unblemished fist. Then I leaned forward, my mouth a breath away from her lips. "Your wrists are locked to that spot."

She glanced up, the question bouncing around in her head evident in the slight crease of her brow and craning of her neck as she tried to see what I was doing.

"Not literally, of course. But for all intents and purposes, they are. I'm not a fan of physical restraints—they're..." My gaze drifted upwards, as if the ceiling held the answer, as I searched for the best way to explain my reasoning to someone who didn't see the world like I did.

And probably never could. "...tactless. Requiring such minimal skill set." Then my eyes dropped back to the woman beneath me as I breathed my next words into the shell of her ear. "You will not move because I'm telling you not to move. Not because an object outside my control makes it impossible to do. And not because you're deprived of the option. Do you understand?"

The girl nodded. The action was slight. Just a quick dip of her chin down and up again. Barely discernible to anyone who wasn't looking but present nonetheless.

"Good girl," I hummed as if the two words were instrumental, my left hand traveling down the base of her throat, over the mound of her breast, along the slight protrusion of each of her ribs before thrumming against her hip and slipping away to push myself off the mattress and onto my feet. "I'll be back."

I didn't repeat my instructions. But they hung in the air without me having to say them. *Do not move. Or you will not like the consequences, little molly.*

CHAPTER FOUR

I watched her for an hour, my ass firmly planted in the chair and my camera angled so that the outline of her body was in its sights, and started to wonder if the screen had frozen. A quick slap against the side of the monitor told me shit was working just fine, though.

The girl lay motionless on the bed. Other than the gentle rise and fall of her breasts—the only visible proof of life she offered whoever cared enough to be looking— she appeared the perfect image of self-discipline. I hadn't told her how long I'd be. That was part of the test of wills. The game I enjoyed when it came to breaking them. And I didn't know what to make of her, whether I'd found the ideal submissive or the girl who'd break me instead.

Both possibilities sent a chill down my spine. I was growing impatient, another emotion I wasn't used to dealing with. I enjoyed delayed gratification as much as the next guy. Most of the time anyway. And right now, *this delay* was meant to aggravate her, not me.

Instead, she lay there in comfortable silence—like some Disney princess just waiting for her white knight to kiss her stupid—while I paced the adjoining room like a canine in heat. My hands raking through my meticulously combed hair and digging into the flesh of my scalp.

The slight sting centered me, deadened the unease crawling up the back of my neck and whispering in my ear. Until my gaze zeroed in on the girl on the screen. The girl who seemed to stare back at me through the glass. No, not at... *through*. Her eyes searing into me. As if she *saw* me.

She couldn't, of course, and I knew it was my mind playing tricks on me... yet I couldn't quite figure out what about her was so unnerving. She was like all the others before her. She smelled the same, tasted the same. Her porcelain skin even felt the same. Untouched. Supple, like that veal I was already picturing. And pink.

However, there was something different about her eyes and the way she looked at me. Almost as though she were dissecting me from the inside out. They were innocent, yes, bright and shiny and so very naïve. But beyond that, there was more...

I powered off the screen, yanking my shirt from my shoulders and jerking my belt from its loops before tossing both onto the floor. Then I stalked back into view of the girl with the dark, haunting eyes. There was a hint of green to them but only in the right light. Why I knew that, I wasn't sure. Didn't make the observation any less true, though.

She watched me enter the room, approach her, but

she didn't move. Her stillness to the point of unsettling. Even as her neck slowly pivoted to follow my path to the edge of the bed. Like one of those creepy animatronic dolls in an abandoned funhouse suddenly coming back to life and staring at you.

I unbuttoned my fly and drew the zipper down to its base, my focus on the girl as I stepped out of my pants and kicked them aside. Any other time, I'd remove each article of clothing smoothly before carefully draping it over the side chair, with the kind of precision I used whenever I was playing my hand at the card table. My every action was meant to be refined, controlled, purposeful. But today, my instincts were raw. More primal than restrained.

That didn't mean I was inclined to rush. *I wouldn't rush.* I never rushed. You didn't rush what was meant to be appreciated. That said, something kept me from being able to follow my usual routine.

I removed my boxers in a similar fashion, a slow reveal before chucking them onto the floor. My cock moistened at the tip, prepared to lay waste to the pounds of flesh splayed out in front of me. I resisted the urge to reach down and stroke myself, to relieve some of the tension that had built up over the last hour or so. Longer, seeing as this girl had been testing my willpower since the moment she thought *my* money was *her* fair game.

My palms itched by my sides and my pelvic muscles twitched with the surge of blood flow. But instead of giving in, I climbed up her body, shifting her thighs to each side and resting my tip mere centimeters from her needy cunt. Then I released her hands from their grip on the sheet. The gesture was sensual, nearly affectionate as I plucked them away, a finger at a time, and massaged each pink kitten claw from base to nail, stimulating her nerve endings and returning her circulation.

And not because I cared. But because I wanted her to feel everything I was about to do to her. She might have looked like a doll but that didn't mean I wanted to fuck one. I liked my women inexperienced. Not dead.

CHAPTER FIVE

I t'd taken years of practice. Hours of nearly edging myself to get to this point. Where I could be so close to the end game without going all-in. Poker didn't just teach you patience. It taught you how much sweeter the pot could be if you were just willing to wait for it.

That practice was just as easily put into play here. In the bedroom. When coming wasn't as pleasurable as all the steps that it took you to get there. Each little whimper I elicited was like an appetizer, offering me a taste of what the main course would be. The thing was, I wasn't interested in digging in just yet. Not when there was so much more to savor.

I brushed the tip of my finger over her clit and watched the way the girl shuddered beneath me, those little bundles of nerves begging for all the sensations her body had never experienced before.

It didn't matter how many times I'd seen it. It always amazed me. How instinctual it was to seek out the stimulation. Humans were born and bred to fuck. Whether or not it resulted in procreation was of little consequence. We were selfish creatures. Far more focused on our own enjoyment than ensuring the species' survival. And women weren't any less guilty than men. They just hid it better. Because society told them they needed to.

Deep down, they wanted this as much as we did. They wanted to be fucked and used and left in a pool of mixed bodily fluids. It was what drew them to me. What brought this girl to my table when there were so many others to choose from.

The prey recognized the predator. And this little piece of unplucked fruit wanted to be chewed up and swallowed. She wanted all the dirty things I planned to do to her.

That first swipe of my tongue up her center told me I was right, while the way she tried not to buck beneath me confirmed this was as new to her as her taste was to me.

Experienced women leaned into you, met you thrust for thrust in a practiced rhythm they'd learned over the years. Using their hips to guide you this way or that. Because they knew how they liked it. How to get from point A to point B without any of the fumbling they were forced to endure between—*from the type of men who didn't know what they were doing.*

I didn't enjoy a girl who knew what she wanted. I enjoyed showing her what she needed. How much better it could be when we took our time. I didn't want to retrain a saddled mare. I wanted to break in that new foal.

Did that make me selfish? Maybe. Then again, the way they cried out my name that first time—how their bodies gave in to that first internal orgasm because there was a fucking difference—suggested I was a giver by nature. And these girls were lucky to be on the receiving end.

She was scared. Her prickled skin speaking to her natural instincts to appear more intimidating while her shallow breaths were meant to keep her hidden from view. The perfect example of fight or flight working in tandem.

It made her taste both sweet and salty, a hint of soap burning the tip of my tongue as I dragged it just above where she needed me most. Where I could feel that ache building in her lower stomach as I pressed two fingers on top of that spot I could find with my eyes closed and applied the slightest hint of pressure.

She tensed—they always did, so unfamiliar with their own bodies they couldn't discern the difference between pain and pleasure—before she melted against the mattress. So agonizingly wound up and relaxed at the same time as I inhaled her scent deep into my lungs.

The next lap of my tongue started at the apex of her left thigh, slowly trailing its way across her smooth skin, over to the right in a zigzag motion that had her squirming against the bed.

"You move," I warned between clenched teeth. "I stop moving. And I promise you it'll be much better for both of us if I warm you up first."

Her only response was a whimper. Not exactly the compliance I was looking for. But for once in my life, I was too fucking worked up to follow through on my threat. Instead, I dove in face-first until I was up to my nose in her juices while mine leaked through the sheets and onto the mattress. Like I was some teenager who didn't know how to keep from coming in his pants.

What the fuck.

CHAPTER SIX

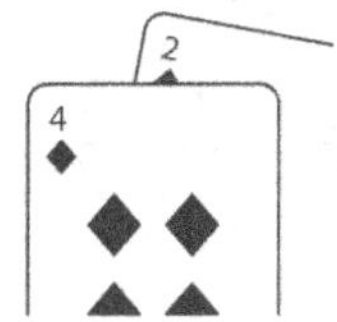

Sheer stubbornness had me clutching her thighs in each of my palms and dragging her down the mattress until I was kneeling on the floor, her ass teetering on the edge of the bed as I spread her pussy lips so far apart and open for me I could practically see inside her. Each time she tried to shoot back up or reach out and grab on to me, I stopped moving. Pressing a palm on her sternum and shoving her against the sheets again.

I'd tell her when I was done. And I wasn't done.

This was for me as much as it was for her. I enjoyed the taste, the smell, being the first to dive into unexplored territory and stake my claim for every man who came after me. There would be others. I didn't indulge repeat customers. But none of them would ever live up to the permanent mark I'd leave in my wake. The ghost of my touch, the memory of my cock splitting them in two and leaving them in pieces for someone else to clean up and try to put back together.

Another observation that was more fact than opinion.

I knew what I could do. What I did. What I was currently doing with the arousal that was quickly pooling between her thighs. It was the kind of thing that couldn't be faked. The body's natural reaction to everything I did to it. Each new sensation I brought to the surface and sent rushing through her like a wave of ecstasy.

It fascinated me. The expressions she made. The way her brows creased, how her eyelashes fluttered as she struggled to decide if she wanted to pry them open or squeeze them shut. The curiosity and confusion. The thrill and euphoria. Like all that build up before the first drop of a roller coaster—the juddering of the cart, the clicking of the tracks and tension of the cables. The fear of the unknown. It was never the same after that. Not after you knew what to expect.

I waited for her to come down from her second external orgasm before I crawled back over her and got into position. The moment my cock slipped through that first ring of muscle, just the tip testing the waters, her arms shot out. Her palms closing over my wrists like a little resistance was enough to stop me. It wasn't.

My pause had nothing to do with her sudden reluctance, and everything to do with the fact I had no intention of diving all the way into the pool just yet.

CHAPTER SEVEN

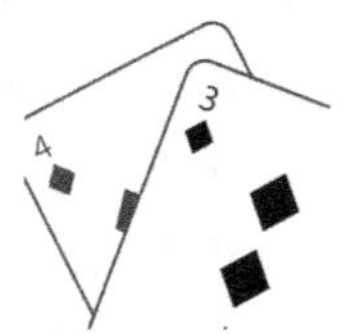

"What are you doing?" she gasped, the way her brows creased in the middle giving her an added innocence that made my dick that much harder as I struggled to keep it in check.

Using one arm to support my full weight, I lifted the other, gesturing between us as I gave the girl an unobstructed view of where our bodies were just barely connected. "Need a little sex education, baby girl? The school system really did fail you, huh?" I grunted, because it was difficult to speak when all the blood meant for my brain was rushing downward at a rate that left my IQ significantly lower than usual.

She shook her head from side to side. "No, I mean aren't you going to use... you know?"

I lifted a questioning brow. *Because, no, I didn't know.*

"Protection—"

I barked out a laugh before the ridiculous word had time to fully form in her mouth. "I fuck virgins, sweetheart. Doesn't get cleaner than that. And if you're worried about getting knocked up, don't. I've been shooting blanks for the last ten years."

Getting snipped was one of the best decisions I'd made. It was far easier than forcing a morning-after pill down a chick's throat and keeping your fingers crossed it stayed there. I had too much to lose to risk being saddled by some teenager who assumed having my bastard would also have her all dolled up in a white dress and strutting down that aisle in my direction.

I didn't want a wife or a girlfriend. I was already in a long-term relationship with the game I loved so much. And I wasn't about to mess that up to raise someone's brat. Even if that brat happened to share some of my DNA.

"And I'm just supposed to take your word for it?" she countered.

"I took yours, didn't I? When you sat down at my table and stamped a price tag on this sweet little cunt of yours." I trailed a hand between us, swiping a finger through the juices collecting on her clit before lifting it to my mouth and sucking it clean. "It's funny that you actually think I'd let anything separate me from slicing through a nice piece of virgin pussy."

"I needed the money," she whispered, barely loud enough for me to hear her.

"We all need something, baby girl." I grinned. "It's what makes the world go round. Supply and demand, a little *tit* for tat." I moved my hand up and pinched one of her nipples between my thumb and index finger for emphasis. "It's an exchange of goods. Like you said, you needed the money. And, well, lucky for you, I needed to release the tension of a long day. That's called fair trade."

"It's not a trade when I go home empty-handed."

I pressed a finger to her lips, just hard enough to exact a twinge of pain as I leaned forward until there was barely a breath separating us. "You'll go home debt free and fully satisfied. Which far surpasses the terms of our little agreement."

I was losing my patience now. I didn't appreciate back-talk. Not when there were far better uses for that smart mouth of hers. I pinched her cheeks together before pushing off the bed and rising to my full height, my cock primed and at the ready. Just waiting to sink into whatever warm hole was prepared to take it. There were different types of virginity after all. Pussy was just the one I preferred over the rest.

I crooked a finger in the girl's direction. "Come here." Once again, it wasn't a request. It was a command. "On your knees. In front of me." I waited for her to scurry off the bed and do as she was told, glaring down at her as I asked the question presently bouncing around inside my mind. "You ever sucked a cock before?"

CHAPTER EIGHT

The girl shook her head. I could see the panic rising in her chest, her labored breaths more indicative of fear than the mounting pleasure I'd already offered her. It didn't matter. I could work with either. And I enjoyed the look of both.

I grabbed her chin, gently stroking my thumb over her jawline as I forced her eyes to meet mine. "Then it's about time someone teaches you, baby girl."

I could feel her swallow beneath my grip and could already imagine her drinking down so much more. My cock twitched at the thought, imagining what it would feel like to be jammed so far down that throat of hers it was hard to breathe. For her. Not me. I was breathing just fine.

The fantasy was good. But the reality was always so much better.

It took the slightest bit of pressure to pry her mouth open. Just wide enough to take the width of me as I fisted my cock at the base and eased it forward. For my own benefit and not hers. Having to knock someone's teeth out was not on my list of kinks. And I wasn't sure I could control myself if the girl got frisky and decided to bite down. Just another reason I wasn't as keen on getting sucked off by a stranger. There was a shit-ton of trust involved. And the only person I trusted was *me*.

I slowly inched myself forward, her lips curling with the action as I continued to rub the pad of my thumb over the soft skin of her throat. Coaxing her muscles into a more relaxed state while her eyes watered at the corners and her nostrils flared. Shit was uncomfortable, I was sure. And it was about to feel a whole lot worse.

I thrusted in as far as I could go without forcing her breakfast up the wrong way before pulling back and repeating the process. Her mouth was warm and perfectly wet. But it was clear the girl didn't know what to do with her tongue. Whether she should flatten it and tuck it out of the way or use it to lap at my cock like a lollipop.

It was fine though. My favorite part was teaching them anyway. Showing them what I liked while getting myself off.

Whenever her jaw would start to tighten, her teeth dangerously close to leaving imprints, I'd press my thumb on her jugular. Forcing her to slacken her muscles and swallow to ease the discomfort. It was another careful dance, but this time it only took my little molly a couple of minutes to learn the steps.

After a few back-and-forth motions—my cock properly slathered in her saliva, my hand now wrapped around a fistful of her hair, and her gagging sounds bouncing off the walls—I could feel myself edging closer and closer to the point of no return. My balls constricted as that familiar tingle traveled up the base of my spine and down again.

I tugged her head back, driving my cock deeper into her curved throat as those honeyed eyes seared into mine, and I came until her cheeks were puffing out at the sides. Her pursed lips keeping me in place as I struggled to stay upright.

I was lightheaded, drunk on the sudden surge of endorphins flooding my system as a smirk tipped up one side of my face.

If her throat was this good, I could only imagine what her cunt would feel like.

I shoved that thought aside as my glare dropped to those plump peach-like cheeks she was currently balancing on the balls of her feet—when they should be bouncing against my dick—as she did her best to keep herself from tipping over.

And then my mouth broke out into a full-on grin. *Her pussy would have to wait, seeing as the next item on the menu was that sweet little ass.*

CHAPTER NINE

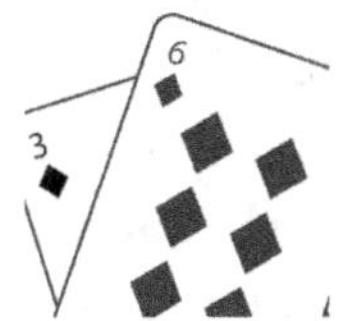

"**B**end over." I didn't wait for the girl to reply before I was tugging her to her feet and pushing her face against the mattress. Her ass in the air and her cunt at eye level as I dropped to my knees and licked her from hole to hole.

I could hear her muffled panic when she tried to lift her head, only to have me reach up an arm and shove her down again. Not all women liked having their starfish eaten out but you never knew until you tried. And she sure as shit wasn't gonna enjoy me fucking her there if I didn't lube her up first.

I circled my tongue around her little puckered hole, flicking and sucking a few times before snaking it forward. She was clenching her muscles when what I needed was for her to relax. So I pushed to my feet and leaned over, my cock knocking against her backdoor as I whispered in her ear.

"You ever been fucked here before, baby girl?" I rotated my hips in a circular motion, precum marking

each of her cheeks just in case there was any kind of...
misunderstanding about which *here* I was talking about.
Of course, I already knew the answer. But I liked to hear
them say it.

She swallowed once. Her anxiety so heightened I
could feel it vibrate across her pebbled skin. "I... no..."
She shook her head from side to side, and I lowered my
mouth again and nipped at her ear.

"Good. Another first," I grunted as I pushed back off
the mattress and crouched behind her. "I'm gonna need
you to relax, though. Or this one's really gonna burn."

This time, she gasped when I started lapping at her
asshole—probably a mix of shock and the sensation of
the warmth of my mouth warring with the cool breath I
blew over her afterwards. If she was more focused on
everything *she was feeling*, she was less likely to think too
hard about what *I was doing*.

I continued eating away at her ass, as my thumb
slinked around her waist and rubbed at her clit. The
sounds I was making were obnoxious. Wet and sloppy.
While the sounds she was making were soft and
guttural. Little whimpers and moans that told me she
hated how much she liked what I was doing to her.

By the time her next orgasm hit her, she was too
dazed to do much else but lie there. Her face still buried
in the sheets as I grabbed a bottle of lube from the
dresser, poured a healthy portion into my palm, and
stroked myself. Once, twice. Then twice more before I
stopped. If I kept going, I was gonna come just watching
her.

She looked so pretty, ass up and cunt out. My saliva

dripping from both as I closed the distance and gave her a solid slap to the cheek to get her blood flowing again. The sudden sting of flesh on flesh had her bolting upright at the same time I pressed myself behind her, my cock already inching into the next hole it was gonna claim tonight.

CHAPTER TEN

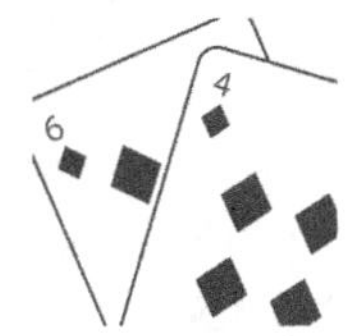

Once you got past the tip, the burn wasn't so bad. At least from what I could tell. They usually stopped crying by that point. And I don't mean full-on sobbing. I wasn't an asshole. Just currently fucking one as a few tears formed at the corners of her eyes.

Shit was painful. I had no doubt about that. But with that came the pleasure of me coming at her from both sides, my thumb on her clit and my dick in her ass, so that she was locked between two different sensations that somehow worked together to stimulate nerve endings she didn't even know she had. Because as much as she bucked against me at first, she leaned into me now. Meeting me thrust for thrust. Her hair wild, back arched, and thighs trembling.

I closed my eyes as the sweat beaded over my forehead before dripping onto my nose. Dropping my hands to the curve of her waist and forcing her against the mattress again. My orgasm was close, her next one was closer if the rhythm of her breaths was anything to go by.

I knew the moment it hit her. She'd had enough of them tonight that I recognized the way her body went limp. How the shivers traveled across her skin and had her convulsing before she went perfectly still. A tiny sigh would part her lips until one side of her mouth tipped up into the makings of a smirk. Like a kid whose hand had been caught in the cookie jar.

Another slap to her ass had her jerking backwards as I tugged her closer, my fist wrapped around her hair, and rode out my own orgasm. I couldn't describe the feeling if I wanted to. No words seemed right when it came to explaining how those rings of muscles clenched around you almost like they were trying to hold you in place. Like they were in a fight for their life and strangling your cock was the only way to survive. Like your soul left your body the moment your cum did the same thing.

An extended orgasm was God's gift to mankind. I had no doubt about that as two more spirts exited my tip and splattered across the girl's back. I reached out a hand and drew a little heart with my fingertip—it was my favorite suit. *The queen of hearts knew how to treat a guy.* Then I pivoted on my heel and went in search of a towel.

Had to clean myself up if I planned on fucking her cunt next. And there was no denying that that was exactly what I was gonna do *next*. It was the last item on my checklist. The last thing we were gonna share together before we never saw each other again.

Unless this little molly was dumb enough to try her

hand at another round of poker at one of my tables. Could only hope she had enough cash on her if she did, though. Seeing as she was one hole shy of having nothing left to offer me anymore.

CHAPTER ELEVEN

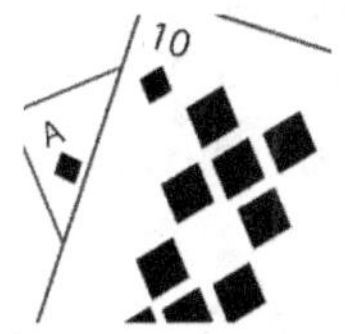

Pussy was a living, breathing organism of its own. Each had a unique scent, flavor... *elasticity.* Like a snowflake or flower petal or brush stroke. And I indulged in all of them. The shape or size didn't matter as long as I was the first one to tear into the packaging. And this girl's was as much the same as it was different somehow.

I couldn't put my finger on it—*excuse the choice of words... or don't.* But something about the way she stared up at me from where I now had her sprawled out on the bedsheets, my cum barely dried on her lips and back, had my cock hard all over again. There was the innocence I enjoyed, of course. The inquisitiveness that came with doing something she knew she shouldn't. But there was also a hint of defiance. A need to both comply and disobey warring with each other beneath the surface.

She liked to be my good little girl at the same time some deeper part of her was dying to be my perfect little slut instead.

That was new, and I couldn't help but wonder what she did in her bedroom, late at night, when no one was watching. Did she fantasize about a man like me climbing through her window and taking her in her sleep? Was her virginity as much of a burden as it was my prize? And why the fuck did I care?

I didn't. I was just curious. The girl had piqued my interests the moment she sat at my table and lifted a challenging brow in my direction. She was asking for trouble and she'd found it.

But that wasn't all she found. She found pleasure too. Hours and hours of thigh-quivering pleasure.

The moment my hand drifted from the curve of her waist, over her soft thigh before brushing along her cunt—wet and fluttering with need—I had to remind myself this was a marathon and not a race. The finish line signaled the end of our evening and I just wasn't ready to step on the platform and hold that trophy over my head.

No, I wasn't ready for the experience to be over yet.

She squirmed beneath my hold, no matter how soft or hard I teased at her swollen clit. She was overstimulated, her pretty pink nipples stiffened to peaks that were just begging to be squeezed and twisted. Licked and sucked.

I bent forward, keeping my body weight trained on one arm as I closed my mouth over the flesh of her left breast while my free hand continued to stroke and torment. She was a wanton little thing now that she'd experienced her first few orgasms, her whimpers just barely audible as she tried to bite her lower lip and keep them in.

Thing was, they weren't hers to keep. They were mine. I'd earned them and I wanted to hear them. I wanted to hear all the sounds I could compel her to make with just a simple twirl of my finger, nip of my teeth, lap of my tongue.

I stilled my movements, gliding my hand back up the length of her body until it reached her chin. Grabbed her jaw and pried it open. "If I wanted to fuck a church mouse, I would have joined the priesthood, sweetheart," I grunted, and waited for my meaning to sink in.

It didn't take long. Girl might have been a shit poker player but there was more than air upstairs. She was sharp and eager to please. Which meant she was teachable. *Thank fuck.*

The little moans she was making grew louder but not too loud. As much as I didn't want that church mouse, I didn't want a porn star either. Or a performance. I didn't want anything I didn't deserve. I didn't count cards or cheat my way to the pot. It wasn't about inflating my ego. I was self-aware enough to know I had flaws. This just wasn't one of them. I was good at what I did at both the table and in the bedroom. Everyone was gifted with certain abilities, indulged in certain vices. Pussy and poker were mine.

CHAPTER TWELVE

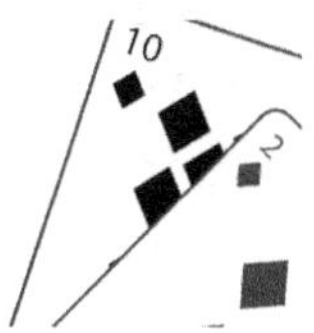

I could hear the clock ticking in the background, reminding me that how we started was very much how we were gonna end. This Cinderella had an expiration date and she was one deep thrust away from turning into a pumpkin—it wasn't my fault I just so happened to prefer my fruit... *unseeded.*

I pushed myself up on my knees, her thighs butter-flied open around me as I grabbed each of her ankles and dragged her down the mattress. Closer. Nothing was better than watching the head of my cock glide forward and disappear between a set of puffy pussy lips. It was my favorite part. That initial penetration that both endeared the girl *to me* and ruined her *for me.*

Her abdominal muscles rose and fell with her quick-ened breaths, as I used my thumb to spread her open. Notched my cock at her entrance and braced myself for that first rush of adrenaline. The same one I felt every time I stepped away from a table with more zeroes in my bank account than I started with.

I could feel the warmth flooding my system, the same time a different kind of warmth flooded my cock. I'd spent the last few hours ensuring her body was ready for me, that the resistance was just enough to grip me from all sides without taking a layer of skin off my dick. Like I said, her pleasure was as much about me as it was about her. Tight, virgin pussies were a luxury... but they could also be painful as fuck. And that just wasn't my thing.

Though it might have been hers if the look on her face the moment I broke through the last barrier separating us was anything to go by. Her body tensed before it melted against the sheets like a deflated balloon. Just as still and shapeless. Until I pulled back and thrusted forward again.

Her hands clawed at the sheets, her legs shaky as I leveraged them against my hips, tugging her ass up each time I drove down. She was a slight thing but that didn't mean her cheeks didn't clap in rhythm with my thrusts. Just audible over the sound of her moans mixing with my own labored breaths.

My abdominal muscles screamed and my biceps ached before I gave up on fighting gravity, tucked her left leg around my waist and dropped onto my thighs. Which had the entire bedframe shaking now, the headboard thudding against the syall hard enough to leave marks. She scrambled to grab my face, drawing it closer as I shoved my tongue down her throat, forcing her to taste herself as much as she could taste me.

She might not have liked me, but she sure as fuck liked what I did to her.

Three more slow pumps, combined with a circular motion that had my pelvic bone grinding against her clit, had her seeing stars again. She sighed into my mouth before prying her lips free and dropping her head back against the mattress. I could almost make out the whites of her eyes as she clung to the headboard and arched her back against me.

There was nothing quite like your first internal orgasm. I might not have been able to experience it directly, but I didn't have to. Not when I could witness it this up close and personal. Just watching her—the way her mouth remained slightly parted, her hair wild and unkempt, her cheeks flush, and her nostrils flared—was enough to send that first spirt of cum deep inside her cunt. Then another and another, until I could barely hold myself upright to stop from crushing her.

CHAPTER THIRTEEN

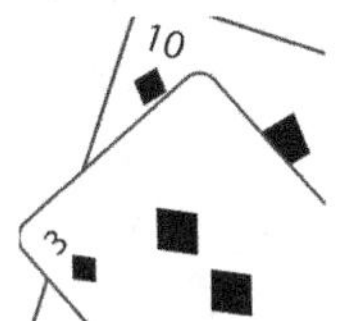

I t was the same every time. The immediate low that followed the highest of highs. My heart beat evened out, my blood pressure dropped—along with the thrill—and then I was left with that familiar emptiness. The one that had me in a chokehold until the next time I entered a room, took my usual spot at the table, and had the first hand of cards thrown out in front of me. Until I holed myself up in my usual suite and made good use of the bleach-white sheets.

I looked up at my reflection in the mirror before chancing a glance over the shoulder at the girl still curled up in my bed. She was such a slight thing I could just make out the shape of her body from here.

That was a problem.

The only thing I avoided more than repeat offenders was slumber parties. Which meant my little pillow princess had to go.

I slammed the bathroom door closed, loud enough that it would wake her if she was in fact sleeping and not just faking it. Turned the tap on the coldest setting and splashed some water on my face before tucking a fresh towel around my waist. What I wanted was a hot shower, something to soothe the sore muscles that told me my night had been well spent. But what I *needed* was help ensuring this girl didn't make a scene when I threw her ass out. Not that I couldn't handle her on my own. I just didn't care to. Especially when I had more than enough cash to pay someone else to do it for me.

I reached out an arm and swiped up the phone that was mounted to the wall to my right. The concierge answered on the second ring, which told me he hadn't been sitting at his desk and had to make a quick dash for it. Hospitality knew I didn't like waiting—*as a long-term guest, I shouldn't have had to.*

"Good evening, Mr. Bettencourt, how may we assist you?" an older man hummed down the line, sounding a little too chipper at this time of night—my eyes flicked to the gold watch I hadn't bothered to remove—or should I say morning? It was already half-past three.

"I have a guest who needs help finding the front door," I grunted into the receiver. I didn't have to say more. The staff knew what was expected of them and security had certain measures in place if things got a little... hairy. It was amazing what a few extra hundred-dollar bills shoved into someone's palm could do for you. How quickly a stiff set of morals could be pushed aside and forgotten about.

I listened to the sound of tapping on a keyboard in the background before the concierge's voice whispered down the line again, "The woman in the green dress?"

He'd been pulling up the security footage, preparing to delete it—as was protocol—until something must have stopped him.

"Yes. Why? Is there a problem?" It wasn't really a question. It was a latent threat. I didn't care if this girl was this fucker's granddaughter. I paid him to turn a blind eye, and that's exactly what he was gonna do. Or he would be heading out the door right along with her.

There was a long pause, my irritation growing in tandem with the rapid clicking sounds and the quick shuffling of steps. And then I heard the pounding of boots. Security, I could only assume.

"I said is there a fucking problem?" I barked between clenched teeth.

"Is she there with you now, sir?" he asked, his voice a little shakier than it was a moment ago.

"Who? The girl?" I couldn't stop myself from glancing over a shoulder again, even though there was still a door between us. "She's in the other room. Why? What the fuck is going on?" By the time I swung it back open, stretching the phone cord as I stepped out of the en suite and into the main living space, security was forcing their way inside.

"You may want to check for your wallet, sir." The breeze from the now-open window left my towel fluttering, chilling my balls while the concierge's words sent a similar chill down my spine. "According to the pit manager, it's the fifth time that girl's *lost her virginity* this week."

ROSALIND

CHAPTER FOURTEEN

I glanced out the window as the streets continued to blur by, the light rain clinging to the glass and giving the outside world a distorted appearance. So that everything looked like blobs of different colors and shapes. It was somehow both pretty and grotesque at the same time. Kind of like the man who was smart enough to clean house at the table every night, but too dumb to keep an eye on his winnings when there was a stranger in his bed.

The rumors were true. I'd give him that, though. That tongue of his knew how to work wonders. It was just a shame it was still attached to the rest of him.

I let out a loud sigh before righting myself in my seat as I drew the ace of diamonds from the hidden pocket in my sleeve. The same card that could have earned me my winnings at the table, instead of at the expense of my opponent's pride. But the satisfied throb between my legs told me that once again, I'd made the right choice by staying in the game until I was able to take the entire pot.

"Where to, Miss?" The older gentleman tapped on the steering wheel while staring at me through the rear-view mirror. He had kind eyes, the sort that were circled by little crow's feet that deepened with his laugh lines when he smiled at me. That smile would earn the man a hefty tip this morning.

I guess you could say I was a little like Robin Hood when it came to how I treated people—rob from the rich and give to the poor and all that.

"The Venetian, please," I replied, using my most polite tone—just like my mama taught me—as my eyes dropped to the compact in my hand. I quickly reapplied my favorite shade of lipstick before flitting my gaze back up to the cab driver.

"Spending the night?" he mused.

My lips, now several hues darker, curled while my perfectly manicured eyebrow arched with the challenge. "No, but I hear they have a killer card table?"

EPILOGUE

SOMETIME LATER. HOW LONG?
LONG ENOUGH FOR OUR GIRL TO GET BORED
ALL OVER AGAIN.

I tapped the back of my nail against the table—*it was a sign of annoyance*. And not a tell. I didn't have any tells. What I did have was another winning hand.

I didn't have to see the other side of their cards to know tonight's crowd was choking on more than the tobacco that darkened their lungs. I loved poker, but I hated the stench of cigar smoke that came with it. Almost like these assholes didn't know how to play the game without a cancer stick shoved between their lips. Or maybe it had more to do with an oral fixation.

In that case, I'd give them something to suck on.

I flicked my eyes up at the man sitting across from me, over the yellowing of his teeth and the crumbs that had made a nest in his beard.

Or maybe not.

The image of letting that mouth anywhere near my lady parts had my pussy clamping shut and closing up shop. Not that she had any customers currently trying to knock the door down.

I slammed my strawberry daiquiri onto the table at the thought. And immediately regretted it. It wasn't the bartender's fault I was wound so tight. It was mine. Sorta.

I guess you could say I was having a bit of a dry spell, and it had nothing to do with how much cash I was raking in every night and everything to do with the fact I hadn't been properly fucked since the last time I wore this green dress. I didn't wear the same thing twice, and not because I was wasteful. It was just smarter to change things up. Eye color, hair color, sometimes height— *finally found a good use for those god-awful six-inch heels, even if I risked an ankle with each step I took in them.*

Today, I'd broken that rule. Call me superstitious, but I thought this dress might bring me a little luck. Instead, all I was getting was a headache and a pair of singed eyebrows.

I didn't look up when a figure darkened the seat next to mine. I didn't need to. The men here were all the same. Old, married, creepy. With the kind of bloodshot eyes that leered much longer than was polite whenever I leaned over the table to toss in another chip. Couldn't fault them though. I had nice... *assets.* The sort that kept the male gaze from focusing too hard on my sleight of hand.

I didn't cheat to win. I didn't have to. I just let the

game play out a little longer when the pot was too small, the table too empty—or let's be honest, when I was just plain bored and wanted to fuck with someone. Kind of like right now.

"I wouldn't do that if I were you... Rosalind," a deep, baritone voice whispered next to my ear the moment my fingertips danced over the card I planned to tuck into my sleeve.

I'd never been caught before, but that didn't mean I hadn't thought about what I would do if I ever found myself in this predicament. Besides, I enjoyed improvising. There was a certain thrill that came with it.

Which was why I still didn't bother looking up as those same fingertips dropped from the card in my sleeve and trailed up the stranger's thigh. He knew my name. Which I admit was a little unnerving. Then again, a quick glance at the ID I had to use to sign in could have told him that.

"I'm sorry. Do I know you?" I asked as my gaze danced over the custom stitching of his suit, the gold buttons of his jacket, and the crisp seams of his dress shirt before landing on a jaw that was so sharp and tense it could cut a girl's pussy in two.

"*Do you know me?*" he hissed. "I would like to think so... Perhaps the wallet you stole would help jar that shit memory of yours?"

"Oh, yeah, I *remember* you now." I grinned, grabbing onto the guy's jacket and smoothing out the slight wrinkle in his lapel.

His arm snapped out before his palm quickly closed around my wrist. Keeping me just out of reach and halting my movements. He didn't trust me. I couldn't blame him. I didn't trust me either. Especially right now.

"But the way I see it... I didn't steal shit, Mr. Bettencourt. I simply took what was owed to me after I *sold* ya my V-card. Would you like to buy it again?"

THE END

FROM THE AUTHOR

THE MORAL OF THE STORY IS:
NO ONE CAN TAKE YOUR V-CARD
BUT YOU SURE AS SHIT CAN GIVE IT AWAY...
AS MANY TIMES AS YOU'D LIKE.
JUST ASK ROSALIND.

II
ROPE PLAY

EAT YOUR HEART OUT
A DARK ROMANTIC COMEDY

SYBIL KNIGHT

The higher the hair, the closer to God.

—Dolly Parton

BLURB:

I DIDN'T EAT PEOPLE. JUST MEN.

FIRST OF ALL, I'D LIKE TO SET THE RECORD STRAIGHT. I WASN'T A CANNIBAL, 'KAY?

I DIDN'T EAT *PEOPLE*. JUST MEN. I ATE THEIR HEARTS OUT BEFORE THEY EVER SAW ME COMING. FIGURATIVELY, OF COURSE. MOST OF THE TIME.

SOMETIMES A GIRL HAD TO DO WHAT A GIRL HAD TO DO. AND SOMETIMES WHAT I HAD TO DO WAS FRY THOSE SUCKERS UP WITH A LITTLE BIT OF BUTTERMILK AND ENOUGH SHORTENING TO GIVE YA CORONARY.

I WOULDN'T EVER APOLOGIZE FOR IT.

WHICH WAS SOMETHING ELSE YOU SHOULD KNOW ABOUT ME. I WAS UNAPOLOGETIC. THEN AGAIN, SO WAS HE. ELSE THE HOTSHOT WITH A BLADE BIGGER THAN HIS DICK WOULDN'T HAVE

BARGED HIS WAY INTO MY LITTLE APARTMENT WITHOUT SO MUCH AS A "MY BAD, SORRY FOR DISTURBING YOU, MA'AM."

AND I WOULDN'T HAVE BEEN FORCED TO TIE HIM TO A CHAIR AND TEACH HIM SOME MANNERS. BUT HERE WE ARE, AIN'T WE?

JUST A SWEET LITTLE SOUTHERN GIRL AND THE BIG BAD PICKLE-DIDDLER WHO THOUGHT HE WAS ABOUT TO GET HIS ROCKS OFF.

GUESS IT WASN'T HIS LUCKY DAY. SURE WAS MINE, THOUGH.

EAT YOUR HEART OUT IS A DARK STANDALONE NOVELLA WITH A **HEA**. FOR A FULL LIST OF TRIGGERS, PLEASE CHECK OUT THE ORIGINAL LISTING.

CHAPTER ONE
CHARLEE

*S*ugar *and spice and everything nice, that was what little girls were made of...*

I glanced down at the severed hand I was tryin' my darnedest to force down the garbage disposal and cocked a hip.

Guess my mama got the recipe wrong. Too much spice and not enough nice. Then again, Jimmy here wasn't being very nice when he tried to grip me up in the Wally's parking lot last night, now was he?

I grabbed on to the flat side of the wooden spatula and did my best to force the rest of his fingers into the drain. But those darn knuckle joints just kept getting caught up on the blades.

I sighed and gave it another go. Using the full weight of my upper body, girls included, to press on the handle and dislodge the pesky piece of cartilage that seemed to be jamming everything up. As soon as I heard the motor rev back to life, I pulled the spatula away to keep her from going down with it.

"Voilà!"

The grinding sound was music to my ears after all the fuss The Mad Grabber was giving me since I had no choice but to *give him* a lesson in manners.

Mighta seemed a little cruel. To leave a man bleeding out in the alleyway behind a hospital, but it was the only way to teach him the most important rule 'round here: If you don't know how to play with your toys, you don't get to keep 'em.

And that included your hands or any other body part that didn't know how to behave itself.

Hearts were a little harder. Couldn't do much with the rest of the body once you took a guy's heart. Well, the docs couldn't. I could do plenty. Which was why my freezer was chock-full of man meat. Rib cages, thigh chunks, flanks and loins...

My stomach growled at the thought, so I turned off the garbage disposal, tossed the spatula into the sink, and popped open the fridge. My eyes bouncing over each of the handwritten labels I'd stuck on the sides of the white butcher paper before they landed on the one in the far left corner.

Philip. Now, that guy was a real sweetheart. 'Cause of the diabetes. Not his demeanor. In that case, he'd been one of the biggest assholes I'd ever met. Which was why I'd turned his rear end into lunchmeat. His torso too. While the rest of him was used as fertilizer for my rose garden.

There was nothing prettier than the roses I could see outside my kitchen window, 'cept maybe the nice sear I got when I dropped a piece of fresh thigh meat onto a hot griddle.

I swiped up a packet of Philip and deposited it on the counter before scouring the cupboards for my favorite pan. I was just about to drop old rusty onto the stove when I heard the rattling of my front door knob, glanced at the monitor for the motion-activated camera I'd set up a few weeks back, and decided I had a much better use for the cast-iron skillet I was currently clutching in my hand.

CHAPTER TWO
JACK

Fucking hell...

My head was pounding and not the kind of pounding that came with a long night of trying to drink my problems away. Or the kind of pounding that told me I'd let some broad use me up and spit me out like the kids I shot down her throat. Nope, this was the kind that came with an ID bracelet, a shit-ton of drugs, and a hospital bill twice the size of Marla's fake tits.

For reference, Marla wasn't some broad. She was my cousin Tony's girl, and it wasn't that I looked at her like that or nothing. She was fucking family, and family was ona the few lines I didn't cross. It was just that when she was in the room, there was nowhere else to look. It was like something outta that *Black Mirror* show.

You turned to the left. Tits. To the right. More tits. Turned all the way the fuck around, and guess what? Fucking tits. Those UFOs of hers practically sucked the eyeballs out ya sockets. Which pissed Tony the fuck off.

Not sure why, seeing as he was the one who'd fronted the bill in the first place.

Didn't matter. Point was, my head was jacked all the way up, and no insurance meant I was probably spread out behind some bar somewhere.

My first instinct was to check for my wallet. Except that was hard to do with my arms tied behind my back and my feet strapped to the legs of a chair. I tried to rock back and forth a few times, tip myself over without bothering to open an eye. Mostly because both were glued shut by the dried blood I now realized was caked all over my black ski mask.

"I wouldn't do that if I were you."

I stopped what I was doing, not because she told me to do it. But because she was a... *she* and I didn't remember if I agreed to some weird bondage shit or if I'd finally pissed off the wrong chick and this was my punishment for not calling her back. Both options were just as likely.

"Yeah? And why's that?" I asked the disembodied voice.

I could hear whoever it was shuffling around what sounded like a kitchen. Banging pots and pans, taking shit out of cabinets and slamming 'em down on the counter before she came stomping towards me. Legit stomping. It was how I knew she was coming. The clanking of high-heeled shoes against what I assumed was a tile floor.

By the time she was close enough that I could smell her perfume—a mix of something sweet and spicy, though I couldn't tell ya what was what—Miss Attitude was already gripping me up. Prying my swollen eyelid open through my mask and staring at me from the other side of the blood-tinted haze.

Blonde hair, all teased out and curled up like one of those beauty pageant girls. Blue eyes, thick lashes, and tits—well, let's just say if Marla's had their own orbit, this chick's could block out the sun.

She dropped my eyelid and I heard the way her hair brushed over her shoulders when she spun back around. " ' Cause all that bruisin's bad for the meat, honey."

CHAPTER THREE
CHARLEE

"**M**eat?"

I hadn't stuttered and obviously my little impromptu dinner guest had heard me well enough to be repeating me. But I couldn't blame 'em for asking. Blows to the head had this way of making things foggy.

Instead of answering him, I strolled over to the fridge and tugged the door open. "Really don't have much room left in the freezer but Mama always said: *Waste not want not, Charlee.*"

"Charlee? Ain't that a guy's name?" he muttered to himself.

I leaned forward, being sure to give my new friend a direct view up my short-shorts as I shuffled a few packages from one shelf to the other, mindful of the dates on the top. Nothing was worse than getting a mouthful of spoiled meat, 'cept if maybe that meat had your name on it.

I paused to glance over a shoulder, noticing the way

his eyes were honed in on my backside. "That's awfully sexist coming from someone who got beat up by a girl."

"Catching a guy unawares ain't exactly fair play, *Charlee*." He grinned through the swelling in his jaw. I could see the movement beneath the ski mask he was wearing like some third-rate Hamburglar.

I slammed the fridge shut and spun around, clicking my pink boot heels against the kitchen floor as I closed the distance. "Breaking into a gal's house ain't exactly fair play either..." I placed one hand on the armrest, the other reaching around and digging into his pockets. Once I tugged his wallet free, I thumbed through that until I found his ID and dropped it on the kitchen table. "Jack Dawson? Really?" I snorted.

He shrugged a single shoulder. "What can I say? My ma was a big Leo fan back in the day."

"Then why didn't she name you Leo?" I yanked the mask off his head and watched a slow trickle of blood trail down his brow, my eyes bouncing from the ID back to the face in front of me.

Same guy. Wasn't all that bad looking either. As far as home invaders went.

"How the hell am I supposed to know? Why don'tcha ask her?" he grunted while trying to blow some of the blood away from his pursed mouth.

Keep doing that and you'll give yourself age lines, sugar.

I tsked my tongue but kept my thoughts to myself as I leaned forward again and flicked my tongue out to clean it up for him, at the same time my hand was plucking his phone from the front of his leather jacket. I'd searched all his pockets before I'd tied him up. It was always much more fun for them to watch me do it, though. Their faces lighting up brighter than a tot at a magic show.

"Okay, I will." I grinned, flipping my hair over a shoulder as I pivoted on a heel and made my way towards the bedroom. Ya know, in case the mama's boy thought screaming out for help was a good idea.

"Wait, what? What are you doing?" he shouted after me. "Don't you dare call my mother!"

CHAPTER FOUR
JACK

She wouldn't, would she? I mean, what kind of lunatic ties you up, clips your phone, and then uses it to call your mother?

"She said you don't call her enough. Oh, and she woulda named you Leo but unfortunately your pa's last name wasn't DiCaprio." Barbie came strutting back into the kitchen with her hands on her hips before tossing my cell on the table beside us.

Who would do that? Oh, right, the lunatic standing in front of me would.

Normally, I'd assume the broad was lying out her ass. But that sounded exactly like something my ma would say.

I glanced from my phone to Charlee's expectant glare. My mouth curling into a grin as I tapped into that Dawson charm my old man and I were both known for. "You've seen my face—you've had a nice little chat with my mother—don't ya think it's time you let me go now, sweetheart?"

She quirked a brow at me, her arms moving from her hips to fold over her chest. I craned my neck to the side and watched the way her cleavage popped out of her crop top. Things weren't looking great for me, but they could be worse, I guess.

"Look, babe, it was nothing personal…" I tried again, and immediately realized my mistake when she swung out a hand to slap me up the side of the head.

"Breaking into a gal's home sounds awfully personal to me," she countered.

"We're back on that, huh?" I grunted, spitting out another mouthful of blood and maybe a piece of tooth.

She turned around and continued stirring something she had out on the stovetop, lifting the spoon to her lips before adding another pinch of seasoning to the mixture. Smelled a little rancid if ya asked me, but I knew better than to critique a woman's cooking.

My old man taught me that too. He'd critiqued my mother's cooking once and only once. Still had a scar from where the side of the plate caught him under the eye before he could dodge it.

"You were gonna come in here and do nefarious things," Charlee hummed without bothering to look in my direction.

Nefarious things? It took a moment for my brain to catch up. "What? No!"

I was a bad guy, sure, but I wasn't that kind of *bad guy.* I didn't need to go prowling for pussy with looks like these.

Charlee glanced at me over a shoulder again, her

bright-blue eyes shadowed by a stray lock of hair. "So you were breaking in to do nice things?"

She gestured to the hunting knife I brought along in case a neighbor got curious (or brave or just plain stupid) and I had to scare 'em. Never had to use the damn thing for more than a little show and tell. Pretty-pretty princess here didn't need to know that, though.

"Well, I mean..." I grumbled.

"Fix the leaky pipe in the basement, hang a few shelves... Just a regular ol' Robin Hood with a rachet, aren't ya?" she huffed, and I cocked a swollen eyebrow.

"How exactly am I supposed to hang shelves with a ratchet?"

"Not the point," she barked, and I couldn't stop myself from chuckling.

"I was here to rob you, sweetheart. Not fuck you."

Maybe it was a heavy dose of brain damage. Maybe it was the fact this broad was cute when she was mad. Either way, by the time she crossed the room again, I was full-blown belly laughing in her face. And she seemed to like that even less than she like the idea of me pillaging her purse straps instead of her pussy lips.

CHAPTER FIVE
JACK

I expected another slap to the face. Would have deserved it too. Ma always did tell me my mouth would get me in trouble ona these days. What I didn't expect was to watch as Charlee dropped to her knees, unbuttoned my pants, reached a hand inside my boxers, and freed my cock.

Didn't matter how much blood was still coming out of the gash in my temple when most of it was redirected to my lap right now.

She opened her mouth, her tongue flicking forward without touching, and I lifted my ass off the chair to meet her halfway. That was all it took for this girl to unhinge her jaw like my cousin Mikey's ball python and swallow me whole like the pinkie mouse he dangled in front of it once a week.

Poof. Now ya see it, now ya don't. Leaving me to watch the up and down motion of her head bobbing against my crotch.

Usually I would be fisting her hair, guiding her

rhythm until I found something I liked. But not too much. I wanted that shit to last. I wanted to enjoy it. Prolong the orgasm so that by the time I did finally nut, I'd have to be careful the force didn't knock her skull square off her shoulders.

Never seen it happen but there was always a first time for everything, am I right?

I swung my legs out as far as they would go and slid my ass lower on the seat. My head tipped towards the ceiling as she did that thing some broads did with their cheeks that turned their mouths into Hoover vacuums and had even the most church-going girl sucking cock like a two-dollar whore.

Didn't know if it was learned, like riding a bike, or just a natural God-given talent. Either way, this Catholic boy would have easily turned heathen given the choice. I mean, if Eve blew Adam before handing him that apple, I sure as shit couldn't blame him for eating it. Guy probably needed the nutrients.

The longer Charlee went, the fewer brain cells she left behind till the fogginess had nothing to do with the pan I took to the side of the head and everything to do with the throat taking my cock to the larynx.

I heard a gurgling sound, and I didn't know if it was me choking on blood or Charlee choking on my dick. I didn't care either 'cause I was five... four... three... two seconds away from coming. My balls rising as quickly as a church pew on Sunday when the game was on. Charlee taking me down—all the way down—gliding her mouth all the way back up again and...

Gone. I opened my eyes. She was gone. Not gone, gone. But not... *on*.

She used a thumb to wipe the saliva from the sides of her lips and pinned me with a smirk. "You said you weren't here to fuck me. I'm just making an honest man outta ya, Mr. Dawson."

CHAPTER SIX
CHARLEE

"I ... what?" Jack sputtered. "I wasn't... That wasn't..." He shook his head from side to side. "That's not the same."

"It's not?" I clutched a palm to my chest, those imaginary pearls nowhere to be found. "Well, butter my buns and call me a biscuit... Guess I always assumed someone named it oral *sex* for a reason."

"I, no, I wasn't the one who... You were the one who was..." He squirmed in his seat while I pried a stray pubic hair out of my teeth with the end of my pink polished nail. I flicked it off before tapping that same finger against my temple.

"Ohhh! I get it now. It's not about the motion of the ocean." I rotated my hips—slow, sensual-like—and raked my teeth against my lower lip before adding, "It's about whoever's steering the bow. And here I was, thinking it was more about penetration. You and your little..." I gestured a hand towards his lap. "...corn cob entering my... corn hole."

I grinned. There was only one thing more amusing than a guy who needed to pound his chest and scream about what big a man he was, all while acting like a *man-sized* toddler. And that was a guy who pretended like he had the higher moral ground.

Kick the box out from under him, though, and he'd land on his ass like the rest of us.

I glanced down at the matching red friction burns on my lower legs. Ass? Knees? However you landed, it was all the same. I mean, I knew I wasn't perfect. What I was, was reactionary. Take from me, I take from you. In some form or another. And right now, I was taking that orgasm this here pickle-diddler claimed *he didn't want.*

"The thing is..." I hummed. "An open door doesn't mean someone's inviting you in any more than an open mouth means I'm willing to blow you. To completion at least."

"I don't understand..." he muttered while trying to hide his discomfort.

The way his rooster was throbbing and bobbing between us was a clear sign he wasn't doing a good job of it. Thing looked so red and angry it might as well climb up onto the rooftop and start crowing.

"What does that have to do with anything? Your door was closed," he tried to rationalize.

"Actually it was locked." I shrugged, crossing the room to lower my boiling pot to a simmer. Then I tugged open the drawer to my right, fumbled around with the contents until I found what I was looking for, and waved the bundle of plastic zip ties in the air.

Jack glanced from my face to my hand, his body

deflating in more ways than one. "Charlee, what are you gonna do with those?" he asked, even though we were both well aware he wasn't gonna like the answer.

I quirked an eyebrow, a smirk teasing at one side of my mouth as I yanked a single zip tie free and looped it together before rotating it around the tip of my finger a few times.

"Wrangling myself a rooster," I replied.

CHAPTER SEVEN
JACK

I stared down at the makeshift cock ring currently strangling the fuck out of the base of my dick and yanked at the bindings around my wrist for the millionth time. They didn't budge.

When I glanced back up, Charlee was watching me, her fingers plucking a thin strip of fabric from somewhere inside her booty shorts and dragging it along one leg, then the other, before she kicked it off her ankle with the end of a boot heel. Neon-pink, triangle-shaped fabric that covered about as much as me standing up and trying to wrap that dishtowel dangling over the edge of the sink around my waist instead.

The crotch part was soaked. I could smell it from across the room. The distinct odor of thigh sweat and pussy juice. Which told me she liked sucking me off almost as much as I liked her doing it.

I didn't hate the idea of being used like a human fuck doll. At least not at first. Chick was edging dangerously close to the "not worth the trouble" side of the crazy-hot scale, though. The kind of hot that had a guy wetting himself twice over and the kind of crazy that had him waking up the next day with no memory of how he ended up in that ice bath—*ya know, the dark web kind of crazy.*

I opened my mouth, a few choice words making their way up my throat when something soft and frilly was shoving 'em back down again. That same piece of fabric she called underwear as Charlee rested a hand behind me and lowered herself onto my lap. Her shorts shoved to one side and her pussy lips sucking me up inside her like the nozzle attachment of my ma's old horizontal vac.

Only tried that shit once as a teen but once was more than enough for me to make the comparison. This was a lot warmer if I were being honest. Wetter. But just as painful as she began bouncing up and down on top of me.

The harder I got, the faster she went, and the better and worse it felt. The little piece of plastic keeping my cock from being able to deflate, no matter how much pain I was in, and the smirk on her face telling me she wasn't stopping.

Charlee looped her arms around my neck, humming to herself as she shucked off her boots and used the tips of her manicured toes to guide her back-and-forth motion. Grinding instead of pounding until my cock turned the same shade as a lump of hamburger meat. The purple kind of red. Her juices seeping passed the opening in my fly and soaking my thighs when she rose up one last time and sank all the way down to my balls, while her cunt throttled me just as tightly as the piece of plastic that was still preventing me from coming.

"Fuck," I hissed out.

Charlee pulled all the way back, rolled onto the balls of her bare feet, and pushed off me. She reached out and flicked my cock with the tip of one of her talon-like nails before pivoting back around towards the hall.

"Hey! Where are ya going?" I called out after her.

"I'm fixin' to take a nap," she called back.

"And what about me?" I nudged the chair forward a few inches, only to have one of the legs snag on the table's edge.

"Why, Mr. Dawson, are you asking to come to bed with me?" She blinked at me over a shoulder. "What kinda girl do ya take me for?"

CHAPTER EIGHT
CHARLEE

A real nutter, that one.

She's certainly a bit touched in the head, ain't she?

Who? Oh, Charlee? Our Charlee? Yeah, girl's crazier than a road lizard. Just ask the Mitchells' boy. Shame what happened to 'em.

Not to speak ill of the dead but I heard her ma killed a fella.

I heard it was two... And ya know what they say... Like mother, like daughter.

Poor girl never had a chance, did she? Bless 'er heart.

I stretched my arms high over my head with a loud yawn, my stomach fussin' as I climbed off the bed and padded my way back into the kitchen. I'd left an entire pot of Philip to rot on the stove. I hated wasting good food. Then again, there *was* more of 'em where that came from.

Plenty of Tyler and Kevin and Bruce too.

I'd also forgotten to flick the switch off before going

to bed, and the overhead light caught on the shiny stainless steel appliances as soon as I stepped around the counter. I glanced up at my reflection in the microwave window and shuddered at the girl staring back at me. Runny mascara, flat curls, bags under her eyes for days.

Yep, I looked about as limp as a dish rag. Which reminded me…

My fingers trailed over the large wooden knife block to my right until they found the scissors. I tugged the handle free and tiptoed over towards the kitchen table, careful not to wake my house guest. His chin touching his chest, slowly rising each time he took a shallow breath and let it out again. His long, black lashes fanned out against each of his cheeks—one slightly more swollen than the other from where he landed on his face after I'd struck 'em with the pan.

Didn't seem fair that men always had the sorta lashes us gals had to paint and pluck and preen for.

But life's not fair, Charlee, my ma's voice reminded me.

I rolled my eyes as I kneeled in front of the chair to get a better look while my hand crept closer to rest the sharp edge of the scissors against the base of the nice serving of man meat that shouldn't have had my mouth watering like it was. And started snipping away.

Jack woke with a start and a shriek. His eyes popping out of his skull as he looked from my hand, to the scissors, and back to his lap. "What the fuck are you doing!"

"Best not to move right now," I hummed as I closed the scissors another few millimeters. He took in a deep breath, the sort that told me an ear-piercing scream was coming next, as I clicked the blades closed and yanked my prize free. "Now that wasn't so bad, was it?" I grinned.

Jack's face turned powder white, his eyes rolled back in his head, and then he was out quicker than the time the neighbor's dog found ma's whiskey stash.

And they said women were dramatic...

CHAPTER NINE
JACK

I woke to the feel of something standing over me with the added pressure of something else—something *sharp*—jabbing into the side of my head. Above my left eye. Which shot open only to be pressed closed by the tip of a pointy finger.

I took a deep breath and tried to relax until I remembered that same finger had been squeezing a pair of scissors against my crotch not all that long ago.

My eyes shot open again, and Charlee stepped back with a huff as I glanced from my lap to the needle in her hand. Back down to my lap one more time and over to the sliver of plastic zip tie curled up on the table.

I forced out a relieved puff of air through my lips and followed it with a chuckle. I was the only one laughing, though. Charlee was about as amused as I was when she came at my dick with that pair of scissors.

"Keep squirming and you're gonna lose an eye, sugar." She popped a piece of chewing gum into her mouth before reaching forward and yanking my head back by a fistful of hair.

I stared up at her with a stupid grin on my face. "Better that than my cock."

"It is a good cock." She nodded once while pressing her nail on my left eyelid, holding it down as she continued to fix me up with what looked to be a pair of tweezers, a sewing needle, and some household thread.

"Glad you agree, babe," I grunted through the pain. For someone so little, girl sure was rough.

When Charlee was done piecing me together like one of those dollar-store craft kits that had more parts than instructions, she tapped the back of my head. I dropped it forward again, my neck muscles stiff as I shifted myself upright in the chair. I then watched as she tossed the needle in the trash bin, stashed her first aid kit in the cabinet under the sink, and started washing her hands. She dried 'em on a dishtowel before opening the fridge and setting a packet of lunchmeat on the counter. She grabbed for the bread next.

I cleared my throat, and she set her carving knife down on the cutting board. "'Preciate the special attention and all, babe, but how 'bout we put Jack Junior away for a bit."

Charlee glanced from the two dishes she was plating up on the counter to where I was jutting my chin towards my open fly and floppy dick. It was still a little red around the base, but other than that, not much worse for the wear. My balls on the other hand...

"Why? Is he shy?" She quirked a single eyebrow,

pivoting around to drop one of the dishes on the table in front of me.

Before I could reply, she was bending forward, tucking me back into my boxers, and zipping me up a little too close *and fast* for comfort.

"Thanks," I grunted as she plopped down across from me with her own plate. And then she was shoving half the white bread and mystery meat sandwich into her mouth with the same finesse she'd used when she'd swallowed down my cock. Landing me with a glare my ma landed me with whenever I was playing with my dinner instead of eating it.

I craned my neck towards the table, as far as it would go, and took a few tentative sniffs. Could have been poisoned but something told me Charlee wasn't the poisoning sort. No, she was the type to look ya in the eye when she stabbed ya, and I was the type who was distracted enough by her tits to watch her do it—*but hey, so were most guys.*

I twisted in the chair so that one shoulder was leaning forward at the same time I lowered my head and stuck out my tongue towards the top of the sandwich. I gave it one good lick before Charlee was sighing, scraping her seat across the floor, and tugging it closer to me. Then her dainty little palm was closing against my throat as she guided my head in her direction while using her free arm to hand-feed me.

The first bite tasted like ash in my mouth. By the second, I didn't even care that the shit was dryer than my prom date's cooch after I told her I'd fucked her mom the morning before the dance.

What can I say? I was a seventeen-year-old boy with the sex drive of, well, a seventeen-year-old boy. And Mrs. Miller looked damn good for a woman pressing forty.

"Bologna?" I asked as I forced down the last bite of whatever the fuck I was eating with a mouthful of my own saliva. I would have sucked a dick for a tall glass of milk.

Not literally. I tried to clear my throat and ended up gagging on a piece of crust. *Okay, maybe literally. But that was a secret I'd take to my grave. Along with whatever was happening here.*

"Not bologna." Charlee shrugged as she licked her fingers clean till not even a crumb was left behind. Once again reminding me of the shit she'd done to my cock. It was sore, but I had to admit I didn't hate the idea of going another round. "It does have a first name, though," she muttered to herself.

"What was that?"

"Nothing." She continued to hum the Oscar Mayer jingle as she rinsed the dishes off before setting them in the drying rack.

A few seconds later, she was slamming a glass of tap water in front of me and dropping a straw in the center.

"In case ya get thirsty in the middle of the night." She grinned. Tapped me once on the cheek and pivoted back towards her bedroom again.

"Charlee! Come on, babe. You can untie me!" I yelled out, knowing it didn't matter much. She'd already made up her mind.

Guess this "easy" grab and dash was turning into a slumber party.

CHAPTER TEN
JACK

I waited an hour after I stopped hearing Charlee shuffling around the bedroom before bracing my spine against the back of the metal chair and using all my strength to pop my left thumb out of its socket. I hissed out a breath, sucked in a lungful of air, and repeated the same thing with my right.

It didn't take more than a few yanks of my arms after that to tug my upper body free from the zip ties that had me bound to the seat for the last few hours. I moved on to my legs next and then I was stepping towards the front door. Where my phone and wallet were waiting for me in one of those decorative bowls.

I popped my thumbs back into place and swiped up my stuff, the floorboards unnaturally loud as I paused to tug at the doorknob. It didn't budge. Neither did the bolt above it when I tried to shift it aside.

I squinted my eyes until I could make out the little padlock that kept me in as much as it kept everyone else out.

"Motherfucker," I grumbled to myself.

Old apartments like these weren't usually locked up like Fort Knox. It was why I'd been scoping it out for the last week. Most of the building appeared empty besides this unit. I also didn't think the resident was home. But here we were. In crazy town.

I spun back around and started searching nearby drawers for a key. I could break the door down, sure. But I was looking for a quick, quiet escape that didn't have everyone on the block reaching for their landlines. I mean, I didn't have much of a leg to stand on if the cops came calling, now did I?

Okay, here's what happened, officer. Sure, I was planning on robbing the place, but she kidnapped me before I could do it. So who's the real victim?

One look at my six-foot-three ass compared to her five-foot-whatever would have every pig on the street laughing in my face before tossing me in a jail cell. And not for nothing, I was far too pretty for prison. It was why I was here in the first place. Needed a fresh start. To pay off a few less-than savory characters and start over. Somewhere a hell of a lot less orange-jumpsuity, if ya catch my drift.

Yeah, and how's that working for ya, buddy?

Not so good. Thanks for asking.

It wasn't crazy to talk to yourself. It was crazy to waste your time answering, though. Especially when you needed to be looking for a way out of this *Southern Fried Homicide* house.

The dumbbell Charlee called a sandwich sat like lead

in my stomach as I snooped through all the cabinets in the kitchen before giving up and turning down the hall. I knew I needed to stay focused but that shit was hard to do with a full bladder. So I slipped inside the bathroom, *carefully* opened my fly, and quickly relieved myself.

I wasn't ashamed to admit it felt about as satisfying as a good nut at this point. When I was finished draining one very-full lizard, I tucked 'em back into my pants. And almost ruined everything when I reached for the handle to flush.

I stared down at the yellow-brown pool in the pink porcelain bowl for a moment. It wasn't very gentlemanly of me to leave my piss water behind, but it wasn't very gentlemanly of me to rob a broad either.

Somehow this seemed worse, though.

I shook the weird moral dilemma from my head and crept back out the bathroom door, pausing when I realized there was only one spot left to look for the key. The bedroom.

I rubbed at the back of my neck, as much out of habit as it was to loosen the kinks. I wasn't a creep. I didn't go sneaking into girls' rooms at night. I didn't go rooting through their underwear drawers. At least not when they were home. And only when I was looking for jewelry and shit to hock. Not because I was sniffing it like some perv.

I mean, there was that one time a few years back... But that was different. Annie and me were a thing, and it's not pervy when it's the chick you're fucking. It's romantic.

Decision made, or something close enough to one, I

drew the sign of the cross over my body, mumbled out a low "sorry, ma," and grabbed the knob to Charlee's door. I twisted it, leaning my shoulder against the frame as I quietly swung the hinge open. Just enough to slip through and stand at the foot of the bed.

Charlee didn't move besides the slow rise and fall of her chest. One arm resting above her head, the other tucked against her side. It was hard to picture the woman who'd busted me up the side of the face with a frying pan when she looked like this. So small, angelic, on a king-size bed covered in blankets and frills. Her mouth slightly parting when she sighed in her sleep and her lashes fluttering just enough to tell me she was deep in it.

I chanced a small step forward and peered over her comforter to get a better look at her tits, shaking my head and stepping back again when I realized what I was doing.

"Not a creep, sure," I muttered to myself, and Charlee shot up on the bed and reached for something on her nightstand. "Fuck!" I cursed and lunged on top of her before she could get whatever she was grabbing for.

Best case? Some pepper spray. My luck? A handgun.

I locked both of her wrists above her head in one hand while flicking on the lamp with the other, my full body weight pinning her thighs together and keeping her from wiggling free. I glanced from Charlee's face to the object on the nightstand.

I was wrong. It wasn't pepper spray *or* a gun.

"Are you gonna hurt me?" she whispered, as I tried to make sense of what I was looking at. My glare narrowing in on the fuzzy handcuffs and the rocket ship of a vibrator sitting next to ′em.

"No, I'm not gonna hurt you. Are those—?" I grunted at the same time her knee shot up to hit me square in the balls. My *very tender* balls.

CHAPTER ELEVEN
CHARLEE

"Buck all ya want, cowboy. I happen to be an expert bull rider." I brushed my lips against Jack's ear before leaning up and shooting him a wink as I shimmied lower. Then a little bit lower and lower still, enjoying the friction it caused beneath my nightgown and against my bare bottom.

I paused the back-and-forth motion to eye Jack from where *I* was now the one straddling *his* waist. Each of his arms secured to the metal rails of my headboard. Pinched so tight that the only thing a couple of dislocated thumbs would earn him was an eight-count and a hefty bar tab. And maybe a cold cot in the county lockup if this cowboy couldn't hold his liquor.

The fuzzy pink cuffs I kept on my bedside table weren't just for show. Though a gal could get used to the view.

I tilted my head to the side and watched the way Titanic Boy's shirt lifted to reveal a decent rack of ribs—*I mean abs*—and a deep V that had my fingertips skimming his waistband on their own.

Jack yanked one more time on his left wrist. Hard enough to have me bracing myself on his pec with a palm. I flopped down in response, until I was flush against him, my elbows digging into his upper torso while I kicked my feet in the air between his legs as I stared up at him through my lashes.

He dropped his chin to glare back at me. "This isn't funny anymore, Charlee."

The rumble of his chest traveled up my arm and out my fingers. "From where I'm sittin', I think it's pretty darn hysterical."

Another tug and I was face-first between his man cleavage, cackling the more he cussed in my direction.

I shifted my left hand from where it was resting on his thigh now and trailed it across the front of his jeans until he was groaning and thrusting against my palm without meaning to do either. Then, when he was nice and distracted, his eyes closed and his head thrown back, I slipped two fingers into his front pocket.

"Is that a phone I'm feelin' or are you just happy to see me, Mr. Dawson?" I pulled the device free and tossed it across the room before positioning myself upright. "Oh, look at that! It's both!"

I grabbed for his belt, tugging it by the tail like a rattler in my mama's rose garden, and tossed that aside too. It hit something behind me with a *thwack* I didn't bother checking the origin of as I shucked the pillows off the bed.

His shoes were the next to go, one foot at a time,

followed by his socks and then his blue jeans. Until the only thing standing between me and a full slab of raw, unmarinated man meat was an undershirt and a thin pair of plaid boxers that probably had his name written across the back in block lettering.

I catfished a hand into the little slit in the front and peered up at Jack through my lashes again. "Gotta safe word, sugar?"

He scrunched his nose at me but he didn't say to stop. I shrugged a shoulder and squeezed once.

"Charlee, stop it." *Oh, darn.* He waited until I was looking at him before adding, "How long do you plan on keeping me here?"

I huffed out a breath and crossed my arms over my chest. I quickly dropped them back onto the mattress as I crawled lower on the bed. My lips crotch level. My breath warm and raspy. "Wanna leave so soon, Mr. Dawson? And here I thought we were just getting to know each other."

He lifted his hips to meet me like he did in the kitchen, and I didn't wait for him to argue this time as I nudged my nose inside his boxers and licked him from tip to torso. He growled deep in his throat like a grizzly and I pulled his underwear down his ass. They landed somewhere on my bedroom floor while I landed myself back between his thighs, my mouth spread wide around the base of a nice piece of thick sausage.

My mama always did say that my eyes were bigger than my stomach, and I guess in this instance she was right.

I had a healthy appetite and I enjoyed all flavors... but

I had to admit this particular one left a different sort of taste in my mouth. The sort that had my panties wet and my nipples peaked. The sort that had me moaning and the man beneath me groaning and meeting my face dip for dip. Stroke for stroke. Deep dive for deep dive.

I swiped out a hand, fumbling with the bedside table until my fingers brushed over the silicon top. One quick yank and the suction cup bottom popped off the veneer. Another flick of a thumb and my favorite battery-operated boyfriend was buzzing to life against my lady bits in a way that sent a shiver up my spine and out my mouth on a satisfied sigh.

I wasn't usually the one being spit-roasted alive, but now that I was, I understood what all the fuss was about. My screams more muffled than the ear-piercing shrieks I was used to hearing die out beneath the crackle of the fire. My body burning up in an entirely different way as I ground my hips against my pretty pink vibrator and Jack ground his against my heated cheeks.

I'd just started to taste the hint of something salty in the back of my throat, my legs quaking and my belly clenching when a few quick, hard thumps of metal against wood echoed past the bedroom door and into my ears.

Jack cussed, and I grinned around him as I plopped his wet balls back into his lap like a hound dog playing fetch, wrapped my silky robe around my waist, and went in search of whoever was beating down my front door in the middle of the night.

CHAPTER TWELVE
JACK

I looked at him, and he looked at me. One eyebrow cocked and a smirk teasing at the side of his mouth as he flicked the hot end of his flashlight back in my direction and then over to the fuzzy cuffs around each of my wrists.

"Care to explain what's going on here, son?" The bastard was trying to sound serious; instead, he sounded like he was two seconds away from popping a button on his uniform.

"Nothin' but a little harmless fun between me and the missus, officer." I clenched my teeth into a thin line, something resembling a grin. I think.

The pig standing behind him snorted into a cupped hand, his pen light flickering with the movement and blinding my left eye. I squinted back at them through the right.

"I see that." Officer Chuckles peered at his partner over a shoulder before turning to Charlee. "Care if we have a look around just to make sure everything is in order, Miss…?"

"Dawson," she replied, and I nearly choked on my tongue. "Newlyweds." She grinned at the man, holding up her left hand so that the diamond I sure as shit didn't put there caught the light, while shooting me a sharp glare that I *did* put there out of the corner of her eye.

Her grin was saying everything she wasn't saying. *You started it.*

He nodded once and then he was shining that stupid flashlight on my face again. "Why don't ya put some clothes on and meet us in the living room, Mr. Dawson?"

"Love to, officer…" I wiggled my fingers at Charlee. "Think you can lend me a hand, *dear*?"

Her smile dropped immediately. Mine widened.

"Of course, sugar," she hummed, pivoting on a bare foot to trail a manicured nail down the buttons of the pig's uniform. She flicked his name tag and then stared up at him with what I was certain were doe eyes. "Go on and help yourselves to the kitchen, Officer Bradley. We'll be out there quicker than a cat on a tin roof."

Officer Bradley let out another low chuckle as he waddled down the hall. Charlee watched him go for a moment before clicking the door closed and switching on the overhead light. Blinding me for the third time in nearly as many minutes.

I blinked back the tears as she stomped towards the bed, yanked the drawer open so hard it nearly came off the grooves, and shuffled around until she found the handcuff key.

She dangled it out in front of me as she glanced from the door to my face. I kept my expression neutral. "No funny business," she hissed.

"Ain't that a little pot meets kettle, babe?" I muttered as she climbed onto the bed, using my waist as leverage when she reached up to grab one of my arms. All while making a show of rubbing her cunt against my face.

Had to admit she smelled good enough to eat, though.

By the time my second arm was dropping onto the pile of pillows spread out on each side of me, I'd forgotten what it was I was supposed to be doing.

Oh, right, getting the fuck out of here.

I shook all those dirty thoughts from my head—at least I tried to—and brought my arms around the back of Charlee's waist. She lowered her face to meet mine and kissed me long and slow. Digging her teeth into my bottom lip when I attempted to pull away.

"Fuck me..." I grunted as I picked her up and set her down on her feet next to the bed. This broad was bad for my head whichever way you looked at it.

"Behave and I will," she fired back, curling her finger in my direction as she ushered me out the bedroom door.

A few more steps, Charlee in front and me trailing behind her, and we were standing in the middle of her little kitchen. She flitted around the stovetop, her silky robe twirling around her. Like none of this was weird.

I glanced down at myself and the pants I'd forgotten to put on. *All of this* was weird.

"Cream and sugar, officers?" She fluttered her

eyelashes at the two coppers standing in the living room, shining their flashlights in every dark crevice as if a crime scene was gonna just drop into their laps.

My eyes flicked over the splattering of dried blood darkening one of her kitchen tiles.

Then again…

"Two sugars and a splash of cream," Officer Bradley replied. "Please."

"Straight black for me, ma'am," his partner added.

Charlee set two mugs onto the kitchen table and shoved a third against my chest with another glare. She pulled out a seat for herself and then gestured for the pigs to join her. "So, what brings you to our door tonight, Officer Bradley?"

He crossed the room and slumped his ass in the first chair. "We got a call about an abandoned car out front. While we were running the plates, we caught ear of what we thought might be a disturbance." He cut me a sharp look. "Wanted to make sure everyone was all right."

"Right as rain, sir." I chuckled as I rubbed at the back of my neck. Cops always made me nervous. Cops at what was supposed to be my next burglary job made me suspicious.

"It was Mrs. Davis next door, wasn't it?" Charlee whispered.

"We really shouldn't say…"

"That's okay." Charlee winked as she reached out to run a finger over Officer Bradley's shirt sleeve. "She shouldn't have wasted your time. Y'all are so busy, fightin' the bad guys and keepin' us safe. I'll go over and talk to her tomorrow. Tell her not to bother you again."

"No bother, ma'am. Like you said, it's our job to protect and serve." The younger of the two tucked his flashlight back into his utility belt and dropped into the only open chair at the table. Tipping his hat before taking a long swig from his mug. "So how'd you all end up together?" He waved a hand between me and Charlee. "I'm a sucker for a good meet cute."

"Funny story actually." Charlee sighed, as though her crazy ass could really picture it. "It was kinda like he just showed up one day and never left."

"Charlee... that short for something?" Officer Bradley questioned.

"Nope." She popped her lips and slurped at her mug.

"Really?" I said without meaning to, and everyone's head snapped in my direction.

"Don't ya know your wife's name?"

I reached up a hand and rubbed at the back of my neck again. Didn't mean to do that either. "Heh, you know how it is once ya tie the knot, ya forget stuff."

"Anniversaries, sure. Not names..." Chuckles grunted.

"What kinda name is Charlee for a lady?" the younger guy asked. He took another chug of his coffee, paused, and stared at the inside of the cup.

"See! That's what I said!" I laughed, watching as the kid's head bobbed a little on his neck.

"Hey, Miss Dawson, did you put sugar—" His eyes rolled back in his skull and his forehead hit the kitchen table with a loud *thud* before he could finish speaking.

I looked over to Officer Bradley in time to watch his do the same.

I glanced down at my coffee mug—at the cream

swirling around inside and the little granules sticking to my tongue—as my knees went weak and my stomach lurched up into my throat.

Guess I was wrong. Maybe Charlee was the poisoning type after all.

CHAPTER THIRTEEN
CHARLEE

"Get up, ya idjit." I cocked my head horizontal and kicked a polished toe out at Jack's side. He rolled himself onto his back with a grunt. "Keep fainting like that and I'm gonna think you're sweet on me or something."

"You poisoned me," he mumbled towards the ceiling, his arms spread out and his palms up. A grade-A martyr for the cause if I ever saw one.

Like I said, the guy was dramatic. But endearing in his own way too, I suppose.

"No, I poisoned them." I hitched a thumb over a shoulder. "You just got yourself a poor constitution, Mr. Dawson. Good thing you went and got yourself a fake wife while you were at it. She'll straighten ya out real quick. Now, come on and give a girl a hand."

I turned around and grabbed on to the smaller man's arm, tugging until his body hit the kitchen floor with a loud *thwack,* followed by a muffled *thump* when he flopped onto his face.

Jack scrambled to his feet to chase after me. "You killed a cop, Charlee," he hissed. "*Two* cops!"

I shook my head and spun back around to glare at him. "*No*," I repeated. "I killed two guys dressed up to *look* like cops."

"What do you mean?" Jack was pacing the kitchen now. He was cute when he was frazzled.

Maybe I was the one who was sweet on him? That would be a first.

I quirked a brow. "Who do ya owe money to?"

"What?" His feet skidded to a stop. "I don't know what you're talkin' about. *You* don't know what you're talkin' about."

He was *less* cute when he was lying.

"Check their pockets." I crossed my arms over my chest, tapping an impatient foot while jutting my chin in the big guy's direction.

Jack huffed before stomping towards the table. "Yeah, and what am I checking for, Charlee?"

I lifted a single shoulder. "A wallet, a phone, something that ties them back to whoever it is that sent 'em to find you."

"No one is looking for me, babe. I ain't all that important." He fumbled around in the big guy's pocket and pulled a phone free. Tapping on the screen a few times before looking over at me again. "It's locked."

I rolled my eyes, took a fistful of "Officer Bradley's" hair, and lifted his head off the table. Using my free hand to point at his reddened cheeks. Nature's rouge. Lividity was starting to set in.

"Oh, right..." Jack held the phone in front of the dead

guy's face and waited for the screen to unlock. It didn't take more than a few seconds for his cheeks to take on a blush of their own.

"Told ya so," I sang out while collecting the cups and tucking them against my body with an arm.

"But I didn't say anything."

"You didn't have to." I twirled a finger in the air around Jack's head. *That* said it all. So... who is it?"

"Who's who?"

I could feel him move up behind me as I deposited the cups into the sink. His breath against the back of my neck hot, his crotch region hotter. I grabbed a knife out of the chopping block to my right and spun around, using the tip of the blade to force him back a step.

"This thing between you and me is never gonna work if you aren't honest with me, sugar." I grinned, and Jack flared his nostrils. Gripping up my wrist with one hand and yanking me forward by my waist with the other.

"And what is this *thing* between you and me, babe? Sounds serious."

"Very serious," I hummed. "I don't kill for just anyone, ya know."

"You killed for me, though, huh?"

He squeezed until my fingers flexed and dropped the butcher knife, and I pushed up on my toes, leaning closer as I rubbed my stomach against his growing bulge. The one peeking out and tapping against my belly button.

"Is that your way of telling me you like me, Charlee— I just realized I don't even know your last name..." He lowered his head to meet mine, skimming his mouth over my lips. A kiss that really wasn't a kiss. But it wasn't *not* a kiss either. It was a challenge. A dare? And the thing with me was I didn't back down from dares.

"It's Dawson or did ya already forget, *dear*?"

Jack let go of my wrist, both hands shooting out to squeeze my backside as I jumped up and locked my legs around his waist. He shuffled a step, then another, nearly tripping over our friend on the floor as he spun us around to slam me against the door. And then his tongue was down my throat as he pounded up into me from below. My fingers switching from pulling on his hair to cupping his jaw. From cupping his jaw to clawing at his back. From clawing at his back to wrapping around and clinging to his neck.

I didn't want to just eat this man. I wanted to devour him. Taste him and savor him. Digest and absorb him.

"Ow, fuck," he grunted, and I opened my eyes to find myself teeth-deep in his shoulder. He didn't stop what he was doing, though. Just clenched his jaw and slapped a palm behind me, using the leverage to change up the angle.

I licked my bottom lip, the metallic tingle hitting my tongue as he continued to ram my lady bits against the door like a juicy piece of ribeye getting shoved into a meat grinder. And I relaxed my muscles and let him. I let him get me there all on his own.

One, two, three more flexes of those tenderloins and I was seeing tweety birds and ninja stars and Jack was carrying me back down the hall and dropping me on the mattress before diving back in again.

CHAPTER FOURTEEN
JACK

I was sleeping with a genuine serial killer. Literally. She curled up on top of me last night and fell asleep. Two dead cops in her kitchen and Charlee didn't have a care in the world.

Worst part? I didn't know if I was scared or turned on.

Probably both. I glanced down at the tenting in my boxers. *Yep, the answer was definitely both. Fuck, that shit was a lot to unpack.*

I pulled Charlee closer to my side and breathed in the scent of her strawberry shampoo. But I could do the *unpacking* later. Right now, I was content with being slightly less fucked-up than the woman I was holding in my arms. Arms that weren't cuffed to a headboard or zip-tied behind my back anymore.

"How did you know?" I asked, as the morning sun streamed in from her bedroom window, hitting me in the eye like the flashlight from a few hours ago. I squinted it closed and waited for my vision to adjust.

I felt like I'd been run over by a semi-truck but then, instead of putting me out of my misery, the driver of that same semi-truck had jumped down and fucked my brains out in the middle of the street.

So no harm, no foul.

"Know what?" Charlee grumbled against my chest. I knew she was awake the moment her breathing changed. She'd been pretending for the last twenty minutes or so, and I'd been letting her. Because she smelled nice.

"That those fuckers weren't real cops."

"My daddy was a cop," she replied on a yawn, pushing up on the mattress and stretching her arms above her head before peering back at me over a shoul-der. "He taught me what to look for."

"Like what? What'd I miss?"

Charlee appeared to ignore me as she crossed the room, swiped her robe off the floor, and punched her arms through each of the sleeves. She was looping the tie around the middle when she finally looked over at me again. Head cocked and eyes so blue I swear I could have drank 'em up.

Might need to too. Woman damn near drained me dry.

"The patches for starters. There was no city or county listed, just the word police. Also, the badge number by his name wasn't real. It was six-digits. Should have been five—mhmm, maybe four—depending on when he was hired. Oh, and then there was the fact he was wearing Class A's. No real cop wears Class A's on patrol." She paused and tapped a finger on her chin. "Probably picked them up at a garage or estate sale or something, threw on a fake badge, and poof! He's got people like you willingly slapping on a pair of cuffs."

"Right." I dragged myself higher up on the bed to lean my back against the metal rails. "And what if you were wrong about all that?"

"I wasn't."

"But what if you were?" I tried again.

Charlee stopped what she was doing to stare at me. "Better for you to learn now, Mr. Dawson. I'm never wrong."

"Never?" I quirked an eyebrow, and Charlee walked over to my side of the bed, pinching my face between her fingers before giving my cheek a light slap.

"Never."

"Okay then." I grinned and pulled her down for a kiss.

A short one because she was already pressing a hand to my chest and prying herself free. "We have some bodies to dispose of. Come on now, they don't say the early bird buries the worm for no reason, now do they?"

"Who's they?" I shouted down the hallway, but she was already banging around in the kitchen. "Charlee, no one says that!"

I tugged my shirt higher up on my nose, trying to block

out the smell of fresh blood. It didn't do much but it made me feel a little better.

"How d'ya know how to do that?" I pointed to where Charlee was bent over on the floor. Her mess of hair tied up out of her face and a pair of plastic glasses propped on the bridge of her nose. She wasn't wearing her robe anymore, having replaced it with a disposable rain jacket.

"My daddy was a butcher." She grinned at me from over a shoulder, red streaks splattering her face as she deconstructed our boys in blue as though they were Lego towers instead of full-grown bodies. Cutting the larger guy's limbs at the socket and popping them off just as easily as I popped off the wheels on my toy cars when I was little.

"Thought you said your dad was a cop?"

"Oh, Mr. Dawson, that's real unprogressive of ya to assume I only had one daddy."

"Riiiight," I muttered under my breath. Somehow a broad with her hands gut-deep in a guy's chest cavity was calling me the problem.

How the fuck did I get here?

"You broke in, remember?" she said even though I hadn't asked that shit aloud.

Charlee lifted the giant knife over her head and started hacking at the guy's throat with a lot less finesse than she used on his arms. A few more whacks and that was tumbling free and rolling across the room too. I stopped it with my foot and held my breath.

They didn't smell how I thought dead people

smelled, but then again, they hadn't been dead all that long.

She jumped to her feet, grabbed Officer Bradley by the hair, and lifted him off the floor. "Now where do you think you're going, Mister." She laughed, and I snorted. "What's so funny?"

"Nothing," I told her.

She was cute. Even when she was just as fucking crazy. Which meant my ass was crazier.

"Sure seems like something, don't it, Chuck?" She looked from the head to me.

"Chuck?" I repeated.

"He looks like a Chuck, don't he?" Charlee shrugged, extending her arm so the head was dangling in front of us.

"Yeah, sure." I pushed the head back in her direction. "Officer Chuck Bradley. You got it, babe."

CHAPTER FIFTEEN
CHARLEE

"The knee bone's connected to the thigh bone," I hummed to myself while chucking *Chuck's* leg into the closest plastic tub. It rolled once and then settled in next to his torso. I tried to squash it down and it popped back up, a trickle of red leaking over the side. "The thigh bone's connected to the hip bone."

I took a step back, my palms braced on my hips, and eyed my handiwork. There were lot more pieces than I was used to keeping.

Lucky for us, I'd stocked up on those black hardware store bins with the neon-yellow lids and left 'em stacked in the shared basement *just in case* I was feeling particularly wronged by the male species on any given day. We'd hefted three of them up the stairs. But apparently, three wasn't enough for my friend here. Officer Bradley was thicker than a tick on a lake leech.

I brushed the cobwebs off my hands and stared at the stack of body parts piled up over the lip before glancing towards Jack, who was watching me warily out of the corner of his eye. His arms crossed and his shirt stretched out around the collar from where he kept using it like a noseguard for no reason, seeing as the only thing rotten was his mood.

Kidnappin' and assault with a deadly weapon was peaches and cream. But kill a couple of fake cops and suddenly a guy starts lookin' at ya differently.

I sighed. Wasn't his fault, I suppose. This was new to him. It was just another day at my daddy's butcher's counter for me.

My gaze flicked to the side, and I grabbed Chuck's arm from the top of the pile and waved it in Jack's direction. "I sure could use that hand now."

He shook his head at me.

"I'm being serious." I flopped the arm disapprovingly, blood splattering across the tarps we'd laid out on the floor, before I tossed it back into the tub. "They ain't gonna keep like this."

When Jack continued to glare at me from where he was standing by the kitchen table, I took two steps forward and closed the distance, draping my arms over his shoulders. He lifted my safety goggles up onto my head. I smiled, and his cheek indented itself on one side.

"Yeah, and what do you suppose we do? Disposing of dead guys ain't exactly my area of expertise, sweetheart."

"I'm gonna have to phone a friend." I didn't like to do it if I didn't have to—independent woman and all—and it was much more lucrative to preserve the organs and keep 'em whole. But I knew a couple of quacks who were always looking to add a few spare parts to their human chop shop. Couldn't tell ya what they did with 'em. Just that they didn't ask questions. Which meant I didn't ask 'em either.

Two birds, one stone. And that stone came with a stack of cash.

"Mmm, pretty certain the fewer people who know about that..." Jack stretched his neck and peered over my head at the tubs, shaking when a shiver went up his spine. "...the better."

"Don't go mansplaining murder to me, Mr. Dawson. One of us is a professional. The other one still has a frying-pan sized lump on the side of his head." I tapped his temple with my index finger for good measure, and Jack winced.

"Speaking of..." He cleared the frog outta his throat, and I watched the way his Adam's apple bobbed in front of me. "How many times have you done this, exactly?"

I blinked up at him, my lashes fluttering like mama taught me to do whenever I wanted a new toy from the corner store and daddy said we had to tighten our purse straps.

"Are you asking me my body count?" I gasped while pressing a hand to my chest.

"Ah, yeah, you could call it that?"

I grabbed Jack's cheeks and gave them a quick squeeze between my fingers before pushing off him and walking towards the bathroom. "A lady doesn't kiss and tell! What I will *tell* ya is that I've never done two in the same sittin'." I winked at him over a shoulder and kept walking.

"Charlee, I didn't ask if you kissed them," he yelled out by the time I was reaching an arm inside the stall and turning the shower on. He appeared behind me a few seconds later. One hand on the doorjamb as he swung himself into the room. "Wait... did you kiss them? Are you into that kinda thing?"

"What kinda thing? Gettin' my rocks off with dead guys? No one likes a sour pickle, Jack." I had to pinch my lips to keep from laughing. I took a deep breath and schooled my features.

His eyebrows scrunched up in the middle like he was thinking too hard. "Aren't all pickles sour, Charlee?"

"It's just a saying." I rolled my eyes, a hand on my hip and my hot water swirling down the drain. "Seriously? What's next? Ya gonna ask me if I cook 'em up and eat 'em too?"

He paused to stare at me for a moment, his eyes bouncing from side to side like a ball across a ping-pong table. Then he shook his head. "'Course not."

"Good, 'cause I gotta get all this blood cleaned up unless you'd prefer to lick it off?" I quirked an eyebrow at him, and Jack backed me into the shower stall. Clothes and all.

"Haha, very funny," he grunted, and then he was lifting me up by the hips and pressing me against the tile. The hot stream pelting against his back and the water turning pink as it bounced off my raincoat and dripped off my legs.

I wasn't joking. He didn't need to know that, though. Sometimes it was better to not know where all the bodies were buried. Most times it was better not to leave any bodies around in the first place.

CHAPTER SIXTEEN
JACK

"I'm sorry but I'm gonna have to kill ya."

My neck snapped in Charlee's direction as she stood over the stove and swatted at a fly buzzing around her head. I took a deep breath and nearly jumped outta my skin when she stabbed the insect into her cutting board with a paring knife. It kicked its little insect legs around a few times, and Charlee watched it struggle until it stilled.

Then she looked up and smiled at me. It wasn't the creepy smile you would think it to be, though. It was soft, her eyes sparkling and her cheeks pink and puffy like someone had just pinched 'em.

I shot her a wink, and she continued stirring the pot on the stove, only to glance towards the entryway a few seconds later when her little camera panel beeped, letting her know someone was at the door. Musta been how she got the drop on me that first night.

Of course my dumb ass would break into a serial

killer's house with a state-of-the-line security system. *Why the fuck not?*

"Kaz!" Charlee squealed at the same time she swung the door open and jumped into some blonde, tatted-up fucker's arms. She wrapped her legs around his waist, and he cupped her ass a little too familiarly as he walked her back inside.

"Hey, sugar tits. Heard ya got some..." His glare flicked to me before adding, "...parts for us."

She jumped down and gestured towards the storage bins we'd piled up in the corner, a bare foot sticking out of the one on top and a couple of fingers gripping the edge. Charlee said rigor mortis had set in. I didn't care to find out what that looked like.

"That's not parts. That's the whole damn thing." He laughed, and Charlee cocked a hip like she did whenever she was about to get sassy. Which was more frequent than not.

"And what are whole things made out of?" She quirked a brow. "*Parts.*"

"Got me there." The guy grinned, his attention shooting back over my way as he ran a tongue along his perfectly white teeth and jutted his chin at me. "Who's that?"

Charlee grabbed onto my arm and rested her head on my shoulder. "My boyfriend."

"You don't need a boyfriend if you wanna good fuck, sweetheart," he replied, that fucking stupid-ass grin widening. "You always got my number."

Charlee rolled her eyes before whispering out of the

side of her mouth, "He's kiddin'. Our mamas were cousins."

"Second cousins—*distant* second cousins," he corrected her, his eyes on me when he adjusted himself in his pants. "You gonna grab one of these bins or just stand there and stare at my cock all day?"

I stepped forward, my fists clenched at my sides, and Charlee tugged me back. Tony woulda bashed this fucker's face in already. But my girl could take care of herself. And this fucker. And me. Besides, I didn't want to draw any more attention from the nosey neighbors she'd mentioned—especially with a stack of body parts just hanging out in the kitchen.

"Ut-uh." Charlee shook her head. "This one's not allowed to leave."

"And why's that?" the guy asked.

"Because I kidnapped him." Charlee looked up at me and smiled.

"Thought you said he was your boyfriend?" He glanced between us, like suddenly we were more interesting than the crime scene he was here to clean up.

"He is." She shrugged.

"Aw, come on, little coz. You're far too pretty to be kidnapping boyfriends." The fucker closed the distance, pulling Charlee against his chest and spinning her around to face me. "I know your ma taught ya better than that. If a guy wants to leave ya, let him leave. There are plenty of other guys wanting to get into those pretty pink panties of yours."

I shoved him back a step and tugged Charlee into my arms. "Hey, pal, how 'bout you back the fuck off," I gritted out. "I wasn't her boyfriend when she kidnapped me."

He dropped his grin until his expression resembled something that should be on a villain in a horror flick. His mouth pulled straight and his glare unblinking. Then, as if a switch had been flipped, he threw his head back on a loud cackle, one hand clutching his stomach and the other pointing at me. "Now that makes fucking sense."

I turned to Charlee and dropped my mouth to her ear. "This guy fuckin' serious?"

"Never," she said. "*Always,*" she added on a huff.

An hour or so later, Charlee's "cousin" and a big mute guy he brought with him were wiping up the entryway with a mop and some industrial-grade cleaner. When they were done, he reached into his pocket and tossed Charlee a tin can.

"For Mrs. Davis." He chuckled before strolling out the door with a weird skip in his step. My ma would tell me that guy was up to no good. I'd tell her, at this point, so was I.

I looked over at Charlee and the tin in her hand. "He brought your neighbor a can of tuna?"

Charlee nodded as she stepped up to the front door, swung it open, and called out, "Mrs. Davis!"

By the time she stepped back again, a white fluffball

with a few patches of fur missin' was sauntering in behind her. Its tail raised and curled at the end as it rubbed against Charlee's legs.

"Mrs. Davis is a cat?" I asked, just to make sure I was understanding this right.

Another nod and a wider grin. "Also why I knew those guys were lyin'. Everyone on this block knows Mrs. Davis," Charlee explained.

I glanced down at the stray that was currently licking at a spot of blood Charlee's friends had missed on the floor. "Ain't that kind of a weird name for a cat? Does that mean there was a Mr. Davis?"

I laughed, and Charlee just stared at me as she plucked the cat off the floor and tickled its belly. "There was. But she ate him."

CHAPTER SEVENTEEN
CHARLEE

I held out a hand towards my cousin and tapped my foot while doing a grabby motion with my fingers. Like I used to do when we were kids and he skipped off to the corner store with the money he'd stolen outta my piggy bank. He'd always bring me back something too. But that wasn't the point. The point was he should have asked me in the first place.

Kaz wasn't one to ask for permission, though. He was more the type to press his luck and hope ya didn't notice.

He'd just returned from doing whatever it was he did with the bodies over at the crazy house he worked at. I didn't much care for the details and neither did he.

"Where's the rest of it, Kazmir," I said. It wasn't a question. Not really, seeing as we both knew he'd shorted me.

It wasn't about the money. It was the principle of the thing. No one got a pass. Not even family.

"Don't ya think I deserve something for my time, *Sharlotta*?" he countered, in that thick Russian accent he liked to use whenever he was tryin' to get under my skin by sounding like my daddy.

"It's just Charlee now, thanks." I rolled my eyes. "Now go on and hand it over before I serve ya up like your mama's *moskovskaya*." I used the same accent on him, and he tucked his hands into his pockets.

"Now we both know you wouldn't do that, little coz."

"Oh yeah?" I tilted my head to look him over from cheek to round-tip. "And why's that?"

Kaz shrugged a shoulder. "'Cause we're blood."

"Ya know what? You're right. I wouldn't. But blood has nothing to do with it." I grinned while pointing a manicured finger at the ink that covered his throat and climbed up behind his ears. "It's 'cause tattoos taste like the underside of a donkey's rear."

My cousin barked out one of his obnoxious laughs and stuffed the rest of the cash into my open palm, and then he was turning around and walking towards the door again. I stopped him with a quick tug on his shirt, glancing over a shoulder to make sure that Jack was still holed up in the shower. I could hear the water running.

"Wait. I got a question for ya."

Kaz quirked an eyebrow, his gaze flickering over my head and likely doing the same thing. Making sure we were outta earshot of any busybodies. But there wasn't nobody 'round except Mrs. Davis, who was sleeping off her lunch next to my radiator—*and she wasn't telling on me unless I told on her. Girl code and all.*

"Go on and ask it. We ain't got all day, sugar tits." He flicked one of my nipples through my shirt, and I grabbed his hand and twisted until I heard it crack. Kaz didn't so much as flinch. My cousin didn't feel pain like a normal person. Which made breaking his bones slightly less gratifying than it normally would.

"Whatcha know about the Mulligans?" I pressed him.

"Buncha Micks, into the usual mob shit—pills, gambling, great if you wanna get your hands on the white stuff. Why? Finally looking to loosen up a bit?" Kaz nudged me with a shoulder before he gripped his dislocated wrist with his free hand and twisted it back into its socket like a cap on a pop bottle. "You don't need them if you're lookin' to party, Charlee. You know I gotchu."

"Not me," I grumbled as I pushed my cousin out the door.

He grabbed on to the jamb with both hands, his much larger frame keeping me from moving him more than an inch. "Ut-uh, I ain't leaving till the show's over. I wanna watch this."

I cussed under my breath, stomped towards the bathroom, grabbed Jack outta the shower stall by the ear, and led him into the kitchen bare-assed and dripping wet all over my floor.

I shoved him down on a seat cushion and shot him a glare. "Jack Alexander Dawson, what were ya thinkin' getting yourself mixed up with the Irish mob?"

He rubbed a hand over his ear and dragged the chair back to get a better look at me, his limp rooster sticking to a thigh as he spread his legs. "Who's starin' now?" He smirked at Kaz before turning to me. "And how do you know my middle name?"

"Your mama told me." I tapped my shoe like I'd

tapped it at my cousin a few minutes earlier. "You still didn't answer my question."

"It ain't that serious, Charlee," Jack muttered, and I cracked him across the side of the head with an open palm. At least it wasn't a pan.

"*Ain't that serious,*" I parroted, throwing my arms in the air. "It's serious enough for them to track you down all the way out here. How much?"

Jack lifted a shoulder, that dimple deepening in his cheek as he pulled me down onto his lap. Chest to back. "Not much."

I spun around to face him, straddling his thighs and locking my arms around his neck. "How much, Jack."

"Twenty grand," he replied, and my cousin let out a low whistle from behind us. "We don't need no comments from the peanut gallery," Jack hissed at him.

"Wouldn't dream of it." Kaz snorted. I peered towards the entryway and shot him a look that said what I didn't have to. He spun on the heel of his boot and grabbed on to the door. "Oh, but a little word of advice? Might want to ask your new girlfriend what she's got cookin' up in that pot over there."

Then my cousin slammed the door shut behind him, and I could hear 'em cackling all the way down the hall.

There were more than a couple of screws loose with that one. Pretty sure his mama dropped him on the head when he was a baby. A few times.

"What's in the pot, Charlee?" Jack asked, and I turned my head back around to look at him.

"Hm?"

"I said... *what's in the pot, Charlee?*" he repeated.

CHAPTER EIGHTEEN
JACK

"What's in the pot, Charlee?"

"Hm?" She turned her wide eyes on me.

"I said... *what's in the pot, Charlee?*"

She started grinding her ass against my lap, my cock quickly rising to the occasion. I had to grab her hips to stop her.

"Charlee, what's in the fucking pot?" I asked her a third time.

She shrugged a shoulder. "Meat stew. It's my mama's recipe."

It wasn't what she said but the way she said it—like it was a question or there was some double meaning behind it—that had me sliding her off my lap and heading towards the stove. I lifted the lid and stared down at the mixture of meat, potatoes, and carrots. What appeared to be pepper flakes and some green stuff sprinkled on top. It didn't look different from any other stew I'd ever seen. It didn't smell all that different either.

But what the fuck did I know about stew? I grew up

eating pasta seven nights a week while my pops knew better than to complain about it.

I could sense Charlee tiptoeing behind me, and could only hope she didn't have another pan in her hands as I tugged the fridge door open and scanned the contents. It was filled to the brim with packets of meat: sausages, flanks, ground, and chunk.

I swiped up the first thing my fingers brushed and read the label on top. *Tyler*. The next one. *Bruce*. And the next. *Kevin*. Then I turned around to look at her.

"Charlee, why do all these packages have names on them? Do you name your lunchmeat?" It sounded weird. But it was completely reasonable when you remembered this broad had a street cat named *Mrs. Davis*.

Charlee stared back at me with a blank expression on her face. I was joking, but suddenly shit didn't seem so funny anymore.

I assumed her cousin was fucking with me. Or, at the very worst, I'd find out that my girl had a taste for exotic animals like caribou or zebra or some other weird shit. Now I wasn't so sure.

When she didn't answer me, I glanced over into the pot again and watched as something floated its way to the top. It looked like a misshapen carrot or maybe a...

I jumped back from the stove, nearly knocking Charlee flat on her ass. "Is that a...?"

I closed my eyes, shook my head, and blinked 'em open again. Then I chanced another peek into the pot. None of that changed what I thought I was seeing, so I grabbed a ladle out of the little cup thing on the counter and fished around the stew until I found what I was looking for. Dropping it back in as soon as I found it. And jumped back again.

"Yup, that's a fucking finger! Charlee, what the fuck?"

I snatched up each of her hands, counting off one digit at a time and then did the same to myself. All twenty of ʾem were there. Twenty-one if you included the thumb still floating around in the pot.

"Charlee, babe, why do you have somebody's finger cooking up on your stove?"

She shrugged another shoulder. "I told ya I didn't sleep with ʾem."

"I... um... You're right. You did." I combed a hand through my hair, quickly pulling my arm back to count my fingers one more time. Still all there.

Wait... one, two, three, four, five... Yup, all good.

I took a deep breath, my eyes bouncing from Charlee to the pot, from the pot back to Charlee, whose expression remained unreadable.

"You can leave now if you want." She spun around and walked towards her front door, opening it wide and gesturing for me to step through.

Mrs. Davis glanced up from where she was curled up in a ball of white fur, stretched out her legs, and pranced out the door with a swipe of her patchy tail.

I stomped over but instead of walking out with the cannibal cat, I slammed the door shut and slid the lock back in place.

Was I stupid for not following her?

Probably, but I was stupid and curious. It was something that always got me in trouble growing up.

I grabbed Charlee by the wrist and guided her over to

the kitchen table, forcing her to sit down like she had done to me when she'd dragged my naked ass out of the shower. Which reminded me I was still walking around the house in nothing but a towel.

That would have been a hard one to explain if I had decided to walk out of here. Not as hard as explaining a girlfriend who liked to eat people. Literally. But still fucking awkward. Besides, I didn't even know where she'd stashed my car keys.

Maybe her telling me to leave was more of a gesture than anything else? Or a test. Either way, I wasn't too worried about passing it.

I lowered myself onto the chair across from her and took another deep breath. Okay, several deep breaths. This was a lot to take in.

Your girlfriend being a serial killer was one thing, but a serial-killing man-eater was a-whole-nother.

Don't ask me why. It just was. *It was!*

"All right, how 'bout you explain it to me." I nodded once, and Charlee peered up from her hands to look at me. "Do you... uh... like the way it tastes?"

"What?"

"Humans. People, Charlee. Is it a taste thing? Like preferring steak over chicken?"

She tilted her head and appeared to consider my words. "No."

"Okay... then what is it? I am really trying to understand here, babe. Can you explain to me why you do it? Please."

"Why?" It wasn't a dumb question. I was questioning

it myself. But that didn't mean I had an answer for her either. Other than…

"Because I'm starting to like you, Charlee Dawson."

She smiled up at me, those eyes of hers just as bright and blue as I remember them being the first time I saw them. In this kitchen. In this chair.

CHAPTER NINETEEN
CHARLEE

Why?

No one had ever asked me that before. Not my papa. Not my cousin. Not even that one guy I'd made sit and watch me cook up his pinkie toe before I removed the bone and popped the fleshy bits between my teeth like a piece of chewing gum. But that coulda been because he'd passed out from the shock first.

Honestly, I didn't think about it all that much. The reason I did what I did or if I even liked doing it. It was second nature. One girl rightin' all the wrongs everyone else was too scared to right themselves.

It was also my moral obligation. Ya see, Mama had taught me that the higher the hair, the closer to God we'd be. And sometimes God was vengeful. He needed to be, else how was he gonna keep his flock from wandering astray?

I supposed *that* was the part I enjoyed the most.

Teaching 'em all lessons their mamas certainly didn't teach 'em like my mama did with me.

We hadn't had a lot growing up. Me and Kaz. My mama spent so much time scrimping and saving, just to make sure we were fed, and his mama was always working. So were our daddies. That was why nothing ever went to waste in our house and it wouldn't go to waste in mine neither.

It was as simple as that. Or maybe it wasn't simple at all if ya didn't know what it was to go to bed with your tummy rumbling. Sorta made sense now why my cousin was so extra. Extra food in his belly, extra cash in his pockets, extra drugs in his veins. Kaz was making up for everything he didn't have before or was afraid he wasn't gonna have again. At least that was my thoughts on it. Not everyone was as easy to figure out.

I glanced over to Jack, who was looking at me expectantly.

If he had enough cash to give it to the mob, something told me he wouldn't understand where I was coming from. So I pushed up from my chair, grabbed hold of his hand, and dragged him off towards the bedroom.

Sex was universal. It didn't need understanding, which was why it was one of my favorite things to do... when I wasn't doing *other things*.

I took two steps into the room, tugged my shirt off over my head, and then yanked Jack's towel free—darn thing was hanging on for dear life anyway.

He didn't say nothing. Just watched me as I moved around him and shoved him backwards onto the bed with a hand pressed to his chest. And then I was climbing him faster than sin on a preacher.

Jack groaned, grabbing my hips as I ground myself against his waist. "Charlee, we need to talk."

"I'm pretty sure we talked plenty in the kitchen," I told him, at the same time I gripped his rooster by the throat and sank down on it until it was weeping instead of crowing.

"You know what I mean," Jack grunted, but he was already thrusting up inside me, his eyes closed and his brows pinched together in the middle.

"I do know." I laughed as I got us both closer and closer to seeing those pearly gates while also ensuring we wouldn't be allowed past 'em. "And all I heard was how much ya like me, Mr. Dawson."

He thrusted upwards one more time before flipping me over onto my back, never losing traction as he stretched my arms high over my head and held them there with one of his fists.

"I do like you, Charlee. Probably more than I should. Probably more than's good for me," he grunted into my ear.

"Okay..." I gasped when he started pounding me so hard one of my girls bounced up and nearly took me out. "I still don't see the problem."

Jack slid his knee off the mattress and stood to his full height, with two feet firmly planted on the floor and one palm on each of my thighs, as he slowly pulled back and drove in again. All his focus now on the way my lady bits swallowed him up and spit him back out. Swallowed him up and spit him out.

I could do the same thing and he'd be none the wiser. 'Cept, for once, I didn't want to.

He threw his head back and started driving forward faster, his breaths coming out in quick pants. "The problem is..." he huffed. "...you eat people, Charlee, and I'm not sure how I feel about that."

I was close but I could tell Jack was closer. So I sat up on the bed and pressed down on his shoulders, until his rooster popped its head free and Jack was kneeling in front of me.

"Then how 'bout you eat me and we call it an even trade?" I grinned wider, and Jack frowned. "What? Too soon?"

"Yeah, can we lay off the euphemisms till there isn't a finger slow-cooking on the stove anymore?" he grumbled before doing the same thing he was so concerned about me doing to everyone else.

He ate me alive.

Three orgasms later, two for me and one for Jack, I was rolling off the bed and waddling towards the kitchen. It didn't take more than a few minutes for Jack to come padding in after me.

I peered over at him from where I was cutting up a loaf of bread on the counter. "Hungry?"

"Starving." He propped himself up against the wall, crossed his arms, and watched me.

I nodded, grabbed another dish from the cabinet, and set it out beside the cutting board. The stew had at least two hours to go before the flesh was falling off the bones. So I plated up two sandwiches and handed one to Jack.

He took it out of my grip, raised the bread towards his mouth, and paused to look at me. "Hey, Charlee, what was in that sandwich you made me?"

I bit down into my own bread, mustard squirting out and spraying one side of my face. I wiped it away with a piece of paper towel and found Jack still staring at me. His food untouched.

"Charlee... it wasn't bologna, was it?"

I lifted a shoulder. "I already told you it wasn't."

CHAPTER TWENTY
JACK

SIX MONTHS LATER

I hated to admit it, but there were several advantages to being a newly-turned vegetarian dating a cannibal. *Before ya judge me, hear me out!*

First off, our grocery bill was much lower than most people's. And in this economy, we'd take all the help we could get on that one. Secondly, she never stole my leftovers and I certainly never stole hers. It was refreshing to open the fridge and see my Tupperware dish exactly where I'd put it the day before. And thirdly, blood made for great fertilizer, which meant my little homegrown garden was thriving.

Did it freak me out every time I thought about where that blood came from? Sure. So I decided to just not think about it.

I glanced out the kitchen window at where my tomatoes were popping up next to Charlee's rose bushes. They were companion plants the broad at the nursery had explained. Aesthetically different but each served their purpose. Kinda like me and my girl.

Charlee was the twisted chaos, a little prickly on the outside but so pretty to look at. She smelled nice too. And I was a giant lump of tomatoes. Perfect to grind up and throw in a pot of gravy if she got tired of dealing with my BS. Or at least that's what she liked to tell me. I *liked* to think she enjoyed my company too much to do that.

I chuckled at the thought just as Charlee was pushing in through the front door with her usual dramatic flair. One hand on her hip when she slapped a stack of cash on the kitchen table.

"Done! Twenty big ones." She grinned, wrapped her arms around my neck, and tugged my face down for a kiss.

It'd taken us a little over six months to scrape together enough cash to pay back my gambling debts, but we'd done it. And I hadn't had the itch to play the ponies ever since.

Threats on life or limb from a girl I knew could deliver on them would do that to you. Just another reason this woman was good for me. She kept my ass on the straight and narrow, and I kept her from piling up too many of those tubs she had stocked up in the basement.

I placed a palm on each side of her waist and lifted her ass up next to the cash on the table. Charlee giggled, and I muffled the sound with another kiss.

I didn't know why she and I worked so well. Just that we did. Sometimes opposites really did attract. Same as my ma and my old man. No one in our families thought they belonged together either. She was Italian American and he was off-the-boat Irish. The two of 'em might as well have been oil and water when it came to agreeing on just about anything.

But not everything needed to make sense, I suppose. Dating the girl who beat ya upside the head with a frying pan and tied your ass to a chair certainly didn't. Then again, neither did dating the guy who broke into your house to rob you.

Guess we shared something in common after all. Piss-poor dating habits.

"I'll drop it off tonight," I told her while gesturing a thumb to the cash. I had an appointment to meet up with one of the Mulligan henchmen for the handoff.

It could have been a setup for all we knew. Though I was pretty certain that it wasn't. They wanted their cash just as much as they wanted a returning customer. They would only be getting one of those things from me. They just didn't know that any more than they knew what happened to the two guys they sent looking for me.

Charlee had mailed them an envelope with a couple of fingers and a note telling the fuckers to back off or they'd be next. She didn't think I knew about it, and I had no intention of bursting her bubble.

I liked how keen on protecting me she was. I also liked how riled up she got. It was as adorable as it was scary.

"I'll come with you," she insisted, and I gave her that look. The one that said everything without saying nothing. "You know, in case I get hungry." She winked at me.

I shook my head. There was no talking her outta

something when she had her heart set on it. So it was usually just easier to keep my mouth shut and agree.

"Speaking of?" she hummed. "When we gonna have your mama over for dinner?"

"Depends..." I quirked a brow at her.

"On what?" Charlee asked.

"On who's cooking..."

BONUS CHAPTER
SHARLOTTA

TWENTY YEARS PRIOR

My eyes were glued to the lady on the television screen. The way her bright-red lipstick curled across her face when she smiled down at me from the glass. Her eyes circled in blue and her hair white blonde and piled twice as high as everyone I'd ever seen in real life. I had no idea how she got her hair that high. Mine was flat and fell down my back in long waves.

Maybe she was magic. It sure seemed like magic to me. 'Cause whenever she moved, her sparkly costume would move with her, catching the light on the stage so that I was just as mesmerized by it as I was with her voice.

She had such a pretty voice. It was almost as pretty as she was.

My papa said women who dressed like that were stupid. But this lady didn't seem stupid to me. How could you be stupid when everyone was looking at you the way I was looking at her?

If anything, the ones looking were stupid. She was smart enough to be noticed. No one seemed to notice me unless I was doing something bad.

I tugged at the light-blonde curl on my shoulder, twirling it around and around until it started to come loose. I quickly dropped my hand and stared down at the lock of hair in my hand. Now that I thought about it, the color wasn't all that different from the lady's.

I wonder if my hair could be piled high on my head like hers one day?

My papa made a loud sound from his throat, and I glanced over to where he was sleeping on the sofa with an empty bottle in his hands. Last time he did that, he woke up angry and the cops came and took him away for a while.

He was back now, though. I sighed as I watched his chest puff out and flatten down.

Sometimes I pretended my papa was one of those cops arresting bad guys—like the one who was here that last time and showed me all the parts of his uniform while my mama talked to his friend. Or maybe my papa could be like the nice man at the meat market, who always smiled when my mama and I came to visit. He'd sneak me a piece of cheese whenever mama wasn't looking. Or maybe I could just get a new papa. I'd be okay with anyone who wasn't like my real papa.

Sometimes I pretended I wasn't me too. The other kids didn't like me. They said my name was weird and that I talked funny. I was working on talking less funny so they would like me more—even though my mama said I shouldn't do anything just to make someone like me.

My mama was usually right but I wasn't so sure about that one. If the other kids didn't like me, they wouldn't invite me to come play with them.

Papa grunted in his sleep again, and I turned back to the lady on the screen. Dolly Parton. Her name flashed across the bottom of the television in big letters when she was done singing about some other lady who took her man.

If that were me, I'd say she could keep him. Men seemed like a lot more trouble than they were worth. My mama was always tired or sad or angry because of a man. Because of my papa.

Like right now. I could hear her clanking around in the kitchen, making dinner for us. I liked my mama's cooking, especially when we were lucky enough to have some leftover meat stored in the freezer. Didn't matter what kind it was, my mama knew how to make it taste good anyway.

Miss Parton was singing another song. Singing was my favorite way to practice my English so I crept over to my papa's chair and went looking for the remote to turn the television a little louder. Not loud enough to wake papa but loud enough so I could try to hear all the words and say them right.

I liked how Miss Parton said her words. Her accent was much softer than mine was, friendly too, like she was the sort of lady to bake apple pies at Christmas time. My stomach grumbled at the thought.

I took another step closer to my papa, and the floor-board creaked. I didn't think it was that noisy but my papa must have thought differently, because he jumped up and grabbed my arm, squeezing and twisting. I didn't cry though. My papa said crying was weak, and I wanted to be strong like my mama.

I bit down on my cheeks and let out a low whimper before I could stop myself. My mama came running into the room with a giant knife in her hand. My papa started yelling and cursing at her. My mama didn't say a word. She just looked him in the eye. My mama was small but she had a temper. She just never used that temper on me.

My papa lunged forward. He was too slow because of that empty bottle. My mama didn't drink any of that bottle so she was much quicker when she raised the knife high over her head and brought it down into my papa's chest.

He looked at it and then back up at my mama before he tipped over and dropped onto the floor. Landing on that same creaky board with the nail sticking out of it.

My mama nodded once and then turned her head towards me. *"Ty v poryadke?"*

"I'm okay, Mama." I smiled up at her and nodded back. "I'm gonna be just like Miss Dolly Parton when I grow up."

"You can be whatever you want to be, Sharlotka," she said. "But first you have to eat your dinner." Mama glanced at where my papa was twitching on the floor. "We're having meat stew."

FROM THE AUTHOR

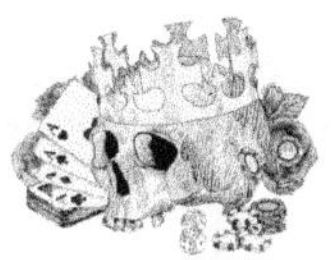

THE MORAL OF THE STORY IS:
DON'T TRUST THE MYSTERY MEAT. OR MAYBE JUST BE
CAREFUL WHOSE HOUSE YOU TRY TO BREAK INTO?

V
ENEMIES TO LOVERS

THE SINS OF OUR FATHERS

A DARK ROYAL ROMANCE

SYBIL KNIGHT & DAHLIA REIGN

BLURB:

For as long as time—for as long as stories have been told—daughters have paid for the sins of their fathers. And, well, my story wasn't much different.

My father's sin was gluttony. The man drank away everything we owned. And I wasn't just his only daughter. I was also his freedom from debt. It would be a simple exchange. One currency in place of another.

Now, I belonged to a king so cruel he reveled in breaking me down to nothing. He turned me into his plaything. His toy. His affectionately named *little fox.*

Silas thought my gilded cage would protect me. It didn't. Not from *her.* His queen wanted me gone. At least she did at first...

That was how I found myself trapped at the center of their twisted affections.

It was the sins of my father that had put me in this

POSITION. BUT IT WOULD BE MY OWN THAT WOULD FINALLY SET ME FREE...

THE *SINS OF OUR FATHERS* IS A DARK STANDALONE NOVELLA WITH A HEA. FOR A FULL LIST OF TRIGGERS, PLEASE CHECK OUT THE ORIGINAL LISTING.

PROLOGUE
TILLIE

My father's last drink was expensive.

It would cost me my freedom.

It would cost me my life.

It would force me to lose a part of myself and become someone I didn't recognize. Someone who'd always lurked skin-deep but hadn't risen above the surface.

That drink handed me over to a ruthless king, ensuring I'd be broken and shattered.

I was just an innocent girl, forced to pay for the sins of man. Of men. Of society.

But no one knew I was a hell of a lot stronger than they gave me credit for. Not even me.

CHAPTER ONE
TILLIE

As I lay awake on the roof of my family's small cottage, I stared at the stars above me and dreamt of a different life. One that wasn't filled with pain and torment, trials and tribulations. One that didn't require me to fight just to survive. I didn't want to starve myself today, so my little brothers would eat tomorrow.

A noise startled me from my daydreams. If you could call them that. They were more like day nightmares. My father was home. He must've cut through the woods, which meant he left the town in a drunken frenzy, likely fleeing from unpaid tabs. Just one more travesty against the citizens of this kingdom, another price on our heads.

I looked to the heavens, asking them to take it all away. Though my pleas remained unanswered, forcing me to contemplate calling out to the devil instead. Perhaps he was as misunderstood as the rest of us.

My prayers faltered as the sound of approaching horses called my attention. I narrowed my eyes and stared off into the darkness as torches glittered in the distance. We never received visitors this far from town, let alone at this time of night. My stomach dropped as dread coursed through my veins.

Four king's guards, two in the front and two in the back, surrounded a rider with a leather jacket, a dark hood obscuring his face. Their armor shimmered against the tall torches lighting up the night sky like a tree during the yuletides. The stranger approached, his posturing confident, assured, as a thick ruby pendent bounced against his chest with the movement. His attire was opulent and beautiful—like nothing I'd ever seen before. A chill of excitement ran along my spine and settled at the base of my neck.

Was this King Silas?

I rubbed at the dirt splotches on my face and tried to adjust my tattered dress. My feet were practically black, and my hair hadn't seen a comb in days. Normally I wouldn't care, unconcerned with impressing anyone. However, these men and their sudden appearance at my doorstep evoked a new sense of self-consciousness.

The front door to our cottage flung open, my father drunkenly falling through the gap a moment later while sending the men on horses into hysterics. One jumped down, his armor clanking as his feet hit the ground with a thud, while the mysterious rider turned his steed, revealing a pair of pale-blue eyes peering out from under the hood. Glaring at me. My heart raced and my body thrummed alive with a strange need—something enlivened between my thighs. My skin seemed to burn and shiver simultaneously, and my breathing increased as though my body had some innate reaction to his presence.

Why did this stranger have such an effect on me?

I didn't have much time to ponder the question before my attention was drawn to my father and one of the king's guards. They were arguing, shouting, though I had to strain my ears to make out the words amongst the ensuing chaos.

"The time has come for you to pay with your life."

I watched as the man raised a blade high above his head and my heart stalled in my chest. We'd never survive without my father's meager wages. My brothers were too young to get decent jobs and Clyde was too sick to do anything arduous. Despite my disdain for our only remaining parental figure, his death would be our imminent undoing.

I turned back to the hooded stranger and his stare held me prisoner once more. The moon was bright overhead and I was certain he could see me clearly. I carefully slid across the rooftop and shimmied down the trusses. All the while, his intense eyes burned into my back. I didn't dare turn around until I heard another pair of heavy boots hit the ground. He walked to his guard and spoke—his voice deep and raspy—matching his overwhelming size. My breath quickened and my hands shook as I concentrated on my descent. I stepped around the corner of the house, my spine pressed against the battered wood so I could listen.

"I-I'm sorry. Please, if you take me away, my family will die," my father cried—though his concern was for himself and not for us. It didn't take a genius to see past his lies.

"I'd hardly consider this living. Death might be preferable."

The deep voice forced my legs together, to stave the need burning in my core. A light sheen of sweat was building on my back and I could feel moisture pooling between my clenched thighs. This was a new sensation to me, but now that I'd felt it, I wanted *more.*

"I'll make you a deal," the man continued, and I was sure they could hear my ragged breathing from the corner but it didn't seem to stop the open discussion. "I'll grant you your life... in exchange for your daughter."

I gasped—I couldn't stop myself—and slapped a hand over my mouth, hoping to strangle the sound while willing my heart to calm its incessant pounding, so I could hear the rest of the exchange. My father's hasty agreement shouldn't have shocked me, but his words filled my veins with ice, sealing off any latent affections I had for a man who never deserved the title of parent. He wanted his debt to be settled, his sins wiped clean, as I paid for it with pounds of *my* flesh. I wasn't naïve to think this man wanted me for anything other than some form of sick gratification. This was no Cinderella story. I wasn't about to be whisked off to a castle to meet my Prince Charming. No, I was cattle, to be used as the king pleased, and then disposed of just as readily when he was done with me.

The stranger barked his commands, his anger filling the space around our tiny home. "James, the girl."

The front door opened, the sound of clanking armor

echoing through the thin walls. My brothers' startled gasps were like a knife stabbing my heart. I'd hoped they'd slept through the racket but they were huddled under the kitchen table while I stood frozen in place, unsure of what I should do. If I went inside to try to protect the boys, I'd be taken. When the guards seemed to ignore my brothers' presence altogether in their pursuit of me, I could breathe again. So, without a second thought, I took off into the darkness as quietly as I could.

"She ran into the woods!" one of the men shouted, the sounds of metal rattling towards the tree line.

"I do love a good hunt." The deep voice was growing closer as several heavy footfalls darted in my direction.

The broken ground and rocks tore at the flesh on my feet despite the well-worn calluses. I slid behind a large tree and paused, tugging at the fabric of my skirt and tossing the shredded material aside so I could run faster. My pursuers were close, but I knew this forest well and the trees offered me protection from the glittering moonlight they would use to guide their paths.

"Come out, come out, little fox."

I stumbled forward, realizing they were closer than I thought as I navigated my way through ivy and prickly bushes, ignoring the sting of thorns and vegetation as it continued to bristle against my exposed skin.

"There she is!" a guard barked from my right. I could hear more rustling of branches and heavy footsteps approaching. I knew any chance of escape was futile, but I refused to make it easy. I was born a fighter, scrapping to survive most of my life. This would be no different. "Your highness, I see her."

Despite the terror spurring me forward, my mind wandered to the men behind me—one man in particular. King Silas. There was no denying it was him anymore. He was a man I knew well, in reputation anyway and never in image. I don't know what I was expecting but it wasn't this. *Him.*

As the stories told it, men feared his blade while women swooned at his feet. King Silas was never one to hide behind his castle walls. No, he led his army head-on into battle, celebrating his victories in local whorehouses until the day he was forced to take a queen. Yes, he was a married man, the move political and decided for him long before his birth.

"Run, little fox. It makes the catch that much sweeter." His voice was practically at my ear, bringing me back to the present.

My lungs burned and my legs threatened to give out. Inhaling deeper, I pushed forward, knowing a large tree was not far ahead—one that's branches could bear my weight and obscure my presence. If I could get to it, I had a chance. Time to figure out my next move. I darted for the lowest branch and swung myself up, climbing as quickly as I could before plastering myself against the bark upon their quick approach.

"She's close. I can smell her fear." His words stalled my breath.

"There!" another voice called out, just as a sharp pain radiated along my side, then another matched it at my shoulder.

I cried out in agony, grabbing the tree for dear life as the men below seemed to go mute. I could hear the roaring of waves inside my eardrum while each beat of my heart intensified the pain. I raised a hand and clutched at my shoulder, turning my head and watching as blood pooled from between my fingertips. Then I dropped my gaze to my side, my eyes landing on the arrow presently protruding from my hip like the last feather on a fowl.

"You motherfucker!" the king cursed under his breath. A commotion at ground level startled me, and I shuttered a step as the pain loosened my grip. "Let go, little fox. I've got you."

"H-help," I cried, my pleas weakened by the pain. My vision was darkening, and I felt the branch slip through my fingertips. A cold breeze floated around me while a sudden warmth seemed to beckon me to follow it into the abyss. I could hear voices come and go with the wind. But they remained ethereal, almost as if they were figments of my imagination rather than tangible exchanges.

"She's losing a lot of blood..."

"It's okay, little fox. You'll be all right."

"Your highness, the men rode on ahead to ready the physician."

"Good. Now lay her over my horse."

"And the archer?"

"I'll deal with him." The voice somehow deepened an octave, though I didn't think it possible, and the sound rattled me to the core. "Sleep now, sweet girl."

"I want to go home," I managed to force the words out between chapped lips.

"That's where we're headed, little fox. Your new home."

CHAPTER TWO
SILAS

"Rest, your highness. We'll handle it." James, my most trusted guard, nodded his respects.

It wasn't my job to deal with matters as trivial as debts and arrests. Especially after I'd ridden through the night to return to my duties at the palace, but I didn't give a fuck. I couldn't stay here... with *her*.

My wife, the queen, was as obnoxious as she was arrogant. The alliance, though it made sense, wasn't one I needed since I could've wiped out her father's entire kingdom with a simple show of force. That being said, the financial strain and potential loss of men weighed heavily on my conscience, when most things didn't. So I agreed to the treaty with her father and the mother-fucker died within weeks of our godforsaken union, leaving his brother—my wife's uncle—at the helm. The bastard didn't give a damn about his niece or the welfare of the kingdom, which left us in a constant state of war. Meaning dear, sweet Agatha was of no use to me. Not really.

My advisors believed that producing an heir would force her uncle to back down. But each new day, each disappointment, only edged me closer to insanity. I could almost feel the woman's blood on my hands, taste the splatter across my face, and hear her muffled pleas as my blade severed her vocal cords.

Fuck the treaty. *If the sick son of a bitch didn't care about his kin, why should I?*

It was far past the expected timeframe for me to start having children, but their intended mother was callous and irritating—qualities she would likely pass down to our shared offspring. I wasn't keen on producing unruly daughters and ignorant sons. I'd worked hard to pull this kingdom from the grip of peril my father left it in. I needed someone strong at my side, preferably someone I didn't loathe.

I returned to the palace early in the eve to find Agatha standing in the hall, blocking the entrance to my wing. She doled out her exaggerated concern and doted on me as our servants milled about and readied my chambers. The moment we were alone, I fucked her from behind like the bitch she was so I didn't have to look at her. It was a quicker exchange when I could focus on something else, anyone else. My kingly duties or so I was told. And that's all it was. My duty to crown and country. I performed like a prized steed instructed to mount the closest mare to secure the bloodline. A fact that would disgust me if I didn't need the release.

Once the ritualistic copulation was completed to the best of my abilities, seeing as my cock liked her cunt about as much as I liked the woman herself, I adjusted my trousers and left Agatha to her ladies-in-waiting and whatever balms and salves were supposed to make a child stick.

I needed to get away from her. So I lost myself to the task at hand, debt collection and punitive matters as deemed necessary—though it was the latter that served as a better distraction. I enjoyed watching blood coat the tip of my blade, the ground turn red, and the fear I saw in their eyes when they realized it was their king at the other end of the hilt.

"I'm coming." I threw my leg over my horse and pulled my hood over my head. Traveling was safer and quicker if I wasn't recognized along the way.

It wasn't until we were riding towards our final stop for the night that something settled heavy on my chest. I had no idea what it was, but my heart beat faster the closer we got to the little shack in the woods.

My eyes remained glued to the rooftop, even as the drunken idiot stumbled out the door to greet us, my gaze focused on the girl who was trying so hard not to be seen. She was thin—*gaunt* may have been a better word —with untamed blonde hair that seemed to cocoon her soiled features. Innocent eyes stared back at me, the dark pools drowning me in their depths.

I swallowed roughly, running a hand over my chest to ease the pain stabbing at my heart. For some reason, one I didn't care to admit, the idea of her being frightened of me burned my throat like acid.

She was mine.

It was the one thought that played over and over again in my head as I watched her navigate the rooftop with the dexterity of a woodland creature and the slyness of a fox.

My little fox.

It was then that the idea came to mind. Though I would have to admit I didn't think long on it and the words were spilling out of my mouth before I realized I'd said them.

"I will grant you your life… in exchange for your daughter."

Something told me this girl was perfect, everything my queen wasn't. That was until my little fox took off, seeking sanctuary in the darkness of the woods, but hell if I didn't love the chase. Torches be damned, I rushed after her, my heart thrumming in my chest as the thrill of the hunt enlivened the blood in my veins. I was right behind her the entire time, playing with her, taunting her.

And then she was gone. Vanished into thin air like a creature out of one of those childhood storybooks.

"She's close. I can smell her fear," I growled while silent promises filled the air between us. And then I saw her. At the same time my archer had her in his sights.

I turned, flinging out an arm to stop him, but I was too late. I watched on in horror as his arrows pierced the air before doing the same to her perfect porcelain skin. I didn't hear her screams. I felt them, pulsing in my ears and sending a chill down my spine, causing it to stiffen on instinct. My palms itched as I clenched them into fists.

"You motherfucker!" I punched him once, knocking

him out with the full weight of my armored fist, then I turned back to the girl. "Let go, little fox. I've got you."

Her fingers lifted from their grip on the boughs above us, and she slipped from the top branch into my arms like an angel falling from the heavens. I shook myself from the trance she seemed to hold over me and inspected her wounds beneath the light of the torches. The first arrow had grazed her shoulder—nothing some thread couldn't fix—while the one to her side didn't appear deep but it was still concerning. As was all the blood darkening her clothing... or what was left of it.

"Help me get her up," I ordered, throwing a leg over my horse as I gestured for James to position the girl across my lap.

The moment we made it through the castle gates, I rushed her to my private wing, far from my marital chambers. As the doctor tended to her wounds, James and I stepped into the corridor. The wind whipping against the stone walls was the only noise that could be heard on the north side. Which was how I liked it. The peace, the solitude.

"What're you doing, your highness?" James didn't often challenge me, but the bastard also didn't hesitate to point out my poor decision-making when and if it was there for public viewing.

"Have Francine tend to her," I said before adding, "And I don't know. But I... I couldn't leave her there."

"What about the queen?" he asked, as the girl continued to call out from behind the door.

"This wing is off-limits. I want you standing guard at

all times. I will deal with Agatha," I growled, my words echoing down the hall.

"Silas." James stopped himself short. "The treaty can be voided. Give her uncle something in return and be done with her. For your sake, the kingdom's... and hers." He nodded towards the bed.

"Send a rider. I want a meeting." I stalked back into the room, leaned over her slight frame, and took her hand in mine.

She was young, innocent, fragile. I wanted to protect her but not nearly as much as I wanted to destroy her— break her down to nothing, all to build her up into what I knew she could be. She bore the kind of beauty that made you stop and stare, forced you to give her attention I wasn't certain she deserved yet.

The girl made me want to give her the world while simultaneously wanting to hide her from it. From everyone. I had no idea what I was doing and felt as if I was unraveling from the inside out, indecision my inevitable undoing. But one thing remained clear.

She was mine. I just needed to handle my *wife* first. Until then, I would show my little fox who owned her, be cruel instead of kind. She needed to learn how to serve, how to submit to more than just her king and relinquish control to the man beneath the crown.

CHAPTER THREE
TILLIE

Voices filtered in and out of my subconsciousness, making me uneasy even in sleep. But when the deep timbre was close, my muscles seemed to relax—as if my body somehow recognized the man I knew as a stranger. I traveled back and forth between a state of semi-wakefulness and oblivion. And I wasn't sure which was more comforting.

I finally opened my eyes, though I was unsure how much time had passed since I'd ventured up the tree, and found sunlight streaming in through a pair of large open windows. Which were flanked by rich burgundy fabric that matched the bedding that currently surrounded me.

"Where am I?" I coughed past my dry throat before meeting a gaze that seemed to stare right through me, reach into my chest cavity, and force me to splutter out my next breath.

"Home."

Chills erupted across my skin at the sound of his

voice. "My brothers, I need…" I forced myself to sit upright, then quickly doubled over with the pain.

His large, calloused hands gripped my arms and pushed me flat on my back again while darkness appeared to dance in the depths of his eyes. I was unsure what was more startling, the fear that look ignited or the silent promises it seemed to make. I pressed my thighs together, biting my lip to silence the moans threatening to break free. Though it was evident my actions didn't go unnoticed as his piercing blue eyes lit with a new fire that threatened to burn down an entire forest.

"I'm not a man with much patience, little fox. You'll learn quickly that my demands are to be met without preamble. Now, you are to stay. In. This. Bed." He ground the words out between clenched teeth and a tight jaw.

"Please, sir. My… my brothers, they need me. They can't fend for themselves," I begged, the sharp pain in my side increasing with each ragged breath I forced through my lungs. "I mean, your highness, King Silas." I was rambling now, and I couldn't tell if it amused or irritated him.

"I like when you call me *sir*." He grinned before adding, "It's how you will address me moving forward." He leaned closer, releasing my hand while dropping his to my hip. "Now lie back and do not move. You've pulled a stitch."

"Please…" I tried again. For better or worse, when my mind was focused on a task, there was little that could dissuade me. It was a blessing and a curse in its own way, entirely dependent on the situation. And I had yet to determine what sort this was.

"Oh, little fox. Save your breath. You'll have plenty of time to beg once you're feeling up to the task." He rose to his feet, impossibly tall and wide, and loomed over me with the sort of authority that demanded my attention.

I couldn't look away even if I wanted to. His dark hair was thick and cut short to his head with a few unruly locks falling onto his forehead, accompanied by a chiseled jaw and high cheekbones. The stories told by the other girls in town didn't do him justice in either appearance or commanding presence.

"Your highness." Those two words broke the tension surrounding us and the static that clung to the air, as a man walked into the room with a large satchel slung over his shoulder and a textbook in hand. He nodded to the king, who in turn gestured to my side.

"She's torn her sutures. Repair them and then give her something to sleep. I want her quiet and compliant." He waved a dismissive hand in my direction as if I were a possession rather than a human being. Which only served to rejuvenate my insolence.

I kicked the soft blankets aside, ignoring the pain in my hip, and climbed out of the bed. King Silas turned, his eyes narrowed and a snarl curling his lips—it was evident the man wasn't used to being disobeyed but I was no loyal subject. Not to a king I didn't know and a crown I didn't respect.

I flicked my gaze to the door, where two knights stood guard, their hands firmly planted on the hilts of their swords. Then returned my focus to the man in front of me. He signaled them to relax their posturing, while I continued to eye him with the sort of disdain that was reserved for a scorned lover and not a stranger.

The physician stepped back—whether fearing my reaction or the king's remained unclear—as my fingers wrapped around a small blade that sat on the table, just within my reach. It wouldn't do much against a sword or the king's size advantage but at least I would go down fighting. I slowly maneuvered myself around the end of the bed while his eyes followed my every step with the precision of a well-practiced hunter. If it weren't for the fire in his eyes and the smirk on his face, one that told me he liked the fight, I'd have struck already.

"Even if you manage to stab me, how will you get out of the room, let alone my castle, little fox?" he taunted, but his words held little weight when my brothers' lives were in the balance. As if he could read my mind, he added, "You should be worried about yourself and not them. Your actions have consequences, girl. And I cannot wait to show you all the tricks I have up my sleeve." He took a step closer and dropped his voice. "I'll have you panting, begging for more. And less. And more again."

"I will not!" I screamed much louder than intended, but my resolve was shattering.

"Well then, show me your teeth, little fox." He smirked, beckoning me forward with a *come hither* motion.

If I were smart, more worldly than a village girl who hadn't traveled much past the boundaries of her modest shack in the woods, the crazed look on his face would've told me this was a game. He was playing with me. The threat of violence excited him, intrigued him. He wasn't a man used to being challenged. And that's exactly what this was.

But I wasn't smart. At least not in this moment. I was mad. Enraged. *Foolish.*

"And if I do, if I bite as hard as I can, what will my punishment be? Will you take me in my sleep? Force yourself on me when I'm drugged and unable to fight back?" I tried to swallow past the excitement as my thoughts took a darker turn. "Will that make you feel more like a man? A king?"

His smile dropped. My shoulders shook despite my attempts to steady them, and my eyes widened as he approached one meticulous step at a time. There was something about the calm, measured reaction that was far more terrifying than a sudden outburst. I watched on, unmoving, as my words seemed to affect him in a way I didn't know how to read. He was the king—surely he'd take what he wanted, when he wanted it. And I was nothing. No one. His property in so many more ways than one.

"Oh, little fox. I don't need to take you in your sleep to feel like a man. Quite the opposite really. I want to feel the way you struggle beneath me, hear your muffled pleas, savor the way your body reacts to me while your mind tries to wrap around the defeat. I want you conscious for all of it. Because I never want you to forget who did that to you." Then he lunged forward. I screamed and struck out with the blade.

He caught my wrist in enough time to turn the tip from his stomach so that it pierced his arm instead. He didn't flinch. He barely registered the fact that I'd breached his leather sleeve and punctured flesh as blood pooled around the open wound, trailed down his wrist, and dripped onto the floor. The first droplet splattered on the ground like the beating of a drum breaking the silence. His grip on my wrist was tight but not yet punishing, a warning before he applied pressure to a spot that forced my fingers to loosen their hold and the knife to clank against the stone floor.

I tried to fight him off, twist in his grip, but all I did was slam my open wound into his hip, his much larger frame hard and unyielding. I looked up to see him watching me with some sort of primal satisfaction. "Fucking perfect," he growled low in his throat before leaning down to bite my earlobe. "Those eyes are like pools of honey, delicious, sweet, and deadly when they want to be."

My fight gave out. It was foolish of me to think I had a chance anyway. The man overpowered me with a flick of his wrist and a castle filled with guards. My legs gave out, exhaustion regaining its hold on my useless limbs. And before I knew what was happening, his arms were closing around me, scooping me up, and depositing me on the bed once again. Our eyes locked, and it was as if nothing else—no one else mattered—despite our audience. I barely registered anything outside of this man and his all-consuming presence. He had to be at least ten years my senior and yet I felt like I knew him all my life. As if something inherent linked us, and it teetered between hatred and need.

He pushed back a sweat-ladened strand of my blonde hair, staring as if he were interring me into his memory.

And a sudden wave of disgust washed over me. At myself. At him. At the difference in our social stature. I didn't have long to consider the worlds that separated us before he rose to his feet and turned his back on me.

"Lock her down. I don't want her out of that bed."

The guards charged forward as the physician pinned me to the mattress by my shoulders. My brain was clouded by a mixture of pain, lust, and confusion. And by the time I realized what was happening, it was too late. The guards made quick work of attaching metal shackles to my ankles and connecting them to the foot of the bed.

I wanted to thrash, cry, fight and beg. But their grips were impenetrable and the metal was unrelenting. I would only hurt myself and lessen my chances of ever escaping the palace that had become my prison. That being said, I wouldn't make it pleasant for them either. I drew saliva from the depths of my throat and spat it in their direction, yelling out every insult that came to mind, all the words my father offered over the years, and repeated them in a slew of less-than-ladylike expletives. Till I was left panting and they were left aggravated by my theatrics.

I sucked in a sharp breath just as liquid was poured down my throat and my nose covered so that I was forced to swallow the concoction. It didn't take long for the effects to take hold as my brain grew foggy and a warm sensation traveled up from my stomach to the base of my neck. As everything else around me dimmed, I could hear his laughter echo off the walls.

King Silas stood between the two posts, at my feet, watching me with unrestrained amusement twinkling in his eyes. He tugged on my ankle straps, a crude smile marring his features as he demonstrated that I had no chance of escape.

"You cannot stretch her arms too wide or the wound will begin to ooze again," the physician instructed.

"James," King Silas muttered. "Add a collar to her neck—and be sure to attach it to the headboard."

"What?" I hissed or maybe slurred. I couldn't be sure honestly. "No! You almost killed me once. Please don't add this to your list of travesties against my family."

"He was dealt with." I could only assume he meant the archer as the king pulled my hair back from my neck, a leather collar with a silver hook in his hand. "Get used to this, little fox. You're my pet now." Then he made quick work of tightening the contraption around my throat before the makeshift hook was tethered in place. King Silas gave the chain a few hasty tugs. Seemingly satisfied, he pulled a small lock from his pocket and secured me in place. "See? A gilded cage can come in many forms. This is just one of them, sweet girl." Then, because of course he liked his games, the bastard reached under his shirt and presented a chain with a large ruby and a key attached. He hung it over the top of the bed, directly above my head. "That is your freedom... if only you could reach out and take it."

He smirked down at me like the cat who got the cream, and I wanted nothing more than to claw his eyes out and feed them to him on his finest china. But that thought was irrational, seeing as I could barely lift my arms at this point, let alone do any real damage in my current state.

Like he said, I was his pet. At his mercy, and something told me no matter how much I fought, he never planned to let me go.

"I want this door locked at all times," he ordered. "Only you, Francine, and the physician may enter without my explicit permission."

"Yes, your highness." One of the men stared at me with a softness I didn't expect. "Rest easy, dear." His eyes were kind, which was disarming, especially as I wanted nothing more than to hate him.

"Tillie," I muttered, my lashes growing heavy. When everyone seemed to stare at me, appearing confused by my statement, I added, "Not *dear*, Tillie."

"Tillie. I like that." King Silas's voice continued to send goosebumps down my spine, even as I willed my body to remain unaffected. Darkness was on the horizon as I heard the audible creaking that told me the door was opened.

"There you are, husband. I've been looking all over for you." It was a woman's voice. The queen, or so I could only assume.

"What are you doing in my wing, Agatha?" King Silas growled in response.

"What is going on in there?" the woman questioned and the door slammed shut, startling me despite the warmth surrounding my body and making it impossible to care about anything other than surrendering to it.

"Sleep, dear—*Tillie*. We won't let her get to you," the kind man whispered as if it were a vow, and I didn't miss the hint of hatred I felt overlying his mention of the queen.

The leather collar constricted my airflow and made it difficult to breathe, swallow, speak... But it did something else too. Elicited a feeling I didn't quite recognize but one I wasn't entirely against exploring. Especially if it helped keep me alive long enough to ensure my brothers were cared for.

I needed to be less impulsive. Think smarter. Have more tact. If the king wanted me to please him, I would do everything in my power to do that. To satisfy his sick obsession with the *village girl* or whatever it was I represented to him. I would earn his favor, play his games, and resign myself to my fate—as long as he promised to protect my brothers in return.

Truth be told, I was a slave long before I was collared to this bed. I was held captive by a life that wasn't of my choosing, forced to submit to a man who didn't deserve the title of father, controlled by a world that told us women were inferior. So, really, while my surroundings were certainly more opulent, not much else had changed.

I was as much caged in this life as I was in my former one. At least for now...

CHAPTER FOUR
TILLIE

I startled awake, choking as the collar tightened around my throat like five ethereal fingers constricting my airway. It served as a little reminder of his presence. That he was here in some form or another, watching me.

"Easy dear," a soft, feminine voice cooed. "If you make too much noise, they'll try to put you to sleep again." Kind brown eyes peered down at me, her gray hair swept into a tight bun while her body was clothed in the same brown dress as the other palace servant women.

"How long have I been asleep?" I asked, coughing around the dryness clawing at my throat. She moved quickly, helping me sip a glass of water.

"Six days," she whispered.

"What?" I shouted, sputtering when the collar pulled tighter. The pain was gone from my stomach and shoulder, more of a distant ache. Though my legs and back were stiff, begging me to stretch the muscles and release the tension.

"Shall I call the king?" The king's guard, James if I recalled correctly, suddenly appeared at my feet.

"No, no. She's fine. She's going back to sleep, aren't you, dear?" The woman glared at me with wide eyes, urging me to comply, and I forced myself to play along, my lashes fluttering closed again.

"You're both terrible liars," James muttered, cursing under his breath when I heard what sounded like the smack of skin on skin. I could only assume she slapped him. A smile tugged at my lips with the thought.

"He's gone, dear. I'm Francine. How do you feel?" Her smile was kind and sincere, comforting, like her voice.

"Horrible," I huffed, shifting awkwardly as the chains clanked against the bedrails, before relenting. "Better than I'd expect, all things considered."

"Yes, the king..." She paused and turned her back to me. "He's been coming nightly to help stretch your legs." The woman's face was flushed when she peered at me from over her shoulder.

"He's been coming in here?" I gasped, appalled by the idea of him being so close when I was so vulnerable. Though I shouldn't be shocked. The man made his intentions very clear. I was his for the taking. His pet, as I recalled him telling me. She nodded, her hands making quick work of changing my bandages until I asked the next question. "Why am I here, Francine?"

"I have no idea, dear." She glanced at the door, obviously hesitant to speak freely. "But I must warn you. I haven't seen him act this way since before he married the queen. He's been miserable, closed off, constantly leaving the castle to deal with trivial things that his men are meant to handle in his stead."

"My... my father owed a debt to the crown," I whispered in cryptic explanation. No more needed to be said as a single tear fell down my cheek.

Francine wiped at my face. "I know, dear. I'm unsure what he plans to do with you. But he's never stolen some unsuspecting woman from her home and felt the need to *protect* her." I know she meant the words to be comforting; however, they were anything but.

Francine stared at the door, uncertainty filling the silence between us, until it burst open as if he'd been summoned from the depths of hell and the devil appeared.

The king eyed me with a look I couldn't decipher while Francine quickly tucked the covers back in place and exited without another word. King Silas kept his gaze locked on mine with each step he took, and when I scowled, he smiled. I rattled the chains at my feet, in a fit of fury and indecipherable lust. Which only made the bastard chuckle.

"How are we feeling, little fox?" He stood within arm's reach now—if my arms could reach out—and my nostrils filled with the floral scent of soap, indicating he'd recently bathed.

"Like I've been pinned to a bed and slept for six days," I spat between clenched teeth, refusing to show him how his proximity was overwhelming my senses, enlivening my every nerve ending in a way a captive shouldn't react to her captor.

"Do you need a few more days to correct that attitude?" His muscular arms crossed over his chest, as he quirked a brow, daring me to fight him. Defy him. Give him a reason to reprimand me. "I've been very kind to you, little fox. Giving you time to heal before collecting on your father's debts. You should be grateful for my generosity, considering all you owe."

It was the voice—that deep, raspy baritone—that rattled my inner beast, one that hadn't existed before him. Not in wanton form anyway. The king looked at me with a ferocity that should leave me trembling, but in reality, it left me curious. Needy. A feeling I despised. A sudden burst of anger took over me before I could stop it.

"You must be proud of yourself, stealing a child in the middle of the night to repay the debt of a father. A life so utterly insignificant when compared to your coffers," I growled, wincing when he stepped closer.

"There is nothing childish about you, Tillie."

A new chill ran down my spine when my name dripped from his full lips. They were so inviting. I wanted a taste, regardless of the poison they promised. His eyes slowly traveled the length of my body, leaving me feeling exposed despite the layers of fabric between us.

"I need to get out of this bed," I said, his demeanor hardening at my challenge.

"You are aware that I am historically the most powerful and successful ruler in this country, correct?" he asked but I didn't dare respond. "I do *not* take orders from anyone. Especially you. Especially in the bedroom."

"I... I..." I stammered, knowing what he wanted, why he was here, while hating and loving the idea of him actually following through. "Please... please release me." The words tasted bitter on my tongue but I took note of how my submission moved him. He liked to hear me beg. It did something to him, something almost as moving as my fight.

If I wanted to survive this, I needed to adapt, force him to fall at my feet. Make him think he was winning, long after he had already lost.

"And if I do, if I release you..." He knelt on the bed, his wide shoulders blocking the sunlight while leaving me with no option but to stare into those piercing blue eyes. "What will you give me in return?" The devil was tempting me, and I wouldn't falter.

"What do you want?" It came out as a whisper, a slow red heat creeping up my neck as I awaited his reply.

"Oh, little fox. You shouldn't ask questions you don't want answers to."

I waited to hear what he would ask of me, but instead of explaining further, he unhooked my ankles—my neck still in the collar. My knees parted of their own accord, the duvet shifting and my bare legs exposing themselves. The king's greedy eyes traveled up the length of my thighs, stopping where the blankets maintained some semblance of modesty. But it was then that I realized something else...

"Am I naked?" I shouted, my arms shifting under the sheets to grope at my bare breasts.

"Naked and bathed," he commented, his eyes now focused on my face. "I wanted you scrubbed clean, to leave your old life at the bottom of that bath water." His chest was inches from mine, as his fingers nimbly disconnected my collar from the headboard. He tugged me forward, forcing my eyes to flick down and take in the leash-like chain in his grip.

"My old life?" I didn't know how he meant for his words to land, but none of them sat well with me. "I'm one of your people. My poverty, my filth, is a reflection of you as a ruler. After my father's accident and my mother's death, we had barely enough to survive. Yet, you came. Knocking on our door, collecting your debts, your taxes. Giving little care for our survival, my family's welfare, all so that you could live a life of lux—" I stopped speaking at his sudden movement, the sound of his growl, his face a breath away from mine.

"Did I force your father to drink away the assistance *my* crown gave him? Money I earned with the blood on my hands, the dirt under my feed, the swing of my sword, to ensure our borders were protected, our country prosperous? *No.* Did I force your father to refuse the jobs he found beneath him in the marketplace? *Also, no.*" His chest was heaving, his features contorted by rage. "Your unfortunate circumstances were his doing, not mine. And I will not apologize for the willful actions of another man."

He loomed over me, unrelenting and unconcerned by the fear he was instilling. I was meant to please him, not piss him off. His face was glacial as he read my silent questions. I had no idea what jobs he was speaking of, what money my father had squandered away.

"You didn't know." He sat back on his heels, forcing distance between us while maintaining his grip on my leash—both literally and metaphorically. This man had me trapped. "I offer money, jobs, to people like your father, those who have lost a spouse by no fault of their own. But we do not force them to take the help. He was offered a job and his pay was given upfront, but he didn't do the work."

I was at a loss for words. I'd spent countless hours so angry at this man and his new queen, flaunting their affluence and turning their backs on their people. If what he was saying was true, then it was my father who was at fault. Not the crown. And my anger had been misplaced all this time.

"Up." King Silas tugged on the leash, forcing me to stumble to the edge of the bed. Which was more of an awkward roll since my limbs hadn't gotten the message that they were free to move about. Once he was standing to his full height, he extended his free hand and tugged me forward so I had no choice but to fall against his chest. "Despite your claims, I still have yet to find anything childish about you." His voice sounded amused. I chanced a glance at him to find he wasn't looking at my face.

"You bastard!" I tucked one arm across my breasts while attempting to use the other to grab the duvet. However, he refused to allow me any semblance of modesty as he tugged me forward once again. My legs shook but thankfully didn't crumble as I followed him. He'd already seen every part of my body, so I dropped my arms and fought him instead. Using both hands, I grabbed hold of the makeshift leash and tugged in like, hoping to at least force him to stumble a step. He didn't move, his muscles taut and his stance wide as he watched me flop around like a hapless fish.

I lifted a palm, looking to slap him instead. He was faster than a man his size should be, catching my wrist before I had a chance to make contact. His look was feral as he yanked me to my knees in front of him. The action was meant to demonstrate his point. I was beneath him, a servant to an unyielding master.

"I do *not* advise you to try that again. Like I've said, Tillie, I've been extremely kind to you. I could've very easily let you die in those woods or sent you to my dungeon. Instead, I'm offering you luxury, protection, pleasure unlike anything you've ever dreamed of having."

Ah, so that's it. The bastard had a savior complex. He acted as if stealing me from my family in the middle of the night was an act of utmost benevolence, rather than the whim of a greedy king wanting to have his way with a poor village girl.

"Thank you, *sir*." The words dripped from my mouth with disdain.

"Well, I guess you need to be taught a lesson." He smiled at me, his enjoyment genuine as he dragged me to the other side of the room.

King Silas sat down on a long, velvet sofa with ornate designs carved into the wood. A tall candelabra stood in the corner behind him, giving his profile an eerie glow. Books and other odds and ends were strewn around the small table, but I was too focused on his penetrating stare. He tugged the chain harder, and my hands flew out in front of me, my open palms landing on his lap as I fell between his thighs. My eyes went wide as realization settled into my bones. I was unsullied, having never known the touch of a man. The sort I was meant to hold on to till marriage. But even I knew what he wanted as I knelt before him, my eyes watching him twitch in his seat. I felt like my heart was in my throat as I tried to swallow past my nerves.

Leaning forward, King Silas pulled my face until it was inches from his. "What kind of lesson do you want, little fox?" He was taunting me, enjoying my fear, feeding off it. "I can smell the innocence dripping off you, which tells me I won't enjoy whatever it is you try to give me right now. But you'll learn. I'll teach you. I'll mold you into the perfect pupil, little Tillie."

My jaw dropped at the crude nature of his words. A messed-up part of me wanted to challenge him, to reach forward and pull his thick length free, make him crumble in my hands. His eyes lit with fire as if he could sense my obstinance, forcing me to bite my lip and sit back on my heels.

"That courage came and went very quickly." He laughed, and I hated myself for being so easily read. "Want to give it a try?" He grabbed his erection. It was hard, straining, far larger than I imagined a man to be.

"I'd rather you kill me now," I gulped.

"I have no desire to end your life, little fox. In fact, I look forward to breaking you down to nothing and rebuilding you into the image of my perfect little pet." The smug bastard tucked a stray blonde curl of my hair behind my ear.

Our eyes remained locked in a silent stare-off, a mix

of heated glares and open loathing. Then he leaned closer still. And at first, I thought he was going to kiss me. And God help me, I really, really wanted him to. The attraction between us was undeniable and I felt moronic as I knelt before him both hating him and needing him in a way I didn't know to be possible. But his lips never met mine. Instead, he pulled me up and placed me across his lap, the leash wrapped tightly around his fist, forcing my cheek to his thigh. My right arm was pinned between our bodies while my left tried to gain purchase on the ground to shove him off. To no avail. My behind was in the air and his free hand was gently stroking from one cheek to another. My face burned with embarrassment as the tightness of the collar had me gasping for air.

"The most amusing part of all of this, little fox? You fight your body's natural reaction to me. But you can't hide it. Not from me, especially not like this." His hand pressed on my thigh, forcing my legs to part, as his hand trailed down to my folds, my arousal coating his fingertips. "I knew it the moment I saw you on that roof, lying there like a fallen angel waiting to be collected. You were made for me."

"Please stop," I whimpered, unsure if I hated the sensation or merely hated the fact that I loved it.

"Do you really want me to stop? Stop giving your body what it swants... from me." The insufferable bastard was grinning again, mocking me.

"Let me go!" I screamed, thrashing my legs and flailing around like a petulant child. Until I cried out in shock at the bite of pain ricocheting across my backside, his hand slapping from one cheek to another. Each hit felt like fire blazing across my skin. The bastard was relentless in his assault. I hated that, as much as it hurt, my arousal was dripping down my thighs. My skin burned and soon my throat was sore from the strain of crying out. I lost count after ten whacks to each side—the pain was too much. Too intense. Too biting. Too... pleasing in an odd way.

I hadn't realized that the pressure on my neck was gone until I sucked in a breath and my lungs filled with air once more. King Silas picked me up in his arms as he rose to his feet and gently placed me on the bed, the soft duvet feeling like razor blades against my raw backside. He stared down at me with desire flooding his eyes, but something else lurked behind it. He wiped away one of my tears, growling as he turned to walk away.

I was still on my back, my legs spread as I put pressure on my shoulders and lifted my ass in the air. I watched my captor stalk towards the door before the rattle of my chains seemed to halt his exit. My neck pulled against the collar as his strong hands gripped my knees and shoved them apart, causing my hips to drop to the mattress. The pain didn't last long as something warm and wet latched on to my folds. My desire increased as I looked down at Silas, propped up on his elbows with his face buried between my thighs. He licked and sucked, tasted and explored, like I was a feast and he was a man starved.

Strange noises filled the room and it took me a moment to realize they were coming from me as I chased the high that was threatening to shatter my resolve. His appreciative growls urged me to let go, to crumble beneath him. My brain no longer registered that I hated him, that I was *his* prisoner. At this moment, the only thing holding me captive was my need and the release that was promised on the tip of his tongue.

He lifted his head, my arousal glistening along his lips as he tugged the leash harder, my core tightening at the pinch of pain. He kissed the apex of my thighs. "You will look at me when you come," he commanded, waiting for my nod of understanding before he returned to the task at hand.

"Please. Please, sir," I begged, feeling myself on the edge of... *something*. I just needed a little more *I didn't know what* to get me there.

"Silas. You will call me Silas. Not sir, not your highness, and nothing between. Do you understand me, girl?"

I mumbled incoherently. Though he appeared less than pleased by the lack of a proper response, he must have deemed it sufficient, because he continued teasing me with several long strokes of his wide tongue. I didn't even feel the pain on my backside anymore. My brain was supercharged, filled with images of me shattering under this man, of giving up all parts of myself to him. He could freely take whatever he wanted as long as this never stopped. I growled in frustration, so close to the euphoria he promised, and yet I couldn't reach it. Whatever it was. But I knew I wanted it.

"Need something more, little fox?" His calloused fingertips trailed up my waist, along the curve of my hip to my chest, as he continued licking. Reaching my hardened nipple, he squeezed one then the other, the delicious pain pushing me closer. "Look at me."

My neck snapped up at his command. Silas yanked the collar aside, gripping my neck and closing off my airway. My body shook, the pain in my nipples increased, and my core tightened. Clenched. Fluttered in a way I didn't know possible. I gurgled behind his hold on my throat and shattered into my orgasm. I screamed a mess of unintelligible things—gasps, pleas, expletives, and moans. I was lost, floating in the waves of pleasure that crashed around me and threatened to devour me whole.

His much larger frame leaned over my body, his erection pushing against the seam of his trousers as it rested above my entrance. My eyes were large with questions, my mind wondering what he planned to do next. But then he dropped his heavy weight on top of me and kissed me breathless, while the taste of myself on his lips acted as the sweetest poison. Clearing my thoughts, then clouding them with something else. He sat back on his heels, shifting down the bed and standing tall. I tried craning my neck, only to stop when the collar pulled tight. Tilting my head back, I realized that the kiss was anything but innocent. My neck and legs were shackled once more. This time, I had no blanket to cover me as he perused every vulnerable inch of my anatomy, like a physician trying to determine where to make the first incision.

"Lessons can involve pain. They can also involve pleasure. Or they can be a mixture of both. You will behave in a way I see fit or your pain will *not* result in pleasure. Learn fast, little fox. I control everything and that most certainly means you." He adjusted himself in his trousers, my eyes snapping to the movement as he responded with a grin. "I told you you'd beg me for it."

And he was right. Yet there was more to it than that. I wasn't the only one suffering. We were both dying of need—a point that was made more evident as he stormed from the room in a fit of apparent rage.

CHAPTER FIVE
TILLIE

"Oh my." Francine's soft voice had my lashes fluttering open. Which was starting to become a frequent occurrence. Being drugged, only to wake to someone new standing in the room. It was an eerie feeling, knowing that no matter what, I was being watched.

The sun was bursting through the windows once again, meaning that another day had passed in my semi-conscious state. My backside was sore and raw, my legs were still shackled, and the collar was breaking open my skin. I was unsure how much longer I would be able to tolerate the confinement. The pain. I was emotionally depleted and needed to relieve myself. My cries for help had gone unnoticed, until I succumbed to exhaustion. And now, hours later, I was in agony.

I wanted to be strong, to come out on top of all this. But after the events of last night set in, I was left with the unsettling realization that my resolve was bravado more than anything else. I wasn't going to survive *him*. If a part of me did, she wouldn't resemble the same woman who was carried into this castle. That night that felt like a lifetime ago now.

"Water, please," I croaked.

"Here." Francine's face popped into my line of sight, and I could see the wrinkles of concern traveling across her forehead. She tried to tilt a gold chalice towards my lips, but I couldn't lift my neck to help her. Instead, the crisp water spilled out the sides and dropped down my chin. "Oh no." She tugged on the chains around my ankles, but even I could see they were locked in place by a key.

A second later, the blanket was covering me again and the pitter-patter of feet fled out the door. I wanted to cry, beg Francine not to leave me. I had to go so badly I was close to wetting myself. I was unsure the last time I ate, and those few droplets of water served to tease rather than refresh my tastebuds.

"Please," I cried out again, only to realize my pleas would continue to fall on deaf ears. I had been holding it in for hours. The urge to urinate on the bed was humiliating but I was seconds away from not having another option.

"She's bleeding, she's dehydrated, and probably needs to... to..." I could hear Francine yelling on the other side of the door.

"And I told you he has the key! What do you expect me to do, exactly?" James huffed, clearly exasperated— though I couldn't be sure what was the tipping point.

"Please, please, please!" I didn't care how pathetic I sounded at this point.

"Then get him!" Francine ran back into the room, her cheeks flush and her movements frenzied.

I choked on a sob as the older woman tried to calm me, but it was too late. My body broke and I urinated all over the covers, myself, and my dignity.

"It's okay, dear. None of this is your fault," she cooed. Her soft hands cupping my cheeks were a sweet relief, as the warmth running down my thighs and moistening the sheets beneath left a cold chill in its wake. "Get out!" Francine hissed, and if I weren't sulking in my degradation, I would have laughed at the scene playing out in front of me as the pint-sized woman shoved a man twice her bulk out the door.

"What is the meaning of all this?" King Silas suddenly appeared at the end of the bed. I hadn't even heard him enter the room. But, sure enough, there he stood... like a creature that had manifested from my nightmares. Only it was daylight and I knew I wasn't dreaming.

"Give me the key!" Francine shoved her open palm in his direction, and I could tell even the king was startled at the woman's tone. "Now! You've already embarrassed her enough!"

"Watch yourself, Francine. This is none of your concern." He crossed his arms over his chest, as if daring her to argue.

"You bet your sweet arse it is." She pointed towards my feet, then to the key around his neck. The king's gaze slowly followed the action. "The girl's been trapped here for hours because you disappeared from the castle."

His brows furrowed. His expression seemed haunted

as his eyes darted between the two of us. I dropped my gaze. I couldn't meet his stare, knowing I had soiled the sheets. It didn't matter that it hadn't been my fault. It didn't matter that it was *his*. There was just something dehumanizing about being treated like a caged animal. Francine put her hands on her hips, waiting for Silas to comply.

"Who left you like this?" he ground out, and I was certain it was a trick question. When I didn't immediately answer, he barked louder. "Tell me, Tillie, now."

"Y-you," I coughed out, my voice raspy and my throat dry to the point I could taste copper. "Af-after we... after we... then you left..." I admitted cryptically, my eyes glued to the ceiling. I couldn't face him. I couldn't face any of them. Not like this.

"No, I didn't," he grunted, though there was a hint of hesitance underlying his words, as he turned to Francine for what I could only guess was an explanation.

"James came to get me when she was crying and pleading to... Well, that part doesn't matter." Francine's petite frame was vibrating with her barely contained rage as she reached a hand out for the key once more.

"Leave," he clipped, but her feet remained rooted in place. "I will make this right. Now leave, Francine."

"No. No. Please, I need her help." I could hardly lift my head, the strain on my neck urging me not to move.

"She... Your highness, please. Let me look after her first..." Francine tried again, but he dismissed her with a look that told the elderly woman she was walking on thin ice. And she was seconds from drowning. I could see the indecision on her face, the inner battle she was fighting within herself. But disobedience meant treason and treason meant death—if Silas decided to push the issue.

I couldn't help but seethe at the thought. This was all because of *him*. The chains, the marks and bruises marring my skin, the dampness of the sheets, the ache in my core—for more than one reason. It was all his doing. And I hated him for it. I hated him as much as part of me didn't. The feeling was both confusing and irritating.

The chains at my feet rustled, as I watched Silas maneuver around the bed until he was close enough to lean across my chest and free my leash from the wall. Regret was written all over his face. He tried to hide it with a scowl but I could read him better than my favorite storybook.

"Water, please." I licked my dry lips as he lifted my head to place an extra pillow underneath it. Then he wandered over to the table, grabbed the chalice, and removed my collar so that I could drink freely.

"Let's feed you." He grabbed the blanket, but I held tight to the fabric, refusing to let him humiliate me further. "Tillie. Enough!" He tugged harder, and my weakened hands were forced to loosen their grip.

I slapped my hands over my eyes, curled in on myself, and hid from his judgmental gaze. But I could still feel his presence, the weight of his gaze, the sound of his breaths.

"Tillie, look at me," he ordered, and I did my best to pretend the man didn't exist. It was childish, I knew. But seeing as that's exactly how I was being treated, it seemed fitting. "Tillie!" he yelled, and I startled at the sound. He was back at my side, tugging my hands from my face. "Move your hands, Tillie," he commanded again, louder this time, before craning his neck and calling out for James. Seconds later, the door was flung open and the man in question stumbled inside. "Have Francine run a warm bath in my chambers, then tell the kitchen staff to prepare a simple broth and a loaf of bread."

No more words were exchanged as the door clicked closed before I could feel the heat of Silas's arm pulling me to his chest.

"Don't!" I cried out, my hands dropping and my eyes springing open. "Don't, please, sir. Don't touch me. I... I didn't mean to... Please!" I was begging now. Not that it mattered. It was already too late for me to salvage my pride.

"It was my fault, Tillie. Not yours." He sighed, and if I didn't know better, I would have sworn a flash of remorse softened his features. As quickly as it appeared, it was tucked away again. Like a lost moment in time I could never get back.

In two long strides, Silas carried me to the door and it opened almost as if by magic. James was standing on the other side. He dropped his gaze to the stone floor and allowed us to pass. Despite my growing animosity for the man who held me, I turned into his embrace, shielding myself from any onlookers who may be lurking in the halls, while my humiliation sat on open display for all those within the castle walls to see.

It wasn't long before I found myself in another larger, more opulent bedchamber. With a bronze tub in the center and a piece of cloth draped across the lip. The steam drifted up like two arms reaching towards the heavens while the scent of floral soap thickened the air. Francine was busy rushing around, gathering various items from different corners of the room.

Moving slowly and with a tenderness I never would have assumed a king—especially this one—could exude, Silas placed me into the warm water. My arms clung to his neck as my sore muscles adjusted to the temperature. I whimpered when steam caressed the broken skin on my backside, biting my lip to hold back the sob, and clawed at his shoulders, wanting him to pull me out. But he pressed his mouth to my ear and whispered soft encouragements as he continued to lower me into the rippling pool.

I sat back and allowed the warmth to consume me, heat my skin down to my bones. Francine handed the king another glass of water before disappearing through the door. Once we were alone, I tried reaching for the cup but he refused to let me have it, tipping the lip towards my mouth instead. I closed my eyes and took small, tentative sips to appease my aching throat. He kept going until the cup was empty while I kept my gaze focused on anything but him.

"Why won't you look at me?" His words echoed off the stone walls, shrouding me with a presence I couldn't avoid, no matter how hard I tried. I suppose, for a man of his size, that was normal.

I didn't answer, nor did I dare to open my eyes. Hiding behind my lids offered me some semblance of peace. He moved around the tub, and without even trying, I could feel the weight of his gaze trailing my skin, memorizing every dip and crevice, consuming me in a way that didn't seem possible at a distance. All this while the warmth of the bath water washed away the sins he'd forced onto my body and relaxed my mind for what felt like the first time in months. I could sense myself drifting off to sleep, despite the monster lurking in my midst.

I was already in hell, so why not embrace the slow burn?

"Tillie!" He startled me awake, reaching out to tug me upright as I sucked in a large gulp of water. My arms and legs flailed until I gained purchase on the sides of the tub. My legs separated and I pushed myself backwards, slapping his hands away from my breasts as I righted myself once more. His glare was directed at me, the prior stoicism replaced by anger.

Good, because I was angry too.

"Oh, dear." Francine gasped when she walked into the room with a large bowl on a silver tray. I could smell the broth across the open space, and my stomach growled in response.

"Put the tray on the table." Silas gestured to his left while his menacing scowl remained focused on me. When Francine didn't immediately move, his neck snapped in her direction. "Leave."

"Small sips." Francine's voice automatically softened when she spoke to me, her eyes kind and warm. Until she turned to Silas, her expression like stone before she darted from the room at his behest.

Once I felt more like myself, I planned to take a page out of Francine's book and give the bastard a piece of my mind too. He'd already proven he was a barbaric monster, so why shouldn't he be treated like one? It would pale in comparison to how he was treating me. But a little payback would feel good at the very least.

Silas pulled the table closer to the tub, the tiny spoon in his large grasp a comical sight. Holding it to my lips, he stared down at me with such intensity I didn't know what to make of it. When I refused to open my mouth, he growled.

"I doubt you ate much before you got here, so stop being stubborn." He chuckled when I didn't move and turned my head away instead. I would sit in this tub until the water turned cold, until my skin wrinkled beyond recognition and hyperthermia took over. "Tillie." He hissed my name—clearly the amusement had worn off.

"Leave it. I can do it myself." I sank further into the water.

"You will eat now, from me, or not at all." He nodded with the declaration, which had my glare burning a hole through his forehead.

If only I could do real damage...

"Apparently I had to destroy your expensive bedding before you thought about returning to free me from my chains. Why not add starvation to the list of atrocities you feel it necessary to bestow upon me?" I smacked the spoon from my face, enjoying the sound of the metal clattering across the floor.

"That... wasn't my intention," he started, but I cut him off.

I leaned forward so that his face was but a breath

away. "Not your intention... It wasn't your intention to leave me strapped to your bed, covered in my own urine, screaming for help that wouldn't come? Begging death to swallow me whole as each hour passed?" I raised a brow, daring him to argue otherwise.

"I informed James to release you shortly after I left. Shortly after..."

If I didn't know better, I'd say the man was at a loss for words.

"Shortly after you took something that wasn't yours for the taking?" Pulling myself up from the tub, I enjoyed the way his greedy eyes watched the water drip down my naked body.

"It *was* mine to take because you are *mine*. Something you would do well to remember. Sooner rather than later." He loomed over me, but I refused to back down. Humiliation had steeled my spine. There was no farther to fall. No disgrace that served to hold me back any longer. "What part of *you are my repayment for your father's debts* did you not understand?" he added on a hiss, his teeth grating and his jaw clicking with the action.

"I was aware of my purpose, of what I am to you. I was just unaware how crude and savage *my* king could be." My chest was heaving as his eyes remained glued to every inch of my smooth flesh. "I heard of your ruthlessness on the battlefield, but as your *possession,* I figured I deserved better. As a human being, I know I do. But I see my mistake now. I see how my position in life makes me undeserving of even the most basic of necessities."

"Tillie..." He wiped a heavy hand down his face, his

brows furrowed in frustration... and perhaps something else. Grief?

"What would you like, *my king*?" I waved a hand up and down my naked form, like an offering to some unfit god. A beast, capable of tearing me limb from limb, yet I refused to tremble beneath his gaze, my own unwavering. Defiant. "I am yours, your highness. To do with as you please, *remember*?" I knew I was pushing his buttons, digging my own grave and waiting for the dirt to rain hell upon me. But at this point, I had nothing else to hold on to except my anger. And it was pulsing in my veins, driving my every word and action.

"Sit down, now." His tone told me he wasn't playing games, yet I waited several moments before doing as I was told. "Small. Sips," he commanded.

My lips wrapped around the spoon, the flavorful liquid exploding on my tongue as I pulled back and swallowed. Before I could stop myself, a cathartic moan escaped from the depths of my chest. Opening my eyes again, I reveled in the sight in front of me. The desire I saw staring back. He'd taken my innocence and in the process created a monster. A girl who just now realized that femininity was a gift—a newfound power—and not a curse.

Those intense blue eyes had morphed into thunderous clouds, holding back lightning bolts just waiting to strike me down where I sat. The quick rise and fall of his chest, the bulge in his pants, it all told me I was on to something. Coming into my own quicker than he realized I would. I *could*.

But that was what happened when you were a

survivor. He'd thrown me into uncharted waters, expecting me to drown. But it was sink or swim. And I would paddle like hell until I pulled myself to shore and faced my demons head-on.

I played up my moans, stopping him with a raise of my hand as my stomach debated on whether or not it was appeased.

"I need you to know something..." Silas focused on the wall behind my head, refusing to meet my gaze. "I didn't expect the other night... I mean, James was instructed to... I didn't know that I had the key. For that, I apologize." Then his eyes flicked back to me, as if he could pin me in place, hold me hostage without ever lifting a finger. Tether me with invisible restraints, nearly as tangible as the ones we'd left behind.

"That must have been painful. It looked it anyway... *if* it was sincere," I deadpanned, swishing the water around with my feet. His only response was a strange noise that rose from the back of his throat.

This was almost too easy if I really thought about it. He had to force himself to leave last night. I had no doubt if he really wanted to let loose, he wouldn't hold back. I needed to keep my wits about me, to tip the scale in my favor without allowing him to realize it was even happening.

"This is nice," I cooed, tilting my head towards the water while peering up at him with what I could only assume were doe eyes.

I moaned again, enjoying the way the soap ran swiftly across my body while plucking and playing with my hardened nipples. Throwing my head back, I got lost in the rhythm as my hands stroked, a small fire igniting between my thighs. My lips parted. I panted out a breath and switched positions in the tub, needing a release I had yet to find on my own.

"Stop that," he ordered, but I kept my eyes closed and ignored him. "I said stop it."

My lashes fluttered open, my mouth still wide as my tongue traced along my bottom lip, curling into a smile when his body tensed. My every nerve ending thrummed to life, chasing the high that threatened to break me from the inside out. My breathing increased. I was close. To that feeling. That euphoria he gave me. And I was thoroughly enjoying watching the way he tried to hold himself back. His hands gripped the sides of the tub, his muscles tight and bulging. My fingers stroked and explored between my legs, shaky and unseasoned. Naïve but determined. A dangerous combination when it came to playing with fire. I was so close and yet so far away.

"I need you," I whined, despite myself.

"Tillie..." he growled, menace dripping from his full lips.

"Please, *sir*." I was toying with him now, again, but he owed me this. "Touch me."

When he continued to stare at me, I pushed up on shaky legs, water cascading down my naked body as I positioned myself on the edge of the tub. I lifted my left leg to the side, giving him a full view of my entrance. My fingers sank into my warm opening, moving in and out the way I remembered him doing last night. I teetered so close to bliss, but frustration had tears forming at the corners of my eyes. I was missing something...

"Now, when I actually need you... *now* is when you find restraint," I goaded him, urging his anger to rise to the surface.

One minute he was standing at a distance, the next he pounced with a near animalistic stealth. His harsh grip seized my arms and he lifted me from the tub, practically tossing me into a large chair. He ripped his shirt over his head and dropped to his knees before I realized what he was doing. And there was something intoxicating about the sound of his weight hitting the floor, watching him lower himself before me.

"You don't command me. I am giving you this as an apology... for last night. That won't happen again, I promise you. And neither will *this*." He tossed my legs over his shoulders, biting down on my thighs and threatening to dismantle the walls I was trying to build. "You are not the one to dictate what I do and when."

I cried out in ecstasy as his warm mouth latched on to my glistening nub.

"I want you to come for me, little fox." He lapped at my folds, then started exploring my depths with his tongue. I was close, ready to let go. Suddenly, he inserted one finger into my entrance, crooking it and throttling me with a delicious form of ecstasy.

"Silas!" I screamed, this new sensation crashing like waves on that same goddamn shoreline I crawled out from.

He pushed to his feet, stepped back, and stared down at me with the most curious expression on his face. He seemed lost in the moment, confused by his own actions. Swallowing past the butterflies clogging my suddenly dry throat, I stood with my head held high before my hands landed on his chest as if a woman I didn't recognize animated my body.

Then I stared into Silas's eyes as I slowly dropped to my own knees. I grabbed onto his trousers, feeling his erection straining through the material. His arm shot out, his fingers curling around my wrist in a painful grip as he halted my movements. I looked up at him with a smirk, my eyes telling him I wasn't taking no for an answer. I would bring him to a heel, no matter what it took.

"Yes, my king?" I questioned, knowing he was beyond his ability to physically stop me. "I want to please you."

Unfastening one button, then the next, I finally reached a hand inside to pull him free. His manhood was red and angry as I struggled to wrap my palm around it. Unsure of how exactly to proceed, I delicately lowered my mouth to the head, sucking and licking around the tip. He was smooth and surprisingly sweet for a bulk of flesh and muscle that was odd to look at.

Pulling back, I ran my tongue around the breadth, tracing a vein that ran from the underside and down the length before returning my efforts to the tip again. I opened my mouth as wide as it would go, struggling to take him fully inside. But I persevered past my extended jaw, not stopping until he hit the back of my throat.

His fists wrapped in my hair, holding tight, his thighs trembling and his breathing ragged. I took a deep lungful of air through my nose, my throat expanded, and I swallowed him down, stopping when my nose hit his pelvic bone. He held me in place, my eyes tearing up and his grip punishing. Relentless to the point I thought I may suffocate.

Silas cursed under his breath, rotating his hips and making me gag around him. His hands pulled me back. He drew himself completely free of my hold, then leaned down before tugging me towards him and capturing my mouth in a demanding kiss. I only had a moment to inhale before he straightened to his full height, shoved his cock past my lips, and plunged inside, stopping when he reached the end of my throat.

Despite his unyielding thrusts, each back-and-forth motion driving me closer to nausea as I tried to suppress my urge to retch, his moans spurred me onward. I did my best to shield my teeth and sucked harder with each stroke. I could tell he was losing his control, and I struggled to keep up as his pace increased. Finally, I felt him grow harder just as something warm and salty filled my mouth and puffed out my cheeks, forcing me to swallow or risk choking.

"Fuck…" He kept himself rooted deep for another moment, though it felt like a lifetime as my fingers struggled to find purchase and push him back.

When Silas finally pulled out and released my hair, I fell forward onto my hands. Panting and trying to slow my erratic heartbeat. I remained on all fours at his feet, too exhausted to look up. Too unsure of myself in this instance to try. He gripped me under my arms and lifted me to my feet before draping a silk robe over my shoulders. He moved quickly, scooping me into his arms and taking me to my room. When he deposited me on the bed, I finally met his gaze again, his eyes the softest I'd ever seen them. Heavy. Sated.

"Francine will see to it that you are fed—something light." I tugged the robe closer to my chest as he spoke, waiting for the next shoe to drop. His next insult or reprimand. He paused as if considering his words before deciding against them and adding instead, "I will also have clothes sent up for you."

"A reward for my obedience?" I threw back, my petulance making a swift return even as I tried to salvage what was left of my shattered dignity.

My hair fell in a blonde curtain of wet curls around my face as I refused to drop my glare. He wanted obedience but something told me he also liked my fire. I wasn't in his employ, merely his captive. Two vastly different positions for a girl to be in. Both just as perilous, depending on the circumstance.

He grinned at me in return, his steps measured as he closed the distance while eyeing me like his new favorite curiosity. Royals liked those. Things foreign to them that they could play with, put on display, then toss aside when they were done with them. My eyes flicked to the tiger pelt displayed on the wall as if of their own accord, my brain trying to remind me that I was no better than an exotic creature fresh for the skinning. Whenever it met this man's fancy.

"Seriously?" I huffed as he latched a cuff to my ankle before I even realized what he was doing. My unspoken question clung to the air between us while his response thickened it.

Nothing I had done had earned me the least bit of freedom.

A firm hand shot out to my throat and squeezed. "I would've liked a little pain with my pleasure, but I wouldn't want you to break your jaw." He kissed me harshly, biting down on my bottom lip, then released me again with a gentle shove. "No collar tonight—you're welcome." With that, his majesty turned on his heel and slammed the door behind him.

I was royally screwed, and the irony of that thought wasn't lost on me...

CHAPTER SIX
SILAS

I was supposed to take away her control, own her wishes, her desires, her thoughts. So that the only thing on her mind was me. Pleasing me. Bending to my will. Yet I found myself entranced instead. Curious as to what made the simple village girl tick.

She was my new favorite puzzle. Both an oddity and a welcomed challenge. Different from the type of women I was used to, the type who brandished their sovereign with fake flattery and false pretenses. I wanted Tillie's world to begin and end with me. Instead, the tides seemed to have turned. I was transfixed by the way her pale skin burned brightly under my palm. I was addicted to her scent and damn near ravenous for her taste. She was making me unravel and I didn't like to lose control.

When she dropped to her knees, I nearly lost my senses. Threw logic and restraint out the window and succumbed to my more carnal desires. Unease settled in my gut like a rotten bowl of porridge. None of this was going how I thought it would. How I planned.

Planned...?

Let's be honest here. I didn't have a fucking plan, other than needing to make that girl mine. The moment I saw her, she clouded my judgement. Bewitched me in a way I didn't think possible. I needed to clear my head and get the fuck out of the castle.

Tillie deserved more—*better*—than being locked down, chained to a bed while my wife lurked in the shadows. Though there was no denying the fact that I liked my little fox there. In bed. At my mercy.

"Highness." My courier stopped me in the halls. "Agatha's uncle welcomes a meeting."

"We ride now," I commanded, ordering my men to ready themselves.

We rode through the night, the moonlight guiding our path as trees blurred by in shades of blue and pitch-black, my mind racing nearly as fast. Once again, I was riding head-on into the unknown. I had no clue as to what I would offer the man in order to dissolve my union with his niece.

Agatha and I didn't have children. I could argue that the woman wasn't capable. It was a valid enough reason to end any marriage. He wouldn't dare blame me for her inability to produce an heir. It would be a direct insult, a declaration of war. And while the man loved his bloodshed as much as I did, he wouldn't like rumors of infertility to spread amongst his bloodline.

It was my only recourse, or so I told myself several hours later when I was escorted into the bastard's opulent throne room. No wonder his people were starving. I liked the finer things in life as much as the next man. However, I earned those luxuries—or stole them from my enemies—never taking from the mouths of the families who served under me.

"Silas, nice to see you," Agatha's uncle gloated as he addressed me informally. Any other day and I would have corrected him. But more flies with honey and all that...

"Let's not waste time on pleasantries. I'm here as a courtesy. To inform you in person that your niece has been unable to provide me with an heir and I am dissolving the union. She will return to your court as your ward." I crossed my arms over my chest, my glare landing on the portly figure situated on the throne in front of me. The sort of man who hadn't seen a battlefield in ages and likely didn't own a set of armor that would fit him.

"I have no need for the wench." He smirked, waving a dismissive hand in my direction.

"Neither do I."

He dropped his leg and pushed to his feet.

"May I suggest you think before you speak? We both know I am more than capable of destroying everything you value."

I became king after my father's death and was left with a pile of debts and a series of broken promises. I'd taken his ruins and built a powerful empire, through the blood and pain of my enemies. One swoop of my sword, and I could cut the bastard's head off before he even flinched.

I knew it. And he knew it too.

"What will you give me... for peace?" He was attempting to feign nonchalance but the slight shake in his hand told me he was rattled.

I could destroy his entire kingdom and take whatever I wanted from him. By force. But I wouldn't put my men or my people's lives in turmoil for something as trivial as his pride. He would give in. I just needed to placate him until I decided what to do. In the meantime, Agatha needed to fucking go. She had always been a mistake. A concession I made to honor a man who was long dead and buried and did little to provide me with a legacy beyond the one I had carved for myself. I'd been young, naïve—though it wasn't that long ago. I'd grown into the man I am today quickly. I had no other choice. My kingdom needed me.

"The port. I will give you access to the port for half a year's time... without fees," I added, and watched how his eyes lit up with greed.

The bastard knew it would increase his coffers tenfold. "If I agree, Agatha comes home, and you won't interfere with what becomes of her?" His question was intentionally cryptic, meaning he already had another union in mind or had more nefarious ideas when it came to his niece—neither of which gave me pause.

"It's your kingdom, your decision." I nodded at my men and they fell into formation. It was a maneuver that

I did frequently. An unnecessary show of force, if truth be told, but I couldn't help the smirk that curled my lips as I took note of the tremor in his hands.

"Let me think on it." He gestured for me to take my leave, but I wouldn't be so easily dismissed.

"That's not good enough." I stepped forward as his personal guards unsheathed their swords.

"I need to figure out what to do with *her*, first. But I have to ask... Why the sudden rush? You have been without a proper heir for months now. Are you ill? Do you fear an early grave before a child can come of age? Or..." He grinned, the expression grotesque as his yellowed teeth sat on display like some sort of ogre that had crawled out of the woodlands and stolen a crown. "... is there another reason? One much closer to the bedchambers..." He leaned forward, his throne creaking with the action. "Who is she?"

"You have three days." I turned on my heel and stalked from the room.

CHAPTER SEVEN
TILLIE

Francine brought me a stew and more bread. My stomach could only handle a small amount, but it was delicious all the same. As promised, his royal pain in the arse also had clothes sent to me. The garments were simple but the fabric was also nicer than anything I owned and definitely preferable to being naked all the time.

James and Francine were my constant companions, in Silas's absence. He hadn't been back in days. But the fire in my room kept burning bright, clean clothes came along with three meals a day, and I was allowed to bathe. My chains were reserved to one ankle and the skin of my neck was finally healing from the aftermath of the collar.

"Where is he? I thought being a captive wouldn't be so... boring," I huffed into my bowl of soup, dropping my spoon with a dramatic splatter when James walked in with more kindling for the fire.

"The king has business to attend to." James spoke like the soldier he was, loyal till the end.

"You mean a wife to attend to, or does his majesty have other captives who require his attention?" I taunted, wanting to get a rise out of him.

"Tillie," James spoke my name on a sigh, as if he was holding back from saying what he really wanted. He had self-control—I'd give him that. "He's... he's never done something like this before and I don't know what his end game is. Honestly, I don't even think he knows."

"Told you," Francine muttered in my direction. She was seated on the sofa, her nose buried in a book as she eyed me with a quick look that reiterated her point.

"As for the queen, well, you should consider yourself lucky that I stand guard." James's armor creaked as he moved, candlelight bouncing along the metal and causing the shadows to dance across the stone walls.

It was like watching a storybook play out as he approached—the ominous shadowy figure equal parts villain and hero until you reached the end and realized the protagonist had tipped one way or the other. The symbolism wasn't lost on me as my eyes narrowed and my spine stiffened, as though my body were preparing for the inevitable fight I saw in my future when these strangers turned confidants stood in the way of my only escape.

When and if that day were to ever arise...

"What do you mean?" I swallowed back my nerves as I considered the woman who was wed to the man haunting my mind.

"She is a bit... vindictive." James glanced to Francine, his eyes pleading for help, but she ignored him. "The queen knows their union was meant to bring peace, and when her father died, his replacement didn't honor the agreement."

"So she's alive because King Silas wills it." I flopped backwards onto the bed.

"And if she keeps up her antics, that will change quickly. His majesty is headed to the battlefield, but he seemed... clear-headed. Which hasn't happened since *her* arrival." With that cryptic message, James pivoted on his boot heel and left, dropping the bomb with no preamble as to what the fallout would be.

"What?" I muttered to the ceiling before shooting upright again, my gaze landing on Francine. "What if something happens to him in battle? What will the queen do to me?" Dread filled my chest like a half-ton weight.

"I realize my words may sound confusing, contradictory, seeing as we are unwilling to act on them now. But I promise you, James and I will get you out of the castle *if* that were to ever happen." Francine rose from her chair, patting my shoulder with something akin to motherly affection.

"Until then, you're loyal to your king," I said without question. "Makes no difference now. Clyde is probably in bad shape if he's even still alive—I mean, what sort of life would I have to return to?"

"Who is Clyde?" A booming voice startled both of us.

Pressing a hand to my chest, I stared at King Silas, who was now looming in the doorway. His jaw tense and his appearance haggard. "My ill brother, if you must know. The one I begged you to save." I settled onto my back, my eyes flicking to the ceiling once more. I focused on the cracks in the varnish, the divots in the wooden beams, the aging of the rafters while I refused to acknowledge yet another royal temper tantrum. That was the irony of our current predicament... when someone took everything you held dear, you no longer cared, knew fear, reacted to threats or intimidation. Because a woman with nothing to lose was a dangerous creature indeed.

"Leave, Francine," Silas ordered, causing the elderly servant to run from the room. "And what will you give me if I help? This brother of yours." He circled the bed, his eyes locked on me no matter which way he turned.

"I am your captive, here at your mercy, under lock and key." I lifted my ankle and waved it in the air, the chain clamoring with the movement. "You can take *whatever* you want." The gauntlet was dropped, the challenge issued, and his subtle growl made me smile internally. The man irked me and I loved returning the favor.

"But it's so, so much sweeter when *you give* it to me willingly, little fox." Silas stretched his arms across the post at the top of the bed, his toned stomach peeking out from the billowing fabric of his shirt.

"Given or stolen? I am here against my will, so how can anything I do be of my choosing?" I sat up, swinging my legs over the edge and landing them between his.

"After my... *misstep* the other day, you still gave yourself to me. You *needed* me to get you off." He grinned through the words, and I wanted nothing more than to knock a few of his pearly teeth loose. "So, I ask again, little fox. What do I get for helping your brother?" He cracked his neck from side to side before pinning me with his glare all over again.

"Favor with the gods for granting kindness to an ill child." I slowly ran my foot up Silas's inner leg, watching as he ground his teeth and tried to focus on what I was saying rather than what my body was doing.

"Try again." He shifted closer, my toes pausing at the apex of his thighs, where his sizable bulge warmed my skin to the touch.

I leaned forward, pushed to my feet, and shoved him back a step, never faltering in my determination. In one swoop of soft silk, I lifted my dress over my head, revealing myself to him before running my hands along the length of his arms. My fingertips teased at the muscles of his neck and shoulders until the stubborn man became pliable beneath my touch. Then I wrapped my hands around his neck, pulled his head down to mine, and owned the kiss that threatened to spill over and consume us both.

One second I was in control, the next my head was pinned between his palms as he ravaged my mouth like a man who hadn't seen bread in days. His tongue explored and commanded me to comply, his teeth sinking into my lip as if to confirm what I already knew. He was starved, dying for a taste. To consume me.

He picked me up and threw me onto the bed. I landed with a bounce and quickly crawled backwards, propping myself up on my elbows while my silence, my gaze, told him what I didn't. This was his moment to pounce. Without breaking eye contact, he ripped off his shirt, giving me a view of his torso that was carved to perfection. His trousers followed before he stalked me, his movements measured, precise. A true hunter preparing for his game.

"Are you going to give me all of you, little fox?" He rested his fists beside my head as he swooped down for a soft kiss. Softer than I was expecting from the tension in his body. "Who do you belong to, Tillie?"

"You..." I whispered, licking my lips as I struggled to breathe through my desire. It was hard to maintain my wits when everything about this man was so unraveling... He lifted a curious brow. "You, Silas."

"Fucking right you do." He dropped to his elbows and I sank into the mattress against his weight. This next kiss was different, filled with so much fire, so much passion. It created a feeling inside my chest that I didn't want to acknowledge.

"Be gentle," I begged, and his eyes closed as he heaved in a breath.

"I'll take care of you, Tillie." He kissed me again. "I told you as much already."

"You've told me a lot of things, not all of them true. So why should I believe this—believe you—now? What makes your word worthy of my trust?"

"Because I say it is..." His reply was gruff, barely contained, as I continued to question his morality. But how could I not? A man who held an innocent girl captive was far from honor-bound.

"That's not how things work, your highness, no matter how much you wish it were." I wiggled beneath his hold, his engorged manhood throbbing against my stomach in a way that suggested it had a heartbeat of its own.

"It's exactly how things work, little fox, or have you forgotten your place—and mine?"

My eyes traveled upward, locking with his gaze in the only act of defiance I had at my disposal. His silent reply came in the form of a smirk and a quick thrust of his hips, his glare as penetrating as the weapon that hung between his legs. Just as lethal too, in the way it destroyed what remained of my innocence. My resistance snapped on a scream and tears leaked from my eyes. He kissed them away, stopping the moisture from trailing down my face. His movements were slow, excruciatingly slow, as I begged and pleaded for him to finish. There was no way for me to find satisfaction amidst the pain.

Several minutes later, he panted through his release and collapsed on top of me. Between his weight bearing down on me and the burning sensation in my core, I was in agony when Silas finally pulled himself free. He unclipped the chains from my leg and carried me from the room before depositing me in the freshly prepared tub. The warm water soothed my sore muscles as I settled into its depths, startling when Silas slid in behind me. His calloused fingertips trailed along my pebbling flesh, causing goose bumps to rise in their wake.

We sat in silence, my back to his chest and the water steaming around us. I think I drifted off to sleep, because it wasn't long before I felt myself being carried back down the hall towards the bedchambers. Panic rose in my chest at the thought of Silas abandoning me to my solitude once again. I didn't understand what was happening between us, even if I knew it was unhealthy, but I did know what it was like to be without him.

I latched on to Silas's hand as he lowered me onto the bed, pleading with him to stay the night, to not leave me alone in the shadows of the candlelight. He hesitated a moment, seeming to waver one way then the other, before lowering himself down beside me. The silence stretched on, to the point I wasn't sure if he was awake or not, until I finally broke it with a question that held several meanings.

"Will it get better?" I asked. When he didn't immediately respond, I assumed sleep had taken over and curled in on myself, shifting my body to the edge of the mattress. A strong arm reached out and quickly tugged me backwards, until I was pressed flush against a solid chest that rose and fell with each heavy breath.

"That depends on you, little fox."

I rolled over to face him, staring into a pair of soft blue pools that seemed to swirl with so many secrets I couldn't even begin to unravel them. "What does that mean?"

"Exactly what I said, Tillie," he huffed, clearly past the point of exhaustion and teetering towards irritation —like a toddler who had missed one too many midday naps. "It will get better if you want it to get better. Worse, if you keep fighting me. In this one instance, the choice is all yours."

I pulled his head towards mine, kissing him softly. It wasn't long before it turned into more as Silas rolled on top of me, his palm instinctively wrapping around my throat as he pinned me to the mattress. This time, I decided to try it his way. I didn't fight. I remained pliable, giving when he took, and taking whatever he was willing to give me in return.

It wasn't until late into the night that I finally started to enjoy it, and when the sun began to peek through the heavy drapes, I found that I was sore and *satisfied.* And alone. Silas had crept from the bedroom while I'd slept. Part of me felt lost, like I was missing something, while another part of me was thankful for the chance to regain my wits. I couldn't think whenever that man entered the same room as me, as if his presence somehow thickened the air and made it hard to breathe.

He was dangerous, more life-threatening than a quick-acting poison, and I had yet to discover the antidote. If there was one...

That was how the next few days passed. Silas would come to me at night, seduce his way into my bed with slow, passionate lovemaking, warming my side when we were both too spent to move. Until I awoke the next morning, alone. Always alone.

He was quickly breaking down the walls I'd tried to build around my heart, removing one stone at a time till nothing was left but the girl beneath. A girl who knew better than to dream that this would ever be more than what it was. That I would ever be more than I was—

nothing. A commoner with only debt to offer a man who had everything. The realization was enough to reinforce the barriers I wanted to keep between us. Ignite the spark that fueled the hatred I swore I held for him and incite chaos. I needed the chaos. I thrived in it. The slow and sweet was too intoxicating. Gave a silly girl silly ideas. When what I really wanted was strength to beat down the thoughts that sought to betray me.

Silas tugged me towards the bed, and I dug my feet into the stone beneath me, refusing to follow him. I reached up a hand and shoved at his chest until surprise had him stumbling back a step. Instinctively, his eyes dropped to the floor as he righted himself before they flicked upward in an attempt to silently chastise me—the man assumed everyone knew or should know what he wanted from them at all times.

He wasn't wrong. Not in this instance. I did know. But I wasn't about to give it to him either.

I narrowed my glare at him, the same way he had done to me so many nights before, and stalked forward, forcing him to step back as he observed me. He wasn't frightened by my sudden change in demeanor. He was curious. It was evident in the slight raise of his brow and the lift of his mouth into an almost smirk.

We continued this dance, me inching forward as Silas slid back, until the underside of his knees hit the bedrail and I shoved him rearward. I tugged his trousers down just past his ass and bunched my dress up on each side. Spreading my legs, I climbed on top of him, my hair falling around us. I straddled his waist as I sank onto his length, stretching deliciously as I sat back to rock my hips. I used him this time, like all those nights he'd used me, and I loved the control, the little grunts he made, and the freedom that came with doing this for myself.

My speed increased, my movements jerky as my muscles tired and I lost my rhythm. His hands reached up and gripped my waist, guiding me up and down with a pace that matched my own until stars began to appear behind my eyelids. And I hissed out his name before I could stop myself, toppling forward on shaky limbs, my body pliant as Silas continued to thrust up into me through his release. His arms fell to his sides as he attempted to regulate his heaving breaths.

I twisted onto my side, enjoying the way he tucked me under his arm as his free hand stroked my hair. My eyes were already drifting shut of their own accord and I was about to fall asleep, when he cleared his throat and my lashes fluttered open again.

"The palace is holding a masquerade ball." It was the most Silas had talked to me in days. Unsure of what to say, of what he meant, I waited for him to continue. "I want you to accompany me." It wasn't a request—more of a statement, a matter of fact, a royal decree.

My mouth opened and shut several times over, my mind convinced this was some sort of cruel joke on his part. Though I didn't think I had ever been more wrong and simultaneously right in my entire life. Wrong because he was serious, deadly so. And right because he wasn't asking me; he was telling me. Which left me feeling conflicted. I couldn't deny that I wanted to go. Much more than I wanted to do anything else besides return home, of course—but that wasn't an option. His majesty had made that very clear.

Before I could think or form words to respond, the moment was ruined by the sound of a fist hammering on the door. "Your highness...?" James shouted from the other side.

Silas darted to his feet, dressing quickly and storming from the room with such haste he forgot to shackle me. I wrapped a blanket around myself, feeling out of place with this seemingly odd taste of freedom. Until the sound of muffled voices had me running towards the door and pressing my ear against it.

"I've told you countless times. This wing is off-limits," Silas roared, his harsh tone sending a shiver down my spine even at a distance.

"You haven't visited my chambers in over a week. I never see you. You're either out on the battlefield training with your men, or holed up in there," a female voice shouted back.

Queen Agatha. I had no doubt.

"Where I am and what I do is of no concern to you."

There was a slight scuffle outside the door and I knew what was coming—so I ducked behind the thick curtain and pressed my spine against the stone wall. I had no idea why I was hiding. I wasn't here by choice. But I wasn't ready to face this situation either. Not now that things between Silas and me felt... *different.*

"What is the meaning of this?" she seethed as the large wooden door slammed against the wall behind it. I held my breath, wondering if she could make out the outline of my body. "Rumpled sheets?"

"Listen to me, Agatha. This little arrangement between us, it's over." Silas's decree was followed by the sound of shattering glass and I didn't know if it was by his hand or hers.

"We're married in the eyes of God, and you need an heir, Silas. There is more at stake here than peace between two countries. Your entire legacy is under threat until you bear a son, a threat that trickles down to your people—all those villagers you care so much about." The woman sounded so self-assured, so certain her husband would relent.

And she was right...

"I will meet you in your chambers," he sighed, and I could almost picture him raking an exhausted hand through his hair.

My heart shouldn't feel like it was breaking. But somehow, despite all the fail-safes I thought I had in place, this man managed to crack open my ribs and stab the traitorous organ, over and over.

The door opened again, James and Silas conversing softly in the queen's wake. And I was more certain than ever that he was ordering me locked down as he tended to his *wife.*

"Tillie," Silas barked but my feet refused to move. "Find her," he called out to James.

"She didn't leave this room," he replied. "I've been

standing guard the entire time. There is no way she slipped past us."

I steeled my spine and locked down my emotions, lifting my head before silently stepping out from behind the curtain—both of their heads immediately whipped in my direction. But I refused to acknowledge their presence as I connected the shackle to my ankle and tucked myself under the covers.

I could feel his shadow looming over the side of the bed but neither of us spoke. I held my breath, waiting for the words that would never come. Instead, he brushed my hair from my face and sucked in a breath, a silent goodbye before the soft click of the door shattered the silence as readily as if he had slammed it shut.

I cried myself to sleep, that night and the several nights following it, all spent alone in that same bed. Each day, I was brought a new meal and each day I declined it—much to Francine's dismay.

If Silas didn't care, why should I?

It was then that I realized he'd won after all. He wanted me broken, and now I was damaged beyond repair. Though part of me insisted I deserved it, for thinking the hunted could ever outsmart the hunter.

CHAPTER EIGHT
TILLIE

Days later, and Silas was nowhere to be seen, but I placated Francine and started eating small bites. One afternoon, she slipped into the room with a happy smile, so bright I couldn't stop my own. I'd almost forgotten that tonight was the masquerade ball.

Okay, I was lying. I'd been thinking about it for days.

I was assuming the king's absence meant he'd rescinded my invitation. I itched to ask James but at the same time I didn't want to know the answer. I had nightmares that the queen had announced a pregnancy, and when their son was born, Silas had murdered me with his own hands.

Francine ranted and raved about the few parties she had attended in the castle. The grandeur, the gowns, the dancing... I zoned out as she pleated my hair and prattled on, my body tense with nerves—even more so when James entered the room with a red dress in tow.

Francine snatched the garment from his arm,

reaching for a pair of shoes I hadn't even noticed before shooing him from the room. She unbuttoned the back of the gown and motioned for me to step inside the pooling fabric. I removed my robe, holding her shoulders as I struggled to stay upright in the center of the red tulle. She adjusted the straps and fastened me up, disappearing underneath the large skirt and helping me into the shoes.

I felt like a princess out of a storybook—one who was being held captive in a tower waiting for a knight in shining armor to come to her rescue. Except I didn't want a knight, or a prince. I fantasized about a king. A man who was already married and it certainly wasn't to me...

Francine grabbed my hand and pulled me towards a tall mirror. I froze, eyeing the beautiful woman before me in disbelief. My blonde hair was curled in perfect layers around my shoulders, the top teased to give it volume while the loose strands were pleated in the back. My eyes were accentuated by black kohl, causing my brown eyes to burn bright. My lips were tinted a deep red while pink stood out against the pale skin of my cheekbones. The dress was cut low in the front, the waist sitting high on my hips as several thick layers of fabric flowed around me. My chest was exposed as the added layers of ruffled material cascaded to the floor. I barely recognized the person staring back at me in the glass reflection.

Surely, she wasn't *me*...

"Francine, we need to leave." James opened the door, stopping as his eyes crept from bottom to top. "Sweet Lord, Tillie, you're beautiful."

My heart softened at the compliment. James and I had grown closer over the duration of my imprisonment. He was free of his armor today, wearing all black with a broadsword at his hip. When he extended his arm, I took it. We made it to the end of the hallway before he stopped, placing a red mask across my eyes. A door opened and King Silas stepped into the corridor, faltering when his gaze landed on me.

"Tillie." He was breathless, his jaw dropped and his chest heaving. "You..."

"Shall we?" I kept my voice cold and neutral. I refused to acknowledge his praise, let alone show how deeply it affected me.

He'd disappeared for days, as if I meant nothing to him, as if those nights we spent together meant nothing, and I refused to give him any part of me willingly.

That game was over. He could take what he wanted—really, what choice did I have?—but my heart was mine. I was a fool for thinking I was anything more than a prisoner to the man who couldn't see past his own selfish whims. I deserved better than all of this and I would make him pay.

In true mistress fashion, I was escorted out the back of the castle, down a dark hallway that smelled of mold and death. Fitting for a street rat playing dress-up. James kept the fabric of my gown from dragging behind me as my shiny shoes splashed along the trail of dirty water. A horse and carriage were waiting at the end of the tunnel, with several of the king's guards surrounding it.

King Silas helped me inside, making sure my gown was situated before James closed the door. I sank into my seat, faltering when something caught my attention. My eyes flicked upward, to a balcony at the far end of the castle, and the silhouette standing in the darkness—it appeared the queen finally had her answer.

"You're in trouble," I hummed, my lips curling into a satisfied smirk just as the horses began to pick up their pace. I pointed out the window, my finger stretching towards the figure eyeing us from afar.

"I will deal with her." Silas's indifference towards the woman he'd spent countless nights placating shouldn't have been as rattling as it was. Neither of us meant anything to him. I shouldn't have been surprised; however, my heart beat a little quicker in my chest with the realization.

"*Her*, as in your wife, our queen?" I questioned, enjoying his sudden flare of anger.

"I wanted to do something nice for you. Don't make me regret it." He shifted his focus, a hand resting on his lower lip as he stared out the window.

The ride passed us by in a blur of trees and rocky paths that led us outside the kingdom. I wanted to toss my emotions aside for just one night and enjoy myself. I wanted to drink wine and dance, actually enjoy his company—if I could bear it.

Just one night, I promised myself and then tomorrow I'd go back to hating him. I'd earned this and so much more.

So that was what I did. I drank and danced, indulged in the way Silas guided me around the dance floor. The other partygoers chatted with us throughout, the masks ensuring everyone's anonymity. Which gave me a glimpse at another side of Silas, one that threatened to ruin me. Because I knew his laughter and lighthearted smiles would be my downfall. He held me close, kissed me sweetly, and made my heart race whenever he tugged me to his chest and whispered in my ear, told me all the things he wanted to do with me. *To me.* And I hated to admit it but I didn't want the night to end.

I wanted to believe in the fairy tale he'd painted for us, the idea that I could be on his arm as more than his mistress. It was cruel the way it felt so natural between us. But once the dream ended, once you woke up, you couldn't hide from reality. And before I realized it, the evening was over and I was being swept out the door under the guise of darkness for a second time.

I'd fallen asleep on the ride home, my lashes fluttering open when Silas quietly carried me back into the castle before setting me on my feet outside my door. He leaned forward and pressed his lips to mine, and much to my dismay, the spell hadn't been broken. No matter what I told myself, this man made me weak in the knees.

I peered up at him, the moisture in my eyes likely shimmering beneath the torch lights. "Stay with me." It wasn't a demand or a request. But a plea. I was begging him not to leave me. Not again.

The thought sickened me, but it didn't stop the words from tumbling out of my mouth. I was a stupid girl in love with a man who didn't know the meaning of the word. And I was both too smart and too dumb for my own good.

His reply was a curt nod, but it still had me breathing easier as I took his hand and guided him into the room. He tensed and I immediately knew something was wrong. My eyes bounced from wall to wall, taking in the destruction in our midst. The tapestries were gone, shredded, then tossed into the fireplace. The bedsheets were slashed and stripped from the mattress. And the tables and chairs were no more than piles of splintered wood and kindling. I spun in his grip, anger replacing my initial shock.

"This is your fault." I pounded my fists on his chest. "What if I had been here? Then what?"

"I wouldn't have allowed that." He tried to pin my arms to my sides, but I slipped from his grip before he could stop me.

"Look around you! Your promises are as worthless as what's left of this room." I shoved him back a step, and he caught my wrists this time.

"Enough!" he roared, but I was too lost to my rage to let it startle me. This woman was taking ownership of her husband, showing me my place. "You're mine, Tillie! Mine," Silas insisted over and over again.

"I am not property! You can lock me down and force me to submit to you, but I will *never* be yours!" I freed a wrist and slapped him across the face, gasping at the red print it left on his cheek.

I took a step back but it was too late. He was on me

before I could breathe. I didn't stand a chance against him. I thrashed, kicked, and clawed as he threw me onto the bed. He pinned my arms to my chest, shredded the dress down the center, and swiftly removed the fabric from my body. Leaving me bare. Then Silas strapped my arms and legs to the shackles, my limbs spread wide on the stripped mattress. He leaned down to kiss me but pulled back when I tried slamming my forehead into his nose.

"Remember that you did this to yourself."

I was prepared to start cursing him to hell and back, all those foul words on the tip of my tongue, when he pulled out the collar, and tears instantly filled my eyes. "No, please, Silas."

"Too late for that now." He secured the device around my neck, attaching the chain to the headboard. I was his by force now, whether I wanted him or not. Truth be told, part of me did and part of me didn't. And it was up in the air as to which side of me would win out in the end.

I suppose I was more broken than even I myself realized.

"You make me crazy, Tillie. I can't get you out of my head." Silas grabbed at his hair with both hands and tugged at the ends. "You put these goddamned thoughts in my mind, make me do foolish things like risk my entire kingdom to ensure you're mine." His eyes shown with a vulnerability that threatened to crumble my already wavering resolve.

But I couldn't. I needed to stay strong. If not, he'd take and take and take, until there was nothing left for me. Until I wasn't human anymore, but a slave to his desires.

"This is the only way you own me. The moment I get my chance, I will leave you." The words tasted bitter on my tongue.

"You can lie to yourself all you want, little fox, but I smell your deceit." He rested on his knees, pressing himself between my spread thighs, while the hunger swirling in the air threatened to drown me. "Don't fucking threaten me, Tillie."

"Go back to your wife…" I hissed in reply. I struggled against my bindings, knowing my attempts were futile but I was far too angry to care. "Fuck me and go to her. Get it over with already!"

I was pushing against the limited restraint of a wild animal. I knew he was ready to attack and his anger was what I wanted. He seemed so unaffected by the clear threat his queen left in my room. He swore he would protect me, but his wife wasn't going down without a fight. I quivered at the thought of what she'd do to me, given the chance.

Yes, men knew how to brutalize, how to impose their wills, and break us all little by little. But women… we knew how to destroy in a way that sank far deeper, that seeped into the marrow of your bones and took root till our rage penetrated every fiber of your being. There was no coming back from that. No, an angry woman was not to be dismissed or ignored.

And this particular woman hated me for a life I was forced into, a life that was slowly devolving my sanity.

"I have spent countless nights pleading with myself

to let you go! To deal with Agatha and forget about the girl I'd left bound to a bed, wet and waiting for me." Silas landed a fist on the side of my head.

At first, I thought the blows were meant for me. But he was too close for the missed opportunity to be anything but intentional. He hovered above me so that our eyes were level, and I could see the indecision flickering behind his.

"Don't tell me you care when you leave me for days on end so that you may tend to your husbandly *duties*," I spat as unwanted tears burned the corners of my eyes.

"My duties!" He threw his head back on a humorless laugh before pinning me with his gaze. "I'm supposed to be leading my people, worrying about the men I sent off to war, and producing an heir to ensure the fate of my kingdom. And you're all I want! All that consumes my mind!" He was unraveling at the seams and I'd be lying if I said I didn't enjoy it.

"And did it work? Disappearing from my bed and running to *hers*? I am a prisoner here, Silas. She has her sights set on destroying *me* and there is nothing I can do but sit and wait for her to unleash her wrath—when it's you who really deserves to be on the receiving end of it." I pulled tight on the chains, lifting my neck as high as I could stretch it. "When something happens to me, it will be on your hands, the same as if you did it yourself..." I allowed my ominous words to trail off on a whisper until their weight thickened the air between us as heavily as smoke.

I hoped he choked on them too.

And it was as if his madness had been unleashed as

Silas transformed into a wild beast in front of my eyes. Latching a large paw onto my throat, he slammed me into the soft mattress. I could see the vein in his neck throbbing with each sharp inhale of breath, and I was certain that at any moment it would burst open and shower me in carnage. Silas was a man who didn't like to lose control, who sought to have it in all things, so that when he finally relinquished the hold on his emotions, he became nothing short of unhinged. Ravenous and insatiable. A sight I both feared and savored.

"I won't let anything happen to you. I... I can't. Tillie, I need you." There was a softness to his voice that was in total contrast to the way his muscles tensed and his chest heaved. Like two parts of the same man were warring with each other.

"God, you are such a good fucking liar. It's almost as if you actually believe what you are saying. I know better. I know everything you say to me is part of the fantasy. But right now, I'm okay with that. So lie to me, Silas. Make me forget. Let me pretend that we have more than this moment."

He didn't hesitate, slamming his lips to mine and devouring me with a wanton abandon. His tongue tasted and explored my mouth, his teeth sinking into my bottom lip hard enough to break skin. The copper tang danced across my tastebuds and mixed with the muskiness of his scent so that everything I felt, smelled, tasted, saw, and heard was him. Until every nerve ending was on sensory overload. And I no longer knew where my tormentor began and I ended.

His hands roamed my body, tugging and plucking

and pinching, as if he really could consume me, and before I realized what was happening, he was thrusting inside me and I was clinging to his back. My nails digging deeper, my arms pushing him away while simultaneously tugging him closer. The bed shook from the force of his thrusts, the frame creaking to the point I was sure the wood would give way and we would plummet to the stone floor. Yet neither of us seemed to care, so lost to this singular exchange.

"Feel it, Tillie. Feel all of me, how perfectly we fit together. How your body responds to me." His deep tone was coming out in harsh, panted breaths. "Deny it all you want, but you're mine. Every part of you knows it, even if you don't."

I couldn't form a cognitive reply. I didn't want to. Truth be told, words were meaningless between us. Like I said before, I knew they were all lies. As much as the lie I told myself every time I said I hated him. But this... this was what we were good at. The physical, the animalistic, fucking and fighting to the point of exhaustion. I wanted to lose control. To ride him to completion. To wrap him in my arms and squeeze the life out of him. Both in equal measure.

Silas was capable of many things, a king who commanded an army. But at the heart of it, he was still a man. One who consumed my every waking thought as I battled to be my own person, to have a life outside this room. The reality of my situation was grim, though. No matter how many times I threatened to leave, I had nothing to go back to. I was a village girl who no longer existed.

There was something cathartic about taking control of a situation where you once had none, something freeing about acceptance and deciding to choose yourself and your own happiness, regardless of the effect it had on other people. And that was what I would do. Screw Silas, the queen, my father... all the people who used me as a method to get what they wanted.

I would show them just how terrifying a woman could be...

My arms shook above my head, threatening to break the headboard as I scratched and pulled on the chains, my shoulders screaming in protest. My mind went blank as I chased the orgasm that was on the cusp of stealing my breath in its wake. All I could think about was running towards that feeling, chasing it down and demanding it destroy me. Piece by piece. Day by day. Silas was destroying the girl I used to be. I might as well become the type of woman to enjoy the ride while it lasted.

"Silas!" I called out his name in both damnation and reverence as I finally dove over that ledge into euphoria, succumbing to the way my muscles relaxed and my heartbeat quickened as pleasure curled my toes and warmed my cheeks.

I had to admit there was nothing like it, nothing like the high of being blissed-out and fucked to the point of feeling numb. It was better than opium, more sedating than the strongest wine I'd ever tasted.

"That's it, little fox. Take it. Take all of me." His powerful thrusts didn't relent, nor did they falter. The pain only increasing my pleasure. He shoved his fingers between the collar and the skin of my throat, forcing my head forward. "You are mine until I say differently. You will take everything I have to give you and you will love. Every. Fucking. Minute of it."

I could try to hide behind the fact that I was being forced to idolize the man as if he were a god—he was my keeper and I was his captive after all. I could list all the reasons why it was wrong. Why I should despise him every time he crept into the room, into my bed, and took what wasn't rightfully his, no matter how much he argued otherwise. But deep down, I knew they were just more lies. Like the ones he told me but worse, because I didn't even want them to be true anymore.

As all those days turned into nights, I knew I loved him. I loved this man. Needed him like I needed air to breathe. It was some sort of sick game that I knew I'd never win. I was merely a pawn that the king controlled, moved across the board, unconcerned with my fate as long as he got his queen in the end.

"Christ, little fox. The things you do to me, I can't... I won't ever let you go." His eyes held so much sincerity, it was like a thousand daggers to my heart.

And I came, again, screaming his name for the entire castle to hear while my body trembled despite its exhaustion. I couldn't move, breathe, speak, or think. His proximity held me captive just as readily as the chain around my neck. There was nothing left I could give to him. He had all of me.

It wasn't long before he found his own release, his palms spreading my thighs as he watched his seed drip from my center and dampen the mattress. Then he collapsed on top of me before rolling onto his back at my side, his focus glued to the rafters as we caught our breaths.

"I... I need you to help my brothers," I whispered, trying not to cry when he growled in response.

"You could've asked for anything in this moment, and there's a high chance I would have given it to you. And your first thought is of them. Why?" He seemed genuinely confused.

"They're my family. They're all I have. I would do anything for them."

"Bullshit, you have me."

"You?" I laughed, the sound bouncing off the walls and mocking us. "We have already established that you are not mine, Silas. You belong to the queen. I've come to accept my fate—a lifetime of misery. A mistress only good enough to warm your bed when you are so inclined to warm mine."

"This is a lifetime of misery to you." It wasn't a question, more of an irritated statement. "Little fox, this isn't even a semblance of the type of misery I'm capable of subjecting you to."

"I have no doubt. I remember the first... incident." I turned my head and stared at the far wall. "Even now, I find myself strapped to a bed, on a pile of shredded linens because *your* queen wishes to punish me for something I have no control over."

"I told you I will deal with her." He pushed himself upright, before draping his legs over the mattress while turning his well-defined back to me. His shoulders shook with angered breaths as he tugged his trousers up his thick thighs. "Your brothers are here. At the palace."

"What?" My eyes widened in shock as my lower lip trembled with the implication.

"I granted your request as soon as you asked." He refused to look at me, his eyes cast to the far corner of the room as he fastened the buttons on his shirt.

"You... you brought them here. And you didn't tell me?" I hissed. "Unhook me, Silas. I want to see them."

"They're safe. You will see them when I say you can, and not a moment before." His tone was dismissive, a king commanding a peasant to do his bidding.

"I don't give a damn what you have to say! I want to see my brothers!"

He ignored my outburst as he stalked towards the door, one heavy bootstep followed by the next. I knew my pleas were falling on deaf ears, yet I couldn't stop myself from calling after him.

"Silas! Now!"

His neck snapped in my direction, and the look of disdain I saw staring back at me should have been enough to have me holding my tongue. Instead, it ignited my fury. He closed the distance between us in three long strides and tugged on my chains, ensuring I was fastened to the bed, then pivoted on his heel. My heart dropped as realization settled in.

"Where are you going? Don't, Silas, don't do this to me again." My voice broke on the last word.

"Do not address me so informally, Tillie. I am your king. And regardless of what transpires between us in this room, you will *respect* me." His eyes were alight with unspoken threats as he exited the room, slamming the door shut behind him.

"No! Please! King Silas, I... please!" I didn't even care how broken I sounded.

He was gone, leaving me *again*. My mind slowly drifted off to sleep, attempting to protect itself from the pain growing in my bladder and the ache forming in my stretching limbs, as I prayed tonight wouldn't end like the last time...

CHAPTER NINE
TILLIE

Francine tried her damnedest to help me, but it was of no use. He did it again. Silas had left me chained to the bed with no choice but to rot in my own filth—like some sort of animal. Worse, because beasts had longer leashes, more freedom to roam than what was my current state. James didn't have the key and the king had fled the castle walls in a fit.

Something was different this time though. The concern evident on the king's guard's face told me as much—he was worried. Francine tipped a cup to allow me a sip of water to ease my dry throat. She'd also grabbed the largest bowl she could find, placing it underneath me. I closed my eyes and cursed Silas to hell as I let go. My bladder was thankful for the reprieve, while rage and humiliation once again reverberated through to my bones.

This was no accident. Fool me once, shame on you. But this was twice now and there was no arguing that this was anything but intentional. A show of force, his way of putting me in my place. Silas was a sick puppet master and I was beyond tired of the strings choking the life out of me each time he tugged me this way, then that.

I was bleeding from my ankles and wrists, my neck was raw, and I was starving. But we learned quickly that the collar was too tight to allow me to swallow much liquid, let alone food. It had been over twenty-four hours while Francine continued to offer me small sips of water and broth. I was past the stage of concern, creeping closer and closer to that ledge of despair—where death seemed a comforting option. Though I was unsure if it would be the physical or emotional pain that would finally be the tipping point.

"This is ridiculous." Francine slammed her hands onto the table next to the bed. "Someone in this castle— hell, in this village—must be able to do something. There has to be a locksmith we can call on." She tucked the blanket around me, ensuring I was covered, then rushed out of the room with a huff. I could hear her and James arguing outside the door, before he turned the key and their voices traveled out of earshot.

They'd help me. I knew they would.

I closed my eyes and drifted off, sleep allowing me a few hours to escape the gravity of my situation. I didn't know how much time had passed when I awakened to the feeling of being watched, as someone shifted the bedding aside.

"I honestly can't see the appeal—I suppose that's why he got bored with you so quickly," a distantly familiar voice sounded from beside me, forcing my eyes to snap open as I stared up at the queen. But this time, it wasn't a nightmare, an apparition my mind had conjured up to torment me. No, she was as real as the pain radiating up in down my limbs, as the throbbing in my head and the ache in my empty stomach.

Her arms were crossed over her chest as she appeared to scrutinize every detail of my bare form, slowly stepping around the bed to assess me from each angle like one would appraise a slab of meat at market. Once she had her fill, she leaned over the mattress, her left hand reaching out to squeeze and tug at my breast. I whimpered, and she laughed.

"Very pale and bland. There isn't much to you, is there?" Though the question seemed to be addressed to me, it was more like she was talking *at* me than *to* me. She certainly wasn't looking for a response. "It must be your spirit. He did always enjoy the hunt, the fight. Yes, that must be what he sees in you. You're a biter too, aren't you? I've seen the marks." She pinched my nipple again, her lips curling into a snarl when I yelled at her to stop. My cries of discomfort fell on deaf ears or perhaps she enjoyed hearing them.

A little too much, was all I could think as she tugged the pleats of her gown up and knelt on the bed.

She positioned herself so that her thighs pinned mine to the mattress and ran a pointer finger across my forehead and down my nose, pinching my cheeks so that my mouth was forced to open. She immediately took the advantage and shoved a finger inside, followed by the top of a wooden spoon she'd found on the bedside table. She pushed two fingers in and out of my mouth, chuckling when she went deep enough to illicit a gag. The spoon stopped me from being able to bite down as she lowered her lips to my ear and whispered filthy insults.

My jaw was overextended, which only added to my panic as the collar pulled tight. I was close to choking on vomit as I retched with each forceful drive of her fingers down my throat and her palm against my chin. Several more thrusts had her tilting her head and pulling away as I choked on my next breath of air.

Agatha left the spoon where it sat between my clenched teeth as she wrapped her lips around mine. Her free hand had lowered to my breasts, rotating between cupping, kneading, and pinching while her tongue slithered, poked, and prodded inside my mouth—like the venomous snake she was. She flipped her dress around me, sitting higher on my pelvis as she continued whatever game she was playing.

At least that's what I thought this was at first. A game, a test, a way for her to see what her husband saw in me. That was until her moans grew louder, unbridled, as she writhed on top of me. That was when I realized none of this was fake. Her breathing was erratic, the grinding of her hips intentional as she chased her own release, causing the chains holding me in place to constrict with each back-and-forth motion. Women had never turned me on before, but my body was responding even as my mind fought to ignore it.

"You have a certain," she hummed to herself. "… sweetness about you. Perhaps it's the kiss of the forbidden that has lured my husband from my bed into yours." She removed the spoon from my mouth, sitting farther back on my waist as she smacked the curved wooden end across my breasts several times, each strike harder than the last.

My skin was red, hot, the pain forcing tears from my eyes as she stared intently at the marks she left behind. No matter how much I begged, how hard I cried, she kept going. Her eyes were dark, slated with lust as my skin bruised from her assault.

"I think I shall tell my dear husband that I'd like to keep you for myself." She dropped the spoon next to my head, slipping her fingers into the collar and tugging my neck forward—forcing me to look down at my reddened breasts. "I think I finally see the appeal of such pale flesh. Look how perfectly raised each mark is, almost radiant, glowing beneath the candlelight like a beacon of depravity. Are you depraved, little girl?" She grinned as if to answer her own question with whatever fucked-up image she had of me in her head.

She shimmied backwards, sitting on my knees now, her hands resting on my shivering thighs as she leaned forward. Her fingertips lazily traced the bruises, pinching my nipples once before she closed her warm mouth around them. My muscles were wound so tightly, odd sensations mixed with a heavy dose of inner turmoil settling deep in my gut. I had no control over how my body responded. I shouldn't be moaning, but I was. She trailed soft, wet kisses down my torso with little bites here and there.

"You've displeased him, you know? And now, Silas wants to get rid of you. Your father is dead, and your brothers are under lock and key. So I think it's in your best interest to please me—I am your only chance to keep your head." Her long nails clawed from my belly button to the apex of my thighs. "You want to please me, don't you, sweet Tillie?"

I couldn't answer. The murderous look that glinted beneath the lust I saw in her eyes had my lips sealed shut. I was too afraid to argue, to make her angrier. And truth be told, what was there to say? She was probably right. I was a stupid, stupid girl for believing the lies Silas spewed, to trust that any part of him had my well-being at the forefront of his mind.

"You're not the first, you know?" Agatha ran a finger between my swollen lips, finding me embarrassingly wet. "Oh, how responsive we are. I like that." Her touches turned aggressive as my arousal coated her hand. She stopped moments before my last string of restraint was about to tug loose, and lifted her two fingers to her mouth. She stared at me with an odd expression dancing across her features as she tasted me. "It's this... here." She lowered her arm and plunged those same two fingers down my throat.

I spluttered and gagged as her lips latched on to my clit, and suddenly I was no longer able to hold back. I came all over her face, crying out a string of expletives— directed at both myself and her. She crawled up my torso, as my body trembled with unwanted aftershocks, and lowered her lips to mine. The taste of the queen's assault was mortifying while the strokes of her tongue in my mouth grew violent as she tried to get a reaction out of me. The collar was crushing my throat and I couldn't breathe around her continued intrusion.

"That's it." She leaned back, rubbing herself harder

and faster against my pelvic bone. My body was still responding as I felt her desire dripping across my folds and sliding down my thighs. Her arm shot up, her fingers curling around my collar, forcing me to look at her. My eyes were large as I watched the evident desire morph into hatred, then switch back again. She pinched and pawed at my chest, her pupils dilating each time I responded to the pain. "I want you to thank me for saving you. How will you thank me, sweet Tillie?" she asked, her tongue darting out to moisten her lips.

"Please," I grunted, though I honestly didn't know what I was asking for. Release, mercy, death—it could be any number of things at the moment.

"Do you need more, sweet Tillie?" Her hand disappeared under the piles of fabric that made up her gown as she plunged two fingers inside me.

I whimpered and arched my back at the sudden assault. She stroked me over and over before making me taste myself again. Repeating the process on herself while forcing me to taste her this time. I spit past the acidic flavor on my tongue and immediately knew that I'd made a huge mistake. Her demeanor completely shifted, her eyes alight with a new rage—something deeper, darker—as my heart seized in my chest. Any chance I had of getting out of here alive, of the queen actually being my salvation was long gone now.

"Guess I was wrong about you," she snarled in my direction. "You don't want to be saved, do you? No, you like to be treated like the filthy little whore you are." She curled my hair around a fist and tugged my head backwards, so that my eyes were forced to the ceiling and my neck muscles extended past the point of discomfort into sheer agony, as she rode me harder.

I could feel her wetness increasing with each tear that broke free, each strike that landed, and each plea I couldn't hold back. I could barely breathe—though it didn't stop Agatha from leaning forward and capturing my lips, her movements uncoordinated as she edged herself closer to completion. I could tell she was at that cusp, and I wanted her to get there, in hopes it would bring this torture to an end.

"Oh!" She jerked a few times, slowing the back-and-forth grinding of her hips as her orgasm pooled on my pelvis. "Oh, little girl." She sighed, kissing me once more before she bit down hard enough to draw blood. I cried out, my tongue flicking out to wipe at the liquid rising to the surface along my bottom lip. "If you think that hurt, you have no idea what pain is." Agatha grinned before rolling over and calling out, "Karl!"

Within seconds, the door flung open, and a large knight wandered into the room. "Your highness." The scar along his jaw and left eye danced when he spoke, while grime appeared to darken his tanned skin. He strode towards the bed, each step purposeful and imposing, as he drank in my naked form with a hunger that sent a chill down my spine.

Agatha slid off the bed, adjusting the numerous layers of her gown, before the two of them openly leered in my direction. The humiliation of the entire situation was long gone, quickly replaced by fear. I couldn't help but wonder if she'd spoken the truth, that I wasn't the first girl to find herself tied to Silas's bed against her will.

Are you, though? Are you really here against your will? My inner voice seemed to mock me, as if I needed more of a reason to hate myself.

But none of that mattered now, not as my fate rested in the hands of a disgruntled wife and her manservant. She was going to send me off, that much I was certain of. However, that wasn't what had my heart nearly beating out of its cavity. It was the fear of what she would do to my brothers once she was done with me. There was nothing left for me to offer. I had no bargaining chips... for her or Silas.

"The king has grown tired of yet another village whore." She crossed her arms over her chest, making her breasts rise even higher out of her corset. "What do you think of this one? What should we do with her?"

"How does she taste?" Karl questioned, licking his lips as he stared at my parted thighs.

"Here." Agatha leaned over the bed, inserting two fingers inside me and stroking in just the right way so that a new wave of warmth flooded her hands, much to my dismay. Once she seemed pleased enough with her efforts, she stopped, holding her hand out for Karl to taste.

He wrapped his lips around her fingers and moaned. "Not. Just. Yet." He ground out each word, shifting his trousers to adjust himself.

"Ah, I see. You enjoy it as well. I suppose we could keep her for a bit longer. Get our fill." She smirked at him before turning her glare back to me, and I could swear that I saw the flames of hell flickering behind her eyes. She was the sort of demon parents warned their children about—though, outwardly at least, her form was much more eye-catching than the creatures that haunted your nightmares.

Agatha held out a hand, and my stomach dropped when I watched Karl place a key onto her open palm.

"She looks broken." Karl chuckled, motioning towards the key before piercing me with his gaze. "It makes sense now, doesn't it, girl? He isn't coming back. He's washed his hands of you."

"Yes, child. You're ours now. I suggest you behave yourself and focus on taking care of us, so that we're more inclined to take *care* of you."

They unlocked me from the bed and pulled me to my feet by the leash. My body swayed and my feet stumbled as Agatha tugged me behind her. My limbs hadn't moved in hours—days now—and I fell to my knees, unable to bear my own weight as blood flooded to the previously restrained parts of my anatomy.

"On your knees already?" the queen asked, cackling when I cowered by her feet. "Are you ready to show Karl your appreciation?" She motioned for the man to step forward.

"I would rather not get bit. I'd like to test her obedience first, my queen." He reached down, tugging my leash tighter and forcing me to sit up on my haunches. "You've got some fight left in you, don't you, bitch?" Before I could answer, he slapped me across the face, his palm heavy and the leather gloves unforgiving.

"Now crawl. Show us you're worth saving." Agatha yanked on the chain and I stumbled onto all fours, following behind her.

Karl positioned himself at my rear. I could feel his gaze drilling into my ass while the unspoken promises of my destruction hung in the air. I prayed that Silas would change his mind, come rescue me from the grasp of the evil queen and her henchman, but I also knew that was nothing more than a fantasy of a girl too stupid to accept her fate. That realization only driven home when Agatha swung the door open and James was nowhere in sight.

No one was coming for me.

Honestly, I wasn't sure I wanted to be saved anymore. There wasn't much left of me to salvage to begin with. If it weren't for my brothers, I would have considered finding the closest window, climbing onto the ledge, and saving myself the only way I knew how— by ending it all. Whatever awaited me on the other side seemed far more bearable than whatever I would be subjected to in the near future.

My knees bled as flesh scraped across stone along the narrow corridor and through several more until we reached the wing of the castle I hadn't seen before—not that I had seen much. The queen's personal quarters, or so I could only assume by the feminine touches that accentuated the various tapestries and wall coverings.

Agatha continued to tug me behind her, yanking on my throat whenever my movements halted or wavered, while various servants ignored my presence altogether, stepping out of sight as we passed. The guards were much more vocal when it came to the sight they saw before them, pointing and mumbling about the queen's "new pet" each time we turned a corner and my ass came into view. My arms were trembling, my knees ready to give way by the time we finally approached a door and Agatha tugged me inside. Karl wasn't far behind us, offering a quick kick to my ribs and sending me face-first into the rug as he chuckled at his own antics.

"Rise," Agatha commanded, and I pushed to my full height at her side. "Welcome to your new home." She grinned as my eyes took in my surroundings.

The room was dimly lit, with torches illuminating each corner just enough to give me a glimpse of the horrors that were awaiting me. A wooden cross with leather bindings attached to each arm, coiled chains, riding crops, a steel cage, a wooden box were just some of the instruments of torture that caught my eye. She planned to brutalize me, use me for her own amusement and pleasure, then toss me aside like a broken toy.

"Now, his majesty has given us clear instructions. He doesn't wish to see you, to even hear you breathe. So, whenever he visits my wing, you will be in *there* until I can trust you to remain silent on your own." When I stared at her in confusion, she grabbed my shoulders and pivoted me towards the box. "When he comes to fulfill his husbandly duties, dear. Women have always given me more pleasure than men, so I will have you watch-ing... waiting... until he's done. "

I had woken up into a brand-new nightmare, one more daunting than the last. Because where Silas sought to break my spirit, his wife wanted to decimate me. So that even if I were offered a chance at escape, my body wouldn't be able to comply.

CHAPTER TEN
TILLIE

My first night as Agatha's lap dog was spent with my hands and leash secured above my head, the chain around my neck latched on to a hook mounted to the wall. I rotated between pressing up on my tippytoes and hanging from my arms. Neither helped the ache in my limbs or the cold that seeped into my bones. The only solace I had was that the lack of water meant I was better able to control my bladder. I could hear footsteps, people milling about the hallways as the sun rose the following morning, but no one came until midday.

"So sorry for the delay, Tillie." The Queen fluttered into the room with Karl hot on her heels. "The life of a royal can be so taxing." She motioned for Karl to move, and he quickly released me from the wall before handing her the metal end of my leash.

Agatha pulled me towards a leather bench across the room, quickly lowering a hand to my back and pushing me onto my knees. When I didn't immediately conform to the top, she shoved me onto my stomach, forcing my bare ass into the air. Then she connected the leash to a hook at the end, secured my hands with leather cuffs, and pinned my knees down with a metal bar.

"Do you know what it's like watching your husband take whores off the streets for his own pleasure? Even if I detest the thought of his touch, the fact that he goes elsewhere is troublesome for my reputation. Do you know what would happen if one of those village girls becomes with child before I do? Do you really think I want my son or daughter to worry about having their throne stolen by some illegitimate bastard born of their father's mistress?"

I could hear the brush of her gown across the floor behind me but I couldn't see her.

"Then to hear your wanton moans all the way down the hall, knowing he couldn't please you like I could. Sad, really."

"My queen." Her henchman stepped to my side and grabbed something off the wall.

"Oh, Karl. I think you're right." She reached for whatever he was holding, stepping to the side and into my view. "Karl is always right when it comes to training." Agatha swatted a wooden cane against her palm.

"We'll break you, then rebuild you… just right." Karl leaned against the table behind me. He was so tall his dick pushed against the back of my head, the meaty girth knocking against my skull with each inhale and exhale of his chest.

"Indeed. Now, tell me, Tillie, did my husband please you?" she asked, and when I didn't immediately answer, her exaggerated sigh sent a trickle of warning through me.

Sharp and firm, a fresh wave of fire lapped across the skin of my ass. The cane whooshed in the air before the pain ignited. Agatha offered me two more swats before repeating her question, but I was sobbing too loud to answer. To form coherent words. I lost count at ten lashes. Across my rear, my thighs, and bruised cunt.

"Be as loud as you want, sweet girl. No one will hear you—not in here. I'm far more careful when it comes to private matters than my dear husband ever was," the queen sneered, then gestured to her sidekick. "Karl, come have a look."

The man in question stepped back into my line of sight, pumping his bare dick in one hand before disappearing behind me. "May I?"

"Yes."

I could sense the grin in her voice—even if I couldn't see it—as his grunts quickened in pace right before warm liquid squirted across the raised flesh along my spine and ass. I gagged and bucked against my bindings. Though I honestly wasn't sure why it mattered now. What was done was done.

"Don't be rude, Tillie," Agatha chided, *tsk*ing her tongue like a mother correcting a spoiled tot.

I could hear the familiar sound of her gown rustling behind me as she sauntered around the bench until her skirt was level with my face.I peered up, noticing how calm and relaxed her expression appeared. Except for her lips, which were pursed in annoyance. She ran a soothing hand up and down my spine, soft, almost sweet but not quite. The moment I took a calming breath, part of me hoping the worst was over, she smacked a palm across my ass with agonizing precision. My body jolted from the unexpected movement, the sticky bodily fluid that had pooled on my back now dripping down my legs.

"Insolence will get you nowhere. You will be grateful for every drop Karl gives you, and you will thank him for his efforts." Agatha unlatched each of the straps on the bench, tugging me to my feet before shoving me towards the bed, where Karl attached shackles to my wrists.

Then she stroked the hair away from my face, curling up beside me while staring silently into my eyes for several long minutes. I couldn't help the tears streaming down my cheeks, and without realizing what I was doing, I leaned into the small comfort she was granting me as she held my racking body.

"Tillie," she whispered, beckoning me to open my eyes. "This arrangement doesn't have to be all bad. There can be enjoyment for you as well. Was my husband your first?" she asked softly.

For reasons I couldn't explain, I nodded. I guess, subconsciously, I was hoping the truth would set me free, would earn me some sort of kindness—as foolish as it sounded. But it was hard to think clearly when you were so broken.

"Men hold all the power in our world. We need them to eat, provide shelter, build families. But not for pleasure— that is the one thing that can be our own. You see, the touch of a woman can be just as satisfying. More so. Women are soft, tender... where men are hard and unforgiving. Don't get me wrong, we all like it rough sometimes. But the female anatomy needs so much more than a stiff cock to... *come* into its own. Do you want to explore that with me, Tillie?" she asked, and I felt myself nodding. "Good girl."

Agatha leaned into me, trailing a fingertip along my jaw before sealing her offer with a soft kiss. My mind and body were so conflicted by the back and forth of her demeanor. It was as if she couldn't decide whether she despised or wanted me. And I suddenly understood her appeal, what Silas must have seen in her. The woman was intoxicating in her own way. She made you work to please her, made you *want* to. Even when you hated her. I wanted to chase the odd sensation, give in to it, even if for just a few minutes. And I wanted the pleasure she promised.

Her lips were soft and full, as she moaned against me, her hands kneading my breasts and pinching my hardening nipples. She pulled away and crawled off the bed, standing next to me as she removed her long silk robe, revealing her naked body. Her breasts were fuller than mine, but surprisingly perky. She had flared hips and a trimmed waist. I wouldn't say that I was overtly attracted to her, but she was a beautiful woman to look at.

"Karl." The queen snapped her fingers, and her henchman moved quickly, grabbing the metal chains and one hand while forcing me onto my back with the other. I hissed as my limbs were yanked this way and that before Agatha crawled over my hips to silence me with a kiss.

"She's secured, your highness," Karl announced as I fruitlessly tugged against my bindings.

"Very well. You may leave us now." She waved a dismissive hand, then quickly added, "Call for lunch and then stand outside."

I could hear the sound of the door opening and clicking closed before I was swallowed up by a barrage of slow, sweet kisses. They trailed from my lips, down my neck, focusing for a few minutes on my breasts, then dipping between my thighs. She licked, suckled, and kissed between my folds, drawing out each unwanted moan I offered her.

It was so wrong, but it felt so good. I just needed this release to make me forget for a little bit. Afterwards, I would return to my despair and self-loathing.

The door crept open again, and a young girl entered with a tray of food. The queen ignored the intrusion, her apt attention on the task at hand as she sucked on my clit, inserting two fingers inside me in motions that shifted between fast and leisurely. I could feel the girls' eyes on us, staring for a moment before Agatha barked at her to leave. Our curious onlooker jumped on the spot and darted for the door. I watched her go until the queen bit down, and my eyes shot to the ceiling as I quivered and cursed the heavens.

"Give it to me, Tillie. Let go," she said between aggressive laps of her tongue. "Let me see how beautiful you look when you come."

A few more strokes, twists of her fingers, and I was overcome with sensations that seemed to sear through my every nerve ending. My body was exhausted, my mind blank, but my orgasm kept burning brighter—wave after wave of bliss—as I trembled uncontrollably.

"There she is. A vision fit for the gods." Agatha pushed to her knees between my spread thighs, tugging my hips while my arms stretched tight. "Are we going to be kind, Tillie?" She motioned to herself, my eyes growing wide in confusion.

"I… I… I don't know," I mumbled, terrified yet intrigued.

I should be fighting her, disgusted by the way she treated me, but I couldn't force myself to do anything other than go along with it. I wanted to blame the exhaustion, the hell I'd endured, the fact that all the fight had been drained from my body. But if I were being honest, all of this was new to me. And the allure of the forbidden was almost as intoxicating as the sips I'd stolen of my father's whiskey when I was eight.

"It's fine, Tillie. I will teach you how I like it." Agatha laughed, and my hackles rose as she shimmied herself up my rattled frame. Then she spun around on all fours, and I could see her glistening folds slowly come into view.

Panic surged through me as I realized what she was doing. Before I could move, yell, plead with her, it was too late. Her warm, wet entrance bore down on my face, earning her a muffled cry as she slowly rocked back and forth.

"Tongue out, Tillie. Be a good girl and please your queen. Do a decent job, and then I will feed you and allow you to rest," she commanded as if I had a choice in the matter.

I could barely breathe as she ground her hips against

my pursed lips, my chin dripping with her obvious desire. I just wanted it to be over, so I opened my mouth and stuck out my tongue. She moaned with the contact, pushing herself down a little harder and sitting back as she put all of her weight on me. Her hips kept up the rocking rhythm and her palms rested on my breasts. She used my nipples as a guide, pinching and squeezing whenever I closed my mouth or displeased her. I twisted my head to the side for a few breaths before she tugged me back in place by my chin. She removed one hand from my breasts and grabbed my wrist, pinning me to the spot as she rode out her pleasure.

"Up and down, move that tongue, Tillie. The harder you work, the sooner it'll be over," she was quick to remind me as her hips demonstrated the various motions.

I flattened my tongue and stroked all the way down, then back up again. Her desire spiked while her juices coated my cheeks, leaving a warm trail to my neck in its wake. Agatha bore down against my jaw, her grip tight on my hair as she rocked harder, faster. Her breathing was raspy, more labored, her movements erratic as she climbed higher and higher up that peak.

She scrambled to reposition her hands, her nails embedding themselves into the skin of my thighs as she shoved my legs apart. Suddenly, her mouth was back on my pussy and she lifted off my face for a few brief moments, allowing me to suck in a few gulps of fresh air. She attacked my core and I was so turned on from the first orgasm that the second ripped through me in seconds. Agatha was skilled when it came to the female anatomy, attentive too, and I couldn't help but get lost to the sensation as she lowered herself onto my face again. I worked my tongue against her cunt and fought to breathe as she pressed into me, her fist twisting around the tangled locks of my hair before she tugged my head up.

"Oh, sweet, sweet Tillie," she moaned. "I'm so close. Faster, Tillie." She slapped a palm down on my thighs like a rider spurring on her loyal steed. Then she arched her back, one hand still in my hair and the other latched on to my collar. She jerked a few more times before she groaned, and a fresh wave of warmth coated my cheeks.

Agatha lifted herself off me, and I sucked in several deep breaths as she rolled onto her side and stared at me with a sated smirk playing against her lips. She gave me a chaste kiss, deposited the tray that the girl had brought onto the bed, and proceeded to feed me from it. Each time she raised a fresh, plump strawberry to my lips, she followed it with a slip of her tongue into my mouth, savoring the taste of the berries as the juices coated my throat.

"No. I don't think I will let you go, sweet Tillie," she seemed to hum to herself before turning to me. "I will have someone start the bath for you." She kissed me once more, then stood to her full height as she tugged her robe back over her shoulders and pushed through the door in a flurry of fine silk and fur cuffs.

The heavy wood clicked into the frame and I was alone with my thoughts. The experience with Agatha wasn't as bad as I feared it would be, and her skilled mouth was definitely a sweet reprieve from the pain of my current predicament.

Several minutes passed before the servant girl returned with a large pot of steaming water; it took her a handful of trips to fill the tub to the brim. Then she topped it off with a few droplets of fragrant oil that carried through the room. A mix of florals, much more feminine than those Silas preferred, and something about that thought gave me pause.

I reminded myself that, that man shouldn't take up any more space in my head, not after everything he'd done. The way he treated, then abandoned me...

The chains at my wrist rattled, and when I looked up, I realized the young girl was unhooking me before lending me her shoulder to lean on. I was naked, a colorful canvas of bruises as the queen's arousal clung to my skin. The servant girl quickly guided me across the room and stood at my side as I slowly stepped into the tub. The warm water seared the fresh wounds closed while cradling my aching muscles. I slid deeper into the pool and I finally felt my body relax. I hadn't realized how cold I was until now. I closed my eyes and turned my mind off, refusing to think of the insanity that had become my life.

"They'll tire of you," the servant girl whispered as she lowered a finger to break the water's surface, then swirled her hand from side to side.

"I hope it's sooner rather than later," I muttered, refusing to open my eyes and play her game.

"Then they'll throw what's left of you to the wolves." I could hear her feet patter around the tub.

"And by wolves, I mean the king's guards," she clarified.

"Leave." I threw a hand in the air and gestured to the door as my teeth set tight in my jaw. When she didn't move, I opened my eyes and glared at her. "I said leave!" My fingers curled around the lip of the tub as my shoulders tensed into posturing that told her I would force her out if I had to.

The girl gasped, faltering back a few steps before she rushed to the door. She slapped her hands against the wooden surface, tugging at the handle when it didn't immediately budge. As soon as it gave way, Karl pushed inside and she scurried under his arm without so much as a backwards glance. The queen's henchman appeared confused for a moment until he shook his head and stalked into the room, his armor groaning with each step he took in my direction.

"What have you done?" he hissed, dropping to his haunches and closing a fist around my hair as soon as he was within arm's reach.

I refused to answer him, my glare hyperfocused on his forehead as if I could see past the flesh and bone and into the deep recesses of his mind, as if I could read all the depraved thoughts running through his head. He wanted what I wasn't willing to give, what I wouldn't allow him to take without putting up one hell of a fight. I might have been the king's whore and the queen's pet but I refused to be this bastard's broken toy.

Karl's large, war-torn hand slowly dipped into the water, disappearing below the surface. And I tensed, waiting to feel his touch. My skin pebbled when his rough palm cupped my bare breast, goose bumps rising along every inch of exposed flesh despite the heat of the water. I slapped at his hand and when he didn't immediately release his grip, I lost all sense of self-preservation and lunged forward.

My nails clawed at his eyes and my teeth gnashed in his face, like an untamed beast refusing to be caged. He stumbled backwards, taking me with him when he landed with a loud thud on his back, and I slid across his chest plate. His meaty palm cocked rearward before connecting with my temple, forcing my world to spin on its axis.

"You fucking bitch." He pushed to his knees, then his feet, latching on to my hair and dragging me to the other side of the room. Where he dumped me next to the bench, kicking me once for good measure.

I was winded, but I managed to suck in another breath and belt out every expletive that came to mind. All the threats and broken promises—since my confinement first started—swirled on repeat inside my head. Urging me to keep fighting. To refuse to give up. To not let one more person in my life use and abuse me.

I did my best to pivot at my waist and claw at Karl's face as he towered over me. It was a useless endeavor. The man was at least double my size, with years of finely tuned muscle at his immediate disposal. At my most fit, I was fast—quick on my feet—but my body had been poorly neglected for weeks now. So it wasn't just an unfair fight; it was certain death. Despite this knowledge, I couldn't stop myself from trying. If I was being cursed to the pits of hell, I was taking as much of his flayed flesh as I could grasp in two hands with me.

"It seems you've yet to learn your place. Guess it's up to me to show you," Karl hissed between clenched teeth, loose spittle breaking free and peppering my cheek as I bucked beneath his hold, attempting to twist so that my feet would connect with his chest while he tried to force me flat on my face.

By the time I was finally able to maneuver myself onto my back, it was too late. He pried my thighs apart, pinning them to the side with each of his knees. And my heart sank into my stomach, where it churned in a mixture of bile and dread with the realization of what was to come.

I had only ever been with one man—if you could call it that. And one woman I suppose—if I were being literal. In the handful of years I had been on this earth. Violence, force, manipulation... it was all I knew. All I experienced, and yet something about the vileness of this moment eclipsed every one of those instances put together.

Karl shoved himself inside me, my body fighting against the action, my entrance dry and aching with the lack of desire he failed to even attempt to elicit. I didn't know enough to understand that, that was part of the attraction for a man like Karl. Though I couldn't fathom how it didn't hurt him too. The friction of the back and forth, the tightness of the intrusion...

Surely there wouldn't be much skin left if he kept up this frenzied pace. It was an odd thought to have in this moment. But one that popped into my head nonetheless.

"What the fuck are you doing?" Karl stopped his

thrusting at the queen's sudden entrance. "Shut her up, Karl!" she yelled. I hadn't even heard myself screaming… hadn't felt the air vibrate my vocal cords or push through my parted lips.

Karl quickly clamped a hand over my mouth, and the moment it was sealed, I was jarred by the sudden silence. Every part of me, inside and out, ached like nothing I'd ever experienced. I could see their lips moving but couldn't make out what they were saying past the waves crashing in my ears.

I watched on in horror as the queen's henchman balled spit around his mouth, swishing from side to side before hurling it at my bare chest. I felt the splattering of the warm fluid but couldn't be bothered to react. It was as if part of me was floating above it all, disconnected from the limp shell of a girl sprawled out over the bench as her body was used like a battered rag doll.

"I'm assuming she did this?" Agatha's voice finally came into focus as my consciousness resolidified. The queen gestured a hand at the various gashes streaking Karl's face, scowling when he nodded. "Oh, you stupid girl…" she sneered, grabbing onto my hair and dragging me across the floor while Karl's limp cock plopped free to hang at his thigh.

I had been too far gone to notice he'd even finished. But when I took a deep, steadying breath, I could feel the tacky substance clinging to my lower stomach and dripping down my hip.

It was then that something came over me. A bout of perseverance. Or perhaps it was madness. Whatever it was, it had my arm shooting out and grabbing on to

Agatha's wrist. With a quick, jerking motion, I pinned her with a glare, and twisted. I waited for the crunch of bone but it never came. Still, I couldn't hold back the laughter that sent my head tipping rearward and my chest heaving when she cried out in pain. I craned my neck to the side and eyed the woman for a moment.

It was funny, ironic even, how the perfectly primped image in front of me was only there to mask the monster that lay within. Then again, it was common practice for predators to appear innocuous in the wild—it was how they lured their prey.

And it was time to decide which I wanted to be...

The queen fell backwards, clutching her wrist to her chest as I lunged forward, raising a fist. More than prepared to strike. However, in all the chaos, I'd lost track of Karl's movements and hadn't realized he was behind me until his fist made contact with my head. My limbs dropped to my sides like a puppet whose strings had been cut, and I slumped onto the ground. Agatha shoved me aside, my unfocused vision trained on the rafters as she smoothed down the wrinkles in her dress and loomed over me.

It was true. She had the upper hand, could do whatever she wanted to me now, as I lay flat on my back. Immobile except for the sporadic rise and fall of my chest. But there was one thing she couldn't do. And that was hide the fear I saw in her eyes or the slight tremble I noticed in her hands as she tried to tuck them against her hips. Because something else was just as eminent as the pain I was sure to endure, and it was the fact that if I were given the chance, I wouldn't hesitate to take her life, and we both knew I'd succeed.

"Did you not think anyone would hear her screams? You left the door ajar, idiot!" Agatha snapped her fingers in Karl's face, prompting him to scoop me up from the floor and position me on the bench. "Teach the girl a fucking lesson, then make sure she's properly stowed away." She cursed under her breath before mumbling to herself. "Someone has likely already informed him of her screams..."

Him. The word repeated over and over again in my head. Like an anthem to my pain, in rhythm with the beat of my heart. Where once it said *thump, thump, thump*, it now screamed *him, him, him.*

There was only one person she could mean, one man whose wrath this woman feared. The king she claimed had abandoned me. Even as my temples pounded, my thoughts clouded by a thick haze, I knew what she meant. What Agatha had so carelessly let slip from her lips, assuming I didn't have the wherewithal to hear her. She'd lied... *been lying.*

Silas never sent me to her, otherwise she wouldn't be so concerned that he might hear my cries for help. I didn't know why it had taken me so long to see it, see past the stories she told me. I could only assume that the blow to my head had also knocked some sense into me.

"You did this to yourself." The queen stood at my side as I was once again strapped to the bench, my eyes following her movements while the rest of me couldn't.

"I... cannot wait... for you to see... what I plan to do... to you..." I forced the words from my raspy throat.

Though my mouth barely moved with the action, I knew she heard me. I saw it in the way her pupils quickly expanded and contracted with an emotion I knew all too well.

Fear.

I hungered for her blood. Karl's too. And I would ensure I got it before taking my last dying breath. Because there was one thing I was certain of in this moment. My wrath was enough to reanimate me, long after my body should be dead and gone.

"Oh, really?" Agatha smirked—an attempt at masking her growing dread. The queen wasn't used to being challenged, and it was clear my insolence left her feeling out of sorts. Unnerved. She lifted an arm, gesturing behind me, before quickly dropping it to her side again. Like an executioner releasing the lever on a guillotine.

I heard the sound of the whip swooshing through the air before I felt the sharp sting of popper meeting skin. Once, twice, then three more times across my raw backside, though my throat was too sore to do much more than swallow the near inaudible gasps. I could feel the blood dripping down my thighs, the scourged flesh peeling back and being ripped away again with each flick of Karl's wrist. But much like how I'd disconnected from my body during his first assault, I grew numb to this one as well. I knew the pain—the agony would be there later, waiting for me when the shock wore off. Though I couldn't be bothered to care.

"I never wanted this marriage, never had any desire to rule my own kingdom. It was all my father." Agatha pulled up a chair and lowered herself onto the seat in front of me, speaking as though we were bedmates rather than captive and captor. Tormentor and tormented. Queen and her less-than-loyal subject. "He had the army to attack but he knew we'd lose in the long run. And there I was, his daughter of marrying age, the ideal offering to a king who favored lineage above all else. So I was forced to wed a man, a brute, and call him *husband.* A stranger, someone who doesn't even like to bed me, all because another man—a father—ordered it to be done."

She scooted the chair closer, leaning against the bench to wipe away my tears as Karl continued to rise the whip and bring it down on what was left of my rear.

"He barely looked at me before, always distant and brash. Then, suddenly, one day, his behavior just switched and he was tolerable. Happy even? Definitely freer, lighter on his feet when he stepped. It wasn't until my spies told me the king had an armed guard in his wing, a locked door, that I knew something was up. You were the reason, sweet girl. You were the one who somehow enlivened the man who never spoke to his wife with anything but disdain in his tone. You see, he had no use for me—except during his futile attempts to produce an heir—and with your arrival to the palace, he didn't even need me for that anymore." Agatha held up a palm, the signal for Karl to put an end to his brutality. Though I wasn't sure that it mattered. The damage had been done.

"My queen!" a voice shouted from the door. "The king is approaching!"

I should've felt a moment of relief, excitement, *some-*

thing. Instead, I was exhausted, my body drained and my tears dry. I could hear them scrambling—Agatha and Karl rushing around the room in an attempt to cover up their deceit. She was hissing at the henchman, demanding that he move faster, hurry.

He was coming.

The fabric of her gown swished from side to side with a flurry of movements that told me this wasn't the first time she'd been forced to act quick on her feet on account of her husband. A cloth was shoved into my mouth and a leather strap draped across it, as Karl pinned my arms to my sides and bound my legs together.

I couldn't do much more than watch as the queen pulled a drawer out from under the bed. Then I felt myself being moved, lifted, before I was deposited inside, like a dirty little secret meant to be hidden from prying eyes. Which wasn't too far from the truth. Agatha slid to the ground and slammed the drawer shut with the force of her back until I was left in total darkness. The sort that didn't just hinder your ability to see; it also dampened all your other senses so that you understood what it felt like to be buried alive. Your only companionship the layers of sediment that ensured no one would hear you scream and the pine box that would serve as your eternal coffin.

"Where the fuck is she?" Silas's voice echoed somewhere in the back of my mind, but I couldn't be certain if it was real or if the madness had finally taken over...

CHAPTER ELEVEN
TILLIE

"Who, my king?" the queen's saccharine-sweet voice carried through the room, breaching the confines of the box like someone poking your eardrum with a needle.

"Don't be stupid, Agatha. You destroyed her room and now she's missing," Silas growled his reply.

Maybe it was the blood loss or maybe I was just put together wrong from the beginning and never really had a chance at being normal. But there was something about the concern underlying his words that had my pulse quickening, my heart pounding in my temples. I despised the man. Hated him. Would spit on his grave given the opportunity. But above all, I needed him more than I cared to admit. Wanted him in a way that made no logical sense. Silas was everything that was messed up in a world created and ran by men and, goddamn, if I didn't love him for it.

"I did not touch the whore, just her belongings.

Which weren't even hers to begin with, now, were they? It's not my fault you lost your toy."

"Don't touch me, Agatha." Silas was pacing. I could hear the back-and-forth motion of his boots on the stone flooring, followed by a struggle. "I fucking mean it. Where is she?"

"I haven't a clue, dear husband. Now, on to more important matters. You haven't visited me in days…"

"Weeks," he corrected, his tone seemingly detached while hers was thickened by desperation.

"See?" Agatha huffed. "Yet you blame me for not providing you with an heir."

Perhaps her royal highness didn't think I could hear from inside the box, or just assumed I'd passed out from the pain. Nevertheless, she was spilling all her secrets, giving me insight into the way her mind ticked.

She didn't hate him as much as she claimed. No, Agatha hated being rejected by Silas, despised feeling disposable and unable to perform a task as inherently feminine as producing a child. Part of me felt bad for the woman and the cross we all had to bear, our worth constantly measured by what we put between our legs, then again by what came out. It wasn't fair, *just*. But neither was life. We were all given a choice as to how we responded to what was deemed our societal shortcomings. And projecting your insecurities onto those you deemed as lesser than you was no way to go about gaining sympathy.

The wood was slick with my blood as I attempted to press an ear to one side, trying my damnedest to overhear the continued bickering between my former lover and his wife.

"You make me fucking sick to even look at, Agatha, let alone touch," Silas snarled.

"The feeling is mutual, my king. But that is what you are. My. King. Need I remind you of your duty to your kingdom? To the people who depend on you, look to you for security."

I kicked harder against the walls caging me in as Agatha seemed to draw closer.

"Continued peace means we need the joining of two great families." She sighed. "It means we need heirs to carry on the line or it dies with us."

"Does it look like I give a fuck about the joining of our families? Your father is dead, your uncle is one step away from declaring war, and you fucking repulse me."

I could hear the defeat in his voice. Silas wanted me but he also wanted to avoid needless bloodshed. The devastation of his people. It was an easy choice. Even I had to acknowledge that much. My life versus that of thousands.

"I promise you I do not have her. Please, Silas, I need you to see reason. I couldn't bear it if everything you built were to be burned to the ground because some silly village girl didn't realize how good she had it and ran off —have you asked the guardsmen? Perhaps she took a liking to one..." Agatha hummed. "You know how fanciful youths can be... they get an idea in their head and off they go without much thought for those they leave behind to clean up their messes."

The bedding rustled, the mattress creaked, and I

could feel the vomit churning in my gut, threatening to rise and choke me behind this gag. She was really playing up the moans as the weight shifted on the bed, and my makeshift coffin vibrated with the movements. My initial thought was…

No, it couldn't be.

Because that's what our brains liked to tell us when something was so far beyond belief that it didn't seem feasible. Long after our hearts knew it to be true. I suppose it was a defense mechanism of sorts, protecting our psyche from realities so brutal they were sure to leave a lasting imprint. Until the moans grew louder and there was no way I could deny it anymore.

"Oh, yes." Agatha slammed a limb down on the bed —an arm I could only assume—right above where she knew my head to be.

"Shut the fuck up," Silas snarled. Then the bedframe shifted back and forth with more force, in rhythm with what I knew to be the thrusts of his hips. Because it was a rhythm I knew all too well. "Where is she?" he hissed between panted breaths, and I could feel the first tear break free and travel down the divot of my cheek.

"I promise I do not know. Now close your eyes, relax your mind, and tell me all about her." The mattress rose, and footsteps echoed to my left as Agatha's voice sounded just outside the box. I was certain she was kneeling next to me. "Keep them closed, Silas, and let me help you rise to the occasion. Go on. What's this girl of yours like?" She was performing, exaggerating the way she sucked and slurped and gagged. Little did Silas know none of it was for his benefit. Not now anyway. This was all meant for me. To show me she owned him and that I was nothing.

I hated to admit it but her little act was working.

"Tillie." My name left his lips on a strangled groan, sending me into a fit of rage. I lifted my legs as high as they could go and slammed them back down on the wooden base. As many times as my growing exhaustion would allow me. "Stop…" Silas hissed. "What was that?"

"What was what?" Agatha feigned ignorance, and I'm sure it wasn't a pretty look on her.

"That noise. I heard banging…"

"Oh, I must have kicked the bedframe. I apologize, my king. I may have gotten a little overzealous in my efforts to please you." Then she started up again, making those god-awful sounds that left my skin crawling, my fingers itching to claw at the surface until the first layer of flesh was gone.

The rag was soaked in a mixture of saliva and blood, and I realized I could finally shift it aside, though just slightly. I concentrated on the task at hand, pressing my swollen tongue against the underside of the material and stretching my jaw muscles until the fabric loosened enough to slip down over my chin. I chose to focus all my energy on this while attempting to ignore his grunts and her enthusiastic wails. He had her bent over the bed now, driving into her cunt over and over again as I struggled to break myself free.

"I swear, Agatha, I will fucking kill you if I find out you had a hand in her disappearance," Silas growled, his voice so close it was like he was whispering in my ear as I doubled my efforts.

"I know, my king."

"I will find her and I will learn the truth."

"I know, my king," she repeated, her words seemingly emotionless.

I could tell my window for escape was closing, Silas's release just on the horizon. If I knew anything about the man, it was that he would be quick to adjust his trousers and walk out that door as soon as the woman in his bed was no longer needed. I chewed at the fabric harder, faster, as his thrusts did much the same.

"What is that?" Silas asked, his heavy boots stepping away from the bed. "Blood? Fuck, a lot of blood. Agatha!" He growled her name, and I felt the bounce of the mattress as she jumped to the other side. Away from him.

"Blood...?" She parroted the word, likely hoping to buy herself time to devise a plan—or a better lie.

"Seeing as you appear alive and well, wife, I can only assume none of this is yours."

"I went a little too hard on—" Her reply died on an audible gurgle and I could picture his hand tightening around her throat. I also knew what it felt like to be on the receiving end of that grip.

"Stop fucking lying," he barked before tossing her onto the bed. The mattress once again dipped with the sudden force of added weight. I grabbed onto a new piece of the fabric and pushed with my tongue until a fresh gulp of air filled my lungs.

"Silas!" I screamed as loud as my irritated throat would allow me, my voice breaking as I sputtered through a cough, followed by several more as I struggled to breathe through the growing pain.

"Tillie?" It was more of a startled gasp than anything else, uttered seconds before he slammed an arm onto the bed in pursuit of Agatha, who must have gotten away. I could hear the fabric of her gown shuffling across the floor, her movements sporadic. Frantic.

"Karl!" she shrieked, and Silas responded by calling out for James. The door opened and heavy footfalls carried into the room, followed by muffled cries and the sound of flesh hitting flesh.

Silas shouted my name louder. I tried my best to answer him, but my voice was weak, barely audible to my own ears. Something heavy landed alongside the box. I turned towards it and started begging for help.

"Your highness," James muttered. "There're handles."

"Run!" Karl grunted, and I could make out the familiar sound of Agatha's gown brushing across the floor, her shoes tapping along the stone in a frenzy of movements.

"Kill him, James. The rest of you, spread the word. The queen is not to leave these walls," Silas ordered. I braced myself as I felt someone tugging at the box.

I fought to stay conscious long enough to see his face. It was all I wanted, to see him looking down at me and know that every word his wife spoke was a vicious lie. I just needed this moment of peace between the two of us. I wasn't delusional. What we shared wasn't meant to last more than a night. Fairy tales didn't happen in real life. But I clung to the idea that I wasn't so foolish as to

believe the man cared for me when he actually felt noth-
ing. And his eyes held the truth his tongue would be
more than willing to deny.

The first stream of light crept passed the darkness,
and I blinked through the tears and dried blood to peer
up at him, immediately wishing that I hadn't. I'd been
wrong. The myriad of emotions that crossed his face left
me more confused than ever. Relief, yes, that one I recog-
nized. Shock and horror too. But it was the last emotion
that gave me pause. Hatred.

"Is she alive?" James asked, stepping up beside his
king, then quickly stepping back again. I could only
imagine what sort of sight I was to behold.

"Help me pull her out." Silas's tone was cold, clinical,
that of a man who had witnessed the atrocities of war
firsthand and had likely become immune to them.

I closed my eyes as two pairs of arms reached
forward and paused. I was so badly beaten it was
obvious neither man knew where to grab, which parts of
me were still attached and which were no more than
lumps of muddled flesh.

"Little fox." The pet name left Silas's lips on a silent
prayer.

"I'll get the physician and send for Francine." James
pushed to his feet and fled the room as fast as his legs
would carry him. I could hear the sound of his boots
rushing down the corridor and echoing off the walls.

"I want her found. Drag my wife back kicking and
screaming if you have to. Just see to it that she's strung
up on that fucking cross!" Silas called out to James,

almost as an afterthought. The shock was wearing off and rage was taking its place.

"Where is… dear lord…"

I couldn't see her, but I knew that voice. Francine knelt at my side as she brushed a strand of blood-matted hair from my cheek.

"No easy way to do this, little fox." Silas quickly rolled me onto my side, laying down a sheet of fresh bedding before placing me on top of it.

I clenched my teeth and hissed through the agony of each subtle movement as he wrapped me up like a newborn babe, scooped me into his arms, and gently placed me on the bed. I relaxed against the mattress until the sudden dip of his weight reminded me of what had taken place here, on this same bed, not all that long ago.

I flailed my limbs and shoved at the blankets while cursing Silas's name. "You know what you did here, on this very spot, as I bled beneath you. I heard every word, every grunt, every lap of her lips. Felt every buck of your hips and thrust of your cock as I prayed for the gods to strike me down where I lay."

Francine gasped and Silas winced, wiping a tired hand down his face. "James. Help," he called out, though I hadn't even heard the king's guard approach with the physician in tow.

James and Silas lifted the ends of the sheet and I was slowly raised into the air. My head rolled to the side and I saw Karl's lifeless eyes staring back at me. As chilling of a sight as it was, my only emotion was regret.

Regret that I hadn't been the one to end him myself.

I felt the glares as I was carried through the halls, heard the whispers—though I couldn't be sure if they were real or imagined at this point. The repeated blows to the head meant that I was seeing double while white noise filled my eardrums. I closed my eyes and threw my head back. I was done fighting to stay awake. I recognized the irony in it, but I finally felt secure enough to drift off.

The queen's biggest ally was dead. Though I didn't know how many more she had at her disposal, I was certain that the king's men presently lining the halls would outnumber them. Whoever they were. The darkness was just starting to pull me under when I heard the sound of footsteps running towards us.

"We haven't found her yet, your highness," the guard announced between panted breaths, his chest plate clanking as he doubled over to suck in a lungful of air.

"Then why in God's name are you here? Go fucking find her!" Silas barked, and each of his men jumped to attention, several rushing off in pursuit of their queen while the others remained steadfast at their posts.

I'm going to kill her. It was the last thought to run through my mind before I gave in and succumbed to oblivion's sweet embrace. Sleep had become a dear friend. There was no pain there. No fantasies anymore either.

CHAPTER TWELVE
TILLIE

"It's the high potential for infection that I'm most concerned about. These cuts are deep and require constant redressing, otherwise the bandages are in jeopardy of adhering to the wounds and reopening them."

"Whatever she needs... make sure it happens."

"Of course, your highness."

"I thought you said this was preventable!"

"Medicine is not foolproof, your highness. We can only do our best to mitigate the risks, which is exactly what we have done. It should have been enough to stave off the infection and give her body time to heal."

"Why do her wounds appear to be getting worse? They're redder and oozing?"

"I don't know, your highness. It doesn't make sense. I've treated men on the battlefield with less sterile conditions who've recovered much faster than your mistress."

"She's not my mistress."

"Of course, your highness."

"Everything points to an allergic reaction, your highness. Almost as if she were bathed in something that irritated the skin and is preventing proper healing from taking place."

"Something like stinging nettle, perhaps?"

"Could be. Why do you ask?"

"Because my fucking wife loves her deadly plants and herbs."

CHAPTER THIRTEEN
TILLIE

The voices came and went over the next few days. Sometimes I recognized them; sometimes I was certain they were angels beckoning me to heaven's gate. Though I wasn't sure I belonged there. But it was whenever I heard *his* voice that I felt most at ease, even when it was raised and sent an unexpected chill down my spine. It told me I was alive, especially on the days I didn't want to be. The days I begged the angels to take me because the pain was too much and my limbs were too heavy to lift to end my own miserable existence. The days when he would somehow sense that I needed him at my side to remind me there was something to live for.

Whether it was love or vengeance had yet to be determined.

"Stop yelling. You're scaring the poor girl."

Francine. She was insistent that I could hear them and she was right. She instructed Silas to talk to me, that it would tether my spirit to this plane. I didn't know what she meant by that. Whether Silas understood her was unclear as well, but for once, he didn't argue with the woman, and it did help. So maybe it wasn't as crazy as it sounded.

"You're not afraid of me, are you, little fox?" Silas taunted, and though my eyes remained screwed shut, I felt it when he reached out to caress my cheek. "No, my girl runs towards danger, doesn't she?" I could hear the grin in his voice. As quickly as it came, it was gone when he added, "Any word on my *wife*?"

To anyone else, the word would be considered an endearment. But there was a certain undertone of disdain Silas emitted whenever he spoke it, suggesting it may as well have been a curse. I guess in a way it was.

"Nothing as of yet, your majesty. Though I have no doubt she's lurking somewhere within these walls."

James. He was another frequent visitor to my bedside. He blamed himself for failing me, admitted as much when he didn't think anyone else was listening.

Part of me blamed him too. At first. But I'd had plenty of time to consider things when I wasn't plagued by harsh, fever-induced dreams. And I realized he was no more at fault than I was when I was taken from my father's home. He was a man following his king's orders, doing his best to watch out for me even when it meant putting his own neck on the line. And truth be told, I couldn't be sure much more could have been done if he had been there when Agatha and Karl came to take me. She was his queen after all, and he was subject to her will whenever his king wasn't there to argue otherwise.

"As if that's supposed to be comforting," Francine muttered under her breath.

"It's better than having lost her scent completely," James countered, and his words were followed by a loud thump. "Ow! What the hell was that for?"

"Better for whom? Certainly not for anyone in this room. That woman—I mean, *her majesty*—is nothing but a threat and the sooner she's gone from this castle, the better. Tillie has been through more than enough. So, you go on and make this right!" Francine's tirade was punctuated by the slamming of a door.

"She smacked me," James grunted.

"And I'll do worse if you don't get this situation handled," Silas growled. "Now, help me figure out a way to wake her up…"

I drifted in and out of consciousness as familiar voices continued to haunt my waking hours. Silas was growing frustrated that I hadn't roused yet, as if me being beaten to the brink of death was some sort of inconvenience for a man used to getting everything he wanted. Which only motivated me to keep my short moments of wakefulness to myself.

"When she's well enough to walk on her own, you'll need to set her free."

"Drop it, Francine."

"No. She's a sweet girl who didn't ask for any of this, who didn't ask for you to complicate her life."

"I can't, okay? Is that what you want me to say? I can't let her go. When I thought she ran off on her own, with another man—no less one of my men—it felt like a part of me was drowning. All the color drained from the world and the air evaporated around me. It's fucking selfish. I know it. I accept it. But I can't... No, I won't let her go."

"Well, then, I hope you remember *that* when she dies. Remember that it was at your hands and you alone could have prevented it."

I could hear the sound of feet shuffling as the stout woman pushed through the door and clicked it closed behind her.

"I know you're awake, Tillie," Silas whispered, his voice tired. Defeated in a way I never knew it to sound before. I opened my eyes and took in his haggard appearance, his jaw unshaven and his pallor gaunter than I was used to it being. "Hi," he breathed the singular word but refused to meet my gaze.

"Hi," I choked out in reply.

"I'm so sorry, Tillie. I know I have no right to ask this of you, but I need you to forgive me. Please."

I bit my lip and curled my fingers into my palms to stop myself from reaching out to him. I couldn't touch him, couldn't let him touch me either. Because I knew what that would mean. I'd fall apart in his arms. I'd give in without even trying to. Silas was everything I knew I shouldn't have. And yet I was drawn to the man like a martyr accepting her fate, a doe caught in the crosshairs, a glutton needing one last bite. It didn't matter how bad I knew he was for me. I wanted more. I wanted it all. And he wanted me.

"No chain? No collar?" I winced as I forced myself upright, propping the top half of my body against the headboard as my eyes flicked around the room. "Where am I?" It was the next logical question, yet saying it aloud sounded foolish even to my own ears.

Silas responded with a soft smile, the kind lovers shared only with each other in the sanctity of their bedchambers. Not that I knew much about love, not when hatred had been the most prominent emotion in my short life.

"No chains and definitely no collar," he said, one arm jutting out to gesture around him. "You're in my room, Tillie. A room I've never shared with anyone. Including my wife."

There were those two words again, spoken with vehemence while his majesty failed to see the significance behind them. He might as well have said *not mine*. Because that was what they meant. He wasn't mine. Not that I wanted him. That would be ludicrous. I just didn't want him to belong to anyone else.

Yes, that made much more sense. Or so I told myself.

"No chains," I repeated, and he nodded. "So I can leave then? Walk out the door and return to my village? Or maybe travel somewhere distant, a far-off land where you'll be nothing but a blip on the timeline of my life?"

His smirk immediately dropped and I could see the rage contorting his features, his jaw ticking and his lip twitching as he fought to subdue his mixed emotions.

He'd assumed I would continue to be his little plaything, the girl hidden away in his bedchambers, at his beck and call but never at his side. He had a *wife* for that after all.

"You're not going anywhere," he barked, quickly clearing his throat to soften his tone. "You need to heal. Then, after you are well, we can discuss a more favorable arrangement—something to your liking as well as to mine."

"Arrangement, hm? An arrangement would suggest terms, a written or oral agreement. You stole me, Silas. You took me from my family in the middle of the night." I coughed past the lump in my throat. "And now look at me. Look at what you've done."

He dropped his gaze, and I reached out a hand, tipping his chin and forcing him to witness the consequences of his actions. The brutality I'd endured because of his selfishness.

"You will look at me, at every inch of my bruised flesh, at every mark that was a result of your decision to do with me as you pleased that night."

He tugged his head away, a single tear breaking free and trailing down his sun-kissed skin. I swiped at his eye with my thumb, my touch gentle, featherlight while my words remained caustic.

"Is this for me? Or yourself?" I brought my hand up to my mouth and sucked the moisture away. "Tastes bitter, doesn't it, Silas?"

"Don't you see? That's where you're wrong, little fox." He lifted his chin to pin me with his glare. "We had terms. We've always had terms. I told you what giving yourself to me would mean."

"Is that what you think happened? Are you really that delusional? I never gave. You *took* and you took and you took and you took again. Then, when I had nothing left, you took more!"

"I'm sorry, Tillie. I promise you, once she's found, she will be dealt with."

"And what about you? What will your punishment be? For what you did to me." I straightened my spine and met his scowl with one of my own.

"Watching you decay in this bed has been punishment enough." He pushed to his feet and swiped at the contents of the bedside table, sending a bowl and various utensils clattering across the floor.

"Says the child currently embodying the man I thought was a king," I hissed in response.

He pivoted on his heel so quickly I felt the air around me twist and whorl. "Is that what you think, Tillie? That I'm a child?"

"You're throwing a tantrum, aren't you? So why don't you answer that one for yourself?" I shifted in the bed so that my face sat but a breath away from his, daring him to correct me. Hit me. I didn't care. I was numb to the pain.

"You're walking on thin ice, little fox..." he growled, and I watched his upper lip curl into a snarl. Fitting for a man who liked to act like a beast.

"Then watch me break it." I ground out the words, tasting copper between my teeth as I forced a breath through my nose and out of my mouth.

His arm shot forward, and before I realized what he was doing, Silas pinched my cheeks with his thumb and forefinger, forcing my lips to part as he lowered his head and darted his tongue inside. He tasted sweeter than I remembered, his mouth both softer and more demanding. I melted into him and the kiss, but only for a moment. That's all I would allow myself. Then I shoved at his chest, kicked the blankets aside, and struggled to pull myself up.

"What are you doing? Tillie, sit down before you hurt yourself!" he yelled, his actions conflicted as he reached out an arm to brace me.

I ignored his warning, sucking in a lungful of air as I attempted to wobble on two feet. The room smelled like him, the air tasted like him, and I hated how that calmed me.

"Take me to my brothers." He owed me this. He owed me so much more. But this was what I was asking of him at the moment.

He shook his head and dropped his gaze again, bouncing between self-importance to shame in the blink of an eye. "They know nothing about your position here, Tillie."

"And what position is that, Silas?"

He placed his arm through mine, and I leaned against his shoulder as he led me to the door. "They believe you were given a job, labor in exchange for their room and board," he said, ignoring my question and offering an explanation instead.

"I need shoes and something appropriate to wear." Part of me wondered if I should wait to see them, afraid that my appearance might frighten rather than comfort my siblings. But it had been proven more than once that tomorrow wasn't promised and we'd been kept apart for long enough.

"How about a bath and a proper meal? I can have Francine prepare those tarts you like, then I will take you to them." When I opened my mouth to argue, he stopped me with an icy glare. "I am not keeping your brothers from you, Tillie. But you look as if you're knocking on death's door. It's been weeks since they've last seen you. Let's not tarnish their image of their sister."

"My childhood was not like yours, Silas. We were starved, left to sleep in our filth, beaten on a daily basis." I grabbed his fingertip and ran it across the divot next to my temple. "That scar is from where my father's knuckle finally broke flesh." I released his palm and motioned down the front of me. "So I see no difference."

Silas's mouth opened and closed a few times, his eye twitching as he fought to rein in his temper. Truth be told, I sympathized with the man. I was feeling a little out of control myself and decided I needed to take him down with me. I reached out a hand, stroking the frown lines along his brow, skimming over the skin of his neck, and trailing a finger over his clavicle before daring to traverse lower.

"Tillie," he grunted, his pupils aflame with a fire that threatened to burn me to the core.

"Silas." It was barely a whisper, his name slinking across my tongue and expelling on a purr. "Make me forget. Take it all away."

"Tillie... your body needs time to heal..."

The look in his eyes told me he could be persuaded,

while the flare of his nostrils insisted his mind had been made up.

"Please," I hummed, and watched as my plea had the intended effect. He was putty in my hands.

Touch by touch. Kiss by kiss. Gentle manipulation by gentle manipulation. I would dismantle this man, much like he'd done to me. Until nothing was left but the dignity he'd stolen from the village girl he hardly knew before he ruined her. Then I'd take that back too.

CHAPTER FOURTEEN
SILAS

It was a strange feeling. Being a man who had everything he ever wanted handed to him on a silver platter, only to realize you had nothing at all —that it could be ripped away from you in the blink of an eye. Almost as if you never had anything to begin with. That was what it was like watching Tillie slowly deteriorate in my bed. It was the one battle I couldn't fight, the one enemy I couldn't defeat.

Death taunted me as I sat at her bedside, awaiting his arrival. My heart thundered in my chest, and I feared sleep, convinced that he'd use that moment of weakness to take her from me. God knew I deserved it, while the devil refused to make a deal. My soul was far too tainted to be of value anymore. So I had no choice but to sit and worry and wait. The walls of my kingdom could fall around me and it wouldn't lure me from this spot. Not without my little fox by my side.

I didn't know who I was before her but I knew I would be nothing after...

And here she was like a dream standing in front of me—a nightmare because I was certain her obstinance and sheer lack of self-preservation would be my demise.

Her eyes pleaded with me, her lips taunted me, all while her body urged me to refuse her. She wasn't ready for all the filthy things I wanted to do to her, things I wasn't certain I'd ever have the chance to do again or to begin with. She could scarcely bear her own weight and yet she was asking me to take more, to bring her to her knees or toss her onto the bed. There was only so much restraint a man, even a man who was thought to be a king could have.

Perhaps I'd fallen asleep and none of this was real, my mind's way of playing tricks on me and conjuring up some sort of fantasy while the demons snuck in and stole her from my clutches. Or perhaps all the stress and lack of proper rest was making me mad. Who could tell anymore?

"Will you refuse me, Silas? Turn me away from your bed, now that the guilt has had time to wear off?" The temptress peered up at me through her fanned lashes, and I was more certain than ever that she knew what she was doing to me. She knew and she liked it. The control, the power she held over me. And I couldn't blame her. It was a heady feeling, addictive in a way that was both terrifying and thrilling in equal measure.

When I didn't immediately answer, Tillie took it upon herself to pull the silk nightgown over her head, watching as my eyes trailed along her naked torso. Her skin pebbled almost as if she could feel the heat of my gaze, as if it seared past the first layer and imprinted on her soul.

There was no escaping me. It was better that she learn that now. Accepted it and the pleasure I wanted to bring her from here on out.

She dropped the material to the ground behind her as she meandered back towards the bed, her heart-shaped ass drawing my eye and forcing me to watch the subtle sway of her hips. They moved like a pendulum, lulling me into submission no matter how hard I fought to keep my senses about me. I didn't understand how she could be standing, let alone attempting to seduce me in the state she was in. Something about this girl was indomitable. It had crossed my mind that she was no girl at all but a mystical creature of sorts, sent to bewitch me and take my kingdom.

Truth be told, she could have it. I didn't care. I just wanted a taste...

She crooked a finger in my direction and I followed before I even realized my feet were moving.

"Who are you to think you can demand anything from me?" I swallowed past my growing desire and lifted a questioning brow. It was difficult to both love and hate the effect something had on you. Not just something but someone.

"Who am I?" She grinned, her dry lips curling in a way that appeared sinister. She'd lost weight during her illness, her frame slighter and her appearance more gaunt. But it seemed her attitude had grown tenfold. "Look me in the eye and tell me who I am," she taunted. "You made me after all? Turned me into your perfect little doll, a monster of your own making, Silas. Don't you like your handiwork?"

I walked around the bed and observed her every movement, her hand trailing down her chest, her fingers tweaking a nipple before continuing lower. Her thighs parted and I could already picture my palms pinning them to the mattress, my cock straining to sink into the warm, wet cunt sitting just out of reach.

A growl rose up my throat and pressed past my lips of its own accord, and I could see how the sound affected her. She squirmed in place as a visible chill traveled down her spine, before she raised a finger to her mouth and sucked on the tip, then returned it to the pretty pink flesh between her legs.

"You have three options, Silas." She moaned my name as she continued to tease the moisture onto the now-glistening folds of her cunt. "You can come here and do as I asked, watch as I do it myself... or leave when I call your wife to do it for me—"

"Goddamn it, Tillie," I ground out, ripping the shirt from my torso as several buttons bounced off the closest surface, rolled across the flooring, and disappeared under various pieces of furniture. Then I lunged for the bed. "If you insist on poking a caged bear, you'd better prepare yourself to get bitten when he breaks free."

"Do your worst," she hissed in reply.

"Oh, I plan to. But not today. I refuse to let you bait me into crossing that line, little fox." I knew what she was trying to do. What she thought she wanted. But I also knew it would just be another excuse she would use to hate me.

I gathered both of her wrists in one hand and held them above her head as she bucked her hips. It was a game we liked to play. She would pretend she didn't want this and I would pretend to force it on her. But we both knew the truth of the matter. She wanted me as much as she didn't, and I wanted her more.

I dropped my free hand between her thighs and coated my fingers in the excitement she would swear she didn't have for me. Her body told me otherwise. My little fox was equal parts sadist and masochist, even if she refused to admit it. I knew her better than she knew herself, could read her like the most detailed map in all my kingdom. She enjoyed pleasure but she needed pain. And I needed to give it to her. There was no better sensation than the feel of this woman submitting to my will. No better ecstasy than the pulse of the vein in her throat beneath my palm.

She attempted to squeeze her thighs shut as my knees pried them wider. The more she fought, the wetter my hands became and the harder my cock grew. And when she cursed my name, I nearly came on the spot. I lowered my mouth to the area just behind her ear, nibbling and sucking until she wore my mark. The flesh there a perfect shade of reddish purple that told the world she was mine, even when her lips screamed that she wasn't.

She tilted her head back, accepting the pleasure I gave her. Her fight dwindling but not completely extinguished yet. She would get there. It would just take time, patience. And I could be a patient man when I *wanted* to be.

When she jutted her hips forward and ground herself against my lower body, I released her wrists. Tillie clawed at the skin of my back, drawing blood in her effort to make me feel a semblance of the pain she had to endure at my hands... and the hands of those around me. I knew I'd wronged her. But that didn't mean I would let her go. I just had to ease her into acceptance.

I wanted to go slow, enjoy the taste of her after being forced to go so long without it. But it was an impossible task as her gentle mewls plucked at the waning threads of my restraint before her tightening grip around my neck severed them entirely. I was an unhinged man given a sudden dose of sanity, when I finally positioned my cock at her entrance and buried myself to the hilt.

No, sanity was the wrong word. Because, if anything, the feel of her cunt pulsing around me, holding me hostage while simultaneously sucking me deeper, propelled me farther over the cliff before plunging me head-first into madness.

I pulled back, almost all the way out, then drove forward again with a grunt. Repeating the action once, twice, three more times until I lost count. Until I didn't care. Until I couldn't tell where Tillie began and I ended as she met me thrust for thrust. She called out my name and I whispered hers like a prayer.

When her muscles tightened, her breath hitched, and her skin pebbled beneath my touch, I knew she was close. So very close to that edge. I wanted—*needed*—to send her spiraling over. There was no better sight than the image of a strong woman crumbling beneath you, coming undone while she both loved and hated you for it.

I lowered my mouth to her nipple, twirling my tongue around the hardened bud, then bit down just enough to have Tillie coming and wincing in the same breath. The sound was nothing short of ethereal, akin to a chorus of angels singing, only far more sinful in nature.

Her body went limp, her arms dropping to the mattress as I used her for my own gratification now, tugging her hips upward as I drove down. Her eyes were nearly closed but I could feel her watching me beneath hooded lids, an onlooker partaking in a cabinet of curiosities. No matter how readily my little fox pretended to embrace her sexuality, the truth was she still had so much to learn. So much I could teach her. If only she'd let me.

She reached up a hand and trailed it along the dips and planes of my chest to my lower stomach, and the light brush of her fingertips had me bracing myself on the headboard and coating her walls like a knight who hadn't felt the touch of a woman since he took to the battlefield.

I'd just collapsed beside her when an impatient knock sounded on the door, causing Tillie to clutch the blanket to her upper body as she curled herself up into a ball and hid behind me.

"Your highness!" James barked from the other side of the wall. "We have her. She's being locked down as we speak."

I threw my legs off the edge of the mattress, shoving my cock back into my trousers while ensuring Tillie's scent was sealed inside along with it. I glanced at her from over my shoulder. "Stay here."

"Absolutely not," she was quick to reply as she scrambled to her feet on the other side of the bed. "She's mine, Silas."

"Tillie, this doesn't concern you. I understand the pain she inflicted on you but Agatha is *my* wife, my queen, mine to deal with," I ground out between clenched teeth.

"Right, *your* wife, *your* queen. If it weren't for your constant reminders, surely I would have forgotten by now." She rolled her eyes and crossed her arms over her chest, emphasizing just how young she really was. It was a fact easy enough to dismiss when she was fighting me with a vigor far beyond her years.

I softened my tone, hoping it would help ease her into compliance. "Tillie, I give you my word. Agatha will pay. But it'll be by my hand. Any wrongdoing committed under my watch and within these castle walls is my responsibility to right, not yours."

"My point exactly," she hissed. "It was under your watch, while you stood idly by and did nothing. Yet you expect me to trust that you'll do something now. Can you not see the error in your logic?" She was pacing back and forth, her bare feet padding along the stone flooring as if she were numb to the chill. "It was your job to keep her in line and you failed. What sort of king can't even handle his own household?"

Before I knew what I was doing, I was lunging forward, my palm wrapping around her delicate throat and closing tight. One quick twist and I could have snapped it, left her head dangling to the side, that smart little mouth of hers permanently shut. I could have and I would have if I didn't think it would ruin me as well. It was a selfish thought, I knew. But a true one all the same. There was no her without me and me without her. We were both too far gone, too stubborn to stop fighting, too fucked in the head to want to try.

She clawed at my hand as I guided her steps towards the bed. It wasn't hard to do. Tillie was a slight thing, weakened by all the damage my wife had enacted on her body and I was fueled by my rage, driven by my need to consume her, and completely powerless to stop myself. As soon as her knees hit the mattress, I dropped my hand and flipped her onto her stomach, her bare ass pushed up and on display—like the sweetest peach, ripe for the taking.

Her skin was still bruised, scars marring the once flawlessly porcelain flesh of each cheek, though it did nothing to take away from her beauty. If anything, it added to it. It was a disturbing thought to have and I was being honest when I said I felt guilty for the pain my little fox had endured. But there was something intoxicating about watching her skin change colors, seeing her wear my mark like a badge of honor, sullying perfection while molding it to your liking.

But these marks weren't of my doing. They were someone else's. That little reminder had me pressing Tillie's face against the bed coverings, as I used my free hand to line up my cock with her slick cunt. She held her breath and hissed through the first punishing thrust of my hips. She needed to remember her place.

Did I enjoy the fire in her eyes, the sharp lashing of her too-quick tongue?

It would be remiss of me to say I didn't. But she had yet to learn how to self-regulate and it was my job, as her king, to teach her. She said as much herself.

If you took a moment to look at it from my point of view, I was merely doing what she asked of me. Fucking her into submission. It seemed to be the only way to keep her from acting out of turn, the only recourse I had to help ease the growing tension between us.

I leaned forward to capture each of her hands in one of mine, driving in and out while holding her arms above her head, as I lowered my lips to her ear. "You will mind your manners and that smart mouth or I will mind them for you, little fox. I may enjoy your company, but I will not tolerate such flagrant disrespect. Not from you, not from my wife, not from anyone."

She whimpered in response and the sound had me coming undone, my seed spilling inside her as I grunted through my release. I reached a hand around and pinched her clit, and seconds later, Tillie was following me over that cliff into orgasmic bliss.

Before she had a chance to catch her breath, I pulled away, grabbed her by the ankle, and tossed her onto her back again. Then I secured a shackle around her free leg, pivoted on my heel, and left the room with my trousers tucked under an arm.

It was for her own good. And, soon enough, Tillie would understand that too.

CHAPTER FIFTEEN
TILLIE

"James!" I kept screaming his name, over and over again, refusing to relent, even when Francine entered the room. The good king might have momentarily fucked me into silence but not into submission. There was a difference between the two—a lesson he'd learn soon enough.

I grabbed everything within arm's reach and hurled it at the door. I didn't care what was shattered, splintered, or wrecked in the aftermath of my adult-sized tantrum. I wanted to destroy it all. Everything and everyone to hurt as badly as I did.

"What! Christ, Tillie." James cursed my name before storming into the room, pausing to step over the debris in his way without giving it a second glance. I guess it wasn't much different from the insanity he witnessed within these castle walls on a daily basis.

"Get me out of these chains, now!" I pointed at my ankle, seething as my chest rose and fell with each staggered breath.

"I can't. I'm sorry." He dropped his gaze and shook his head, having the decency to at least appear ashamed by his actions.

My sanity was hanging on by a thread, slipping and fraying the longer I was in yet another form of forced captivity. Silas didn't realize what the time in that box had done to me, how fragile my constitution had become. I wasn't the same girl he had taken into his bed or even the same one he'd carried out of Agatha's makeshift torture chamber. I was neither myself nor someone else. I felt as though I existed and didn't, all while fighting for the kind of survival I no longer wanted. It didn't make sense, even as I thought it, but that was what happened when you were bred by chaos.

It was as if my limbs were no longer attached to my body when I reached out a hand and grabbed for the metal letter opener that was strewn haphazardly on the bedside table. My fingers curled around the edge and my brain immediately knew what I had to do. I pressed the sharpened end to my ankle, above the chain, just enough to draw blood. I couldn't even feel the sting of pain anymore as I watched the sheets turn a bright shade of red.

Francine gasped and James lunged for my hand. I lifted the blade in his direction before resting it against my own throat. "Don't... don't take a step closer or I'll do it," I hissed.

"You wouldn't." Even as he said the words, I could see the doubt in his eyes.

"Wouldn't I?" I swiped a finger along the pool forming at my ankle, brought my hand to my mouth, and sucked until the taste of copper burst across my every tastebud. I could feel the wasted blood droplets dripping down my chin as my lips curled into a grin. "Now, one of you..." I bounced the letter opener between them. "...is going to figure out a way to get this goddamn chain off my leg or I'm going to cut it off. Silas be damned, I'll bleed out on this floor before I allow your precious king to tie me to this bed again."

Francine had always appeared to be a steel-spined woman, at least during the short time that I had known her, but as I eyed her in this moment, I realized how frail she really was. She was notably trembling, her lips quivering and her nostrils flaring in a way that told me she was on the verge of tears. Whether they were for me or her own welfare, I couldn't be certain. I knew Silas wouldn't take this betrayal lightly. There really was no winning here, not for the king's faithful servant and loyal guard. They could either ignore a direct order or watch me die—watch his majesty's preferred plaything mutilate herself *and then* die.

"Jesus, Tillie, you realize he's going to have your head for this, right?" James asked the question, though he really wasn't asking anything at all. He was telling me. Then he took a tentative step forward, one hand in his pocket as he fished around for what I hoped was the key.

"Don't you see?" I craned my neck to glare at him. "He already has it, my head as well as every other part of me. None of it is mine anymore. Your king made sure of that." Never had truer words been spoken than those. I didn't like the way I felt whenever I was with Silas, but I *despised* the way I felt without him.

A tear began to form under my eye and I swiped at it with my free hand, while keeping the only weapon at my disposal pressed along the underside of my chin.

James looked at me with pity in his eyes as he placed the metal key into my trembling palm, and I hated it. Almost as much as I hated myself and everyone else right now. I wasn't in my right mind. I knew that. But that knowledge did little to dissuade me. It was this, this small act of defiance, or nothing else.

I fumbled with the key in the lock until I heard the audible click. As soon as my ankle was freed, I swept my legs over the edge of the mattress and onto the floor, limping across the room and making my way to the door. A splattering of red droplets revealed my every step like a trail of morbid breadcrumbs. James and Francine watched, their expressions a mix of terror and curiosity. They weren't going to stop me but they sure as hell weren't going to help me either.

Like most things in my short life, I was on my own.

The various corridors were winding, each appearing exactly like the last as exhaustion and blood loss slowed my progress. I didn't know where I was headed, what I thought I'd accomplish looking as I did, but I refused to turn back.

"Where do you think you're going?" a masculine voice had me pausing in my tracks, before a large palm closed around my wrist and tugged me forward.

Silas's men, king's guards, two I didn't recognize had me cornered at the end of a darkened hall. Not that I'd been given a roster of names. But I paid attention, memorized every face ever posted outside my door. Usually it was James. But on occasion, when he was likely off tending to Silas's needs, someone new would appear to replace him. They always wore that same emblem on their uniforms— the family crest. A serpent wrapped around a sword.

I saw the resemblance. Silas was venomous, penetrated my skin and sank into my veins. I succumbed to the man's charms before I'd even realized I'd been bit. And now it was too late. I was infected, slowly decaying from the inside out, just waiting for the predator to gobble me up.

When I didn't immediately answer, the guard turned to his counterpart. "Throw her in the dungeon. We've got better things to do than chase down nosey little girls sneaking into rooms they ought not to be."

"I wouldn't do that if I were you," I sang, still clutching the bloodied letter opener to my side.

The guard narrowed his glare on me before glancing over his shoulder at the man behind him, and I seized the opportunity, striking out with my right hand and penetrating his meaty thigh through a breach in his chain mail.

He sucked in a breath and stumbled back a step, but it seemed to do little else other than annoy him. Like a beast swatting at the fly buzzing around its head. I was a nuisance instead of an actual threat. The man ground his teeth, hissing out various insults as he scooped me up around the waist, threw me over a shoulder, and stomped back down the hall. In a direction opposite from the one I'd come.

I didn't have to take in my surroundings or try to lift my head from where it was still plastered against a plate of armor, left to bounce off the metal every time the guard took a step while my ass was directed at the ceiling. Because the moment we entered the dungeon, I knew it. The air was thick with the stench of piss, noticeably colder too, and the sounds were unlike anything I'd ever heard. Moans, sobs, pleas for help, and then there were the screams... they were loud enough to pierce eardrums if you let them.

I didn't have time to get my bearings before I was dropped on my rear in the middle of a dark cell, the metal door creaking towards me, then slamming shut. I threw my head back and laughed at the irony. I was constantly being passed from one cage to the next. My body continued to convulse with my outward amusement, and more than likely a heavy dose of madness, until I heard someone call out my name.

Unless that was all in my head too...

"Tillie..." There it was again. The sound muffled but the inflection so hauntingly familiar. Like something out of a dream. No, more like a nightmare.

I squinted my eyes into the darkness, trying to figure out if someone else was here with me or if my mind was conjuring up new horrors.

"Agatha." Her name stuck to the roof of my mouth

and festered there until I was left choking on my own words. There was so much I wanted to say... do to her... And yet I was frozen to the dirt floor, having lost all ability to move my limbs.

She was shackled to the wall, her arms stretched far above her head and her hair slipping free from its pins, left to curtain her face as her head slumped forward. A rag was stuffed into her mouth, meant to dampen the volume of her screams, and her gown was gone—her shoes too. They had stripped her down to her undergarments and left her to the mercy of the rats, or perhaps her husband. Whichever got to her first.

The longer I stared, the more I realized how far her majesty had fallen. We stood equals in this cell. No finery or jewels, no servants or titles, just two prisoners of the same man. Not so different when it came down to it.

She kept mumbling my name, repeating it over and over again, as if she thought I would somehow be the one to save her. I took a tentative step forward, then another. Until I was close enough to reach out a hand and lift her chin, forcing her gaze to meet mine. I watched as her pupils dilated. She either liked what she saw or feared it. Maybe even a mixture of both.

I know the feeling, your highness. It was a thought I reserved for myself.

I brushed a few of the loose strands from her face, my fingertips twisting and curling into her hair before delving deeper and tugging hard. She whimpered with the sharp pain as I clawed at her roots just long enough to find what I was looking for. I released my grip to pluck free a metal pin, bringing it into view as the torchlight flickered across the shiny surface.

Agatha gasped through the makeshift gag, likely pulling the fabric deeper into her throat, and watched as I fumbled with the cuff around her left arm. The dull end of the pin rummaged inside the locking mechanism until I felt the telltale shift in gears. The metal clicked open, Agatha's arm dropped to her side, and I repeated the process on the right.

As soon as she was freed, she tumbled forward into my reluctant embrace, and I staggered back a step, trying to bear her weight on my slighter frame. She seemed so much smaller without all the layers of fabric filling her out, younger too. In a different life, we may have liked each other. Been friends even. But we all had to accept the hand we'd been dealt and the reality of the choices we had made to get us here. To this moment in time.

She had chosen to be my tormentor, to look at me like I was less than human, a doll to be played with until it was broken and replaced. And I had decided I'd had enough. That I would cut the strings that left me tethered to a master I had never chosen to serve.

Agatha peered up at me as I fished the fabric out of her mouth and tossed it aside. Her jaw dropped as if she meant to speak, and I silenced her words with a quick jab to the gut, the letter opener glinting between us as it caught a random stream of light. I withdrew my arm before thrusting it forward again and again, not stopping until I saw the linen of her undergarments turn red. She clutched her stomach, doubled over, and crumbled to the floor.

"Wh-why?" she asked, staring up at me as if I had been the one to betray her and not the other way around.

I crouched down next to her head, a palm resting on a knee, as I leaned forward to get a better look at the gaping wound in her abdomen. Her entrails were poking free, the blood pooling around her body before seeping into the soil beneath us. And the air smelled like death and rot. She wasn't long for this world. That much was certain. The rest I would figure out along the way.

"Why?" I parroted her question, and Agatha gurgled in reply. "Because I wanted to give you a small taste of freedom before I ripped it away again." I trailed a fingertip across her pale cheek, humming as she sputtered below me. "I wanted the last thing you saw to be my face as I watched you die on the floor of this cell. By my hand and not his. It was important for you to know that it was me. Someone so beneath you, now standing over you. And I couldn't do that if I left you shackled to that wall."

She didn't respond and I didn't need her to. This was never about her. It was about me taking back some of the power I had relinquished to this woman and her husband. Replacing some of what they had stolen, and rebuilding myself up until I started to resemble the girl I'd lost to them and their depravity.

I watched and waited as she took her last breath, her body unmoving and her eyes open and glaring at me from across the cell. I could still hear her voice—it taunted me as tangibly as the thoughts in my head. Told me I was destined to die in this cage. That I would be forced to sit here as what was left of my tormentor decayed, withered away, and turned to dust. That I would breathe in her remains, and she would infect me from the inside out like some sort of ethereal poison darkening my soul.

My mind wandered off until I imagined becoming her, her spirit somehow possessing my body, her limbs reanimating and rushing forward. I clutched at my throat, swearing that I could feel her icy grip curling around it and taking her vengeance. But every time I glanced back in the direction of her corpse, she lay there. Unmoving and staring. Judging me, insinuating I should have taken the higher moral ground instead of thirsting for revenge.

I knew it was my own conscience whispering in my ear, warning me that if I continued down this path, I would become just like them. The royals. The type of people who took from those who had nothing left to give. But that didn't stop my pulse from increasing or the sweat from dripping down my forehead.

I shouldn't be sweating, not when it was so cold down here...

CHAPTER SIXTEEN
TILLIE

I was startled awake by the sound of my name being chanted. My eyes flung open. But all I saw was nothing. More darkness. My first thought?

She was back. She was taking me back. To that room. To that box.

I could feel the dread sitting like acid in the pit of my stomach, telling me I'd made it all up in my head, dreamed it in my fever-induced state, imagined that I'd killed the woman who'd killed my spirit.

Did I ever leave in the first place? That room. That box.

I willed my body to move but I couldn't feel my limbs, the cold traveling up my spine and holding me hostage. There was an indescribable pressure on my chest, something heavy—it was weighing me down.

I couldn't breathe. I was suffocating. Dying. Inside that room. Inside that box.

CHAPTER SEVENTEEN
SILAS

White noise filled my ears, panicked chatter and raised voices directed at me, asking me what to do. What could be done. The truth was, for once in my life, I didn't have the answer.

I didn't know where she had run off to or where she could possibly be hiding. All I knew was that I had to find her. Sooner rather than later. Before the gossip traveled beyond these castle walls and to the ears of the villagers, then the foreign traders and finally off to distant kingdoms.

It was as if it was all happening around me, bodies rushing from every direction, close enough to whip the air my way but never touching me. Just out of reach.

Until I saw her, lying there, and my world came back into focus. Like I'd found my target on the battlefield and was rushing full-speed ahead, my sword raised high and my armor glinting in the sunlight. I could finally breathe again, content with the knowledge that I could make good on my promise.

She'd never leave me or the confines of these walls. I wouldn't allow it.

Tillie had been screaming for hours now. None of which made much sense to anyone in the room. Especially to me. I'd held her down, tried to persuade her to see reason but the woman was out of her mind, clawing, spitting, hissing like a creature in forced captivity. So I cleared the remaining cells—all inhabitants sans my wife's lifeless body—and told my guards to wait outside the door while I attempted to coax my little pet out of hiding.

Apparently she'd grown quite *stab happy* since her escape from my bedroom. Henrick had a stitched thigh to prove it, though the fault was on him. He should have known better than to touch her. I'd made my orders clear.

"Tillie! Enough!" I barked her name and she immediately fell silent, her jaw snapping shut and her eyes cast to the floor. I appreciated the obedience but despised the despondent look on her face.

Part of me knew it was my fault. She'd experienced too much, too soon. My little fox needed a slower introduction into my world, a gentle but firm hand to guide her into understanding the way things worked. How she was expected to behave in my presence.

Instead, my late wife had gotten to her—*or had she really gotten to my late wife?*—and the two of them together had unraveled all the progress we'd made over the days. Weeks. Months?

I'd lost count. It felt as though she'd always been part of me. I didn't know what it meant to be without her.

She refused to leave the cell, curling herself up in the corner, as far from me as she could get without climbing inside the walls. So I paced in front of the door, back and forth and back again, until I was certain I'd worn a path in the stone. I told myself to be patient, to give her time to come around on her own, but I had a kingdom to run, a funeral to arrange, and a war to prevent.

It was foolish to waste more time on some poor village girl who couldn't stand my presence on a good day, and swore to end my life on a bad one. But I couldn't leave her either.

I raked a hand through my hair, tugging on the roots while attempting to keep my temper at bay. "Tillie, I order you to come out here right now. You're being ridiculous."

Something about what I said finally had her head snapping up and her glare landing on me. "Ridiculous? I'm being ridiculous? *Me?*" she hissed the words like a woman possessed.

I crossed my arms and nodded my head once. Which, apparently, was the wrong thing to do as far as she was concerned and exactly the right thing to do if I wanted her out of that cell.

Tillie rushed forward, her feet moving quicker than I'd ever seen them. Before she lunged. The sudden force sent me tumbling backwards, my boot catching on a nearby stool and causing me to lose my footing. I attempted to brace myself on the cell door, but my hand swiped at air as I landed on my back with Tillie on top of me. Her legs straddling my waist and the dagger she'd swiped from my belt pressed up against my throat.

"Do you know what's really ridiculous, Silas?" she ground out, her nostrils flaring in that adorable way they always did when she was mad. Which seemed to be more often than not since I brought her into my bed.

My Adam's apple bobbed in my throat as I swallowed my reply. I could feel the blade starting to pierce my skin, warm blood trickling down with the slow penetration. When I realized she was waiting for my verbal prompting, I decided to tempt fate and see how far she would take this.

"Do tell, little fox." My lips twitched with a grin while hers curled into a snarl.

"You... believing you could do as you pleased without ever facing the consequences, believing that you could keep people like cattle until you had your fill of cream and decided to send them to slaughter."

It was impossible to hold my smirk back any longer. "Not people, just you, pet," I told her, and she sliced the dagger through the second layer of skin, the blood flowing more like a river now. The wound would require a stitch or two but I'd live. This was more for show than anything else. A way for my little fox to try to assert her dominance.

I wouldn't say I liked it, but I didn't hate it either. My mind drifted to thoughts of her riding my cock to completion as my blood coated her hands, streaking across her chest as she leaned forward to get that angle that would have her cursing my name until her eyes rolled back in her head. That was one thing Tillie had forgotten about me. I liked her fire, needed her fight, and would enforce her fealty.

As soon as she realized it was what was best for both of us.

I reached up a hand to brush a strand of her golden hair behind her ear. She flinched at my touch. "Let's start anew, Tillie. Do things right. No secrets, no lies. Nothing between us but the finest silk sheets. I'll make you my wife, fuck you until you become the mother of my children, declare you my queen, and lay my kingdom at your feet. Give you whatever you want if you give yourself to me, little fox."

"There's only one thing I want, *your highness*."

"And what's that?" I urged her.

Tillie tilted her head to look at me, and it took all my willpower not to flip her onto her back and pull her gown up to her hips, willingly or not.

"I want you to fuck her," she spat the words in my face.

The air thickened between us before I realized who she was talking about. Her eyes flicked back to the cell, and I followed her line of sight to where Agatha still lay sprawled out on the dirt floor.

"What...?"

"I said. I. Want. You. To fuck her." I could hear her teeth grinding in her jaw. "I want to watch you fuck your wife while you call out my name. I want to see what I missed when I was locked in that box beneath you. When I was forced to listen to her moan around your cock as I struggled for my next breath. I want the full picture, Silas. Give me that, and then I will consider letting you live."

"No." Her request was ludicrous and didn't deserve more of an answer than that.

"Silas..."

"I said no, Tillie!"

She recoiled at the sudden harshness of my tone, but not enough to heed the warning there. "Why not?"

"Goddamn it, the woman is dead—if that's not enough of a reason, then maybe you need more help than even I have at my disposal."

"She's no more dead than I am on the inside, yet you have no issue bedding me. So, again, I ask you why not?"

I slammed my palms down and pushed myself upright so that Tillie was sent tumbling onto her ass. Then I crossed my legs in front of me, sitting opposite her as she glared back in a way that told me she still had murder on her mind.

Specifically, *mine*.

"You're not dead, little fox. If anything, you're more alive than you ever were... rotting away in your father's shack in the middle of the woods."

She threw her head rearward on a cackle, the sound otherworldly as it bounced off the stone walls and echoed back at me. "So you saved me, did you? Is that what you really think? That you came riding in like a white knight on his mighty steed?"

"Didn't I?" I quirked a single brow in question.

She shook her head. "Why me, Silas? You could have had any woman in the kingdom, most certainly those in several others, yet you came to my father's house, my home, and took me. Why?"

"Because I only wanted you. You stupid, stupid girl. Loved you. Long before I even knew I could. I still do. Even as you threaten my life. Maybe more so *because* you have that fire in you to do it..." I shrugged.

"And I despise you," she hissed the words like venom could somehow spew from her tongue.

Once again, my lips tipped up into a grin. "You don't. I have no doubt that you want to. Even wish you could. But you don't."

The confused look in her eyes told me I was right, while the clattering of my dagger from her hand onto the floor confirmed it.

EPILOGUE
TILLIE

Once upon a time, in a land not so far away, there lived a ruthless king and his blood-thirsty queen. Or so the history books would come to say...

Truth be told, I would have been crazy not to accept my dear husband's proposal—I don't think we would have both made it out of that dungeon if I hadn't. And he would have been crazier to assume a crown would be enough to quiet the demons in my head and the nightmares that plagued me even in my waking hours.

Agatha's spirit never left my side, and oftentimes, she would whisper in my ear. Instructing me to do this, warning me not to do that. Perhaps my tormentor had found redemption in the afterlife, or perhaps she simply didn't want me to share her same fate. I couldn't be certain, and it wasn't like her ghost was ever forthright with the answer.

Sometimes I would heed her advice; other times, I would remain steadfast in my own. Refusing to be swayed to the whims of the apparition of my husband's scorned lover.

At first, our union was met with unease. I was a commoner who very quickly replaced their fallen queen —a queen they were told had succumbed to the difficulties of an unfortunate miscarriage. And a lie that stressed their king's virility, while easing the discord the lack of an heir brought to the kingdom, until I blessed my husband with a child less than twelve months later. A boy, destined to take his father's place when the time came.

Those who had witnessed or heard whispers of the truth of what had happened in the weeks prior to my coronation were either sworn to secrecy—such as James and Francine. Or silenced on the spot, the regrettable fate of several prisoners, guards, and chatty servants who'd failed to realize the brutality of my husband's hand. Agatha's uncle was more than content to be freed from the burden of her care, as well as avoid the black mark on his family name her presumed sterility would have brought to his door. Thus, we avoided a war between kingdoms.

As promised, my brothers lived out their lives at my side, enjoying the comforts my sacrifices brought them, while my father was never to be seen again, presumed dead by the blade of a vengeful king and husband. They never asked about him or questioned what it was I had to do to bring them here. Though, as they got older, I'm certain they knew. There weren't many options for women of the time other than to be taken as wife or mistress.

It wasn't long after our first anniversary that I became known as the mad queen—a woman of the people to those who supported me—while providing my husband with six more sons to fortify his bloodline. One each year following our wedding night.

There was definitely something akin to love shared between us, Silas and me. Hatred too, on occasion. The throne became my gilded cage, my wedding band my new collar. And I drew fresh blood from time to time, whenever my husband needed a reminder that I wouldn't hesitate to slit his throat in his sleep should he give me reason. He would fall in line momentarily, usually laugh at what he deemed my quirks, take me to bed, and I would bear him a new son several months later.

But deep down, I knew he knew...

It didn't matter what a good king, husband, father he was or became, what jewels he offered me, or what luxuries I'd grown accustomed to. Because, at the end of the day, we both knew I had no qualms about burning it all to the ground just to prove that I could.

FROM THE AUTHOR

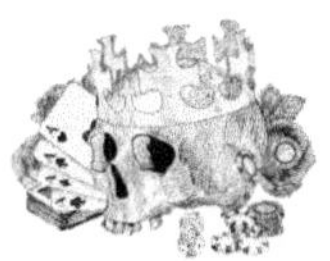

ALSO BY SYBIL KNIGHT

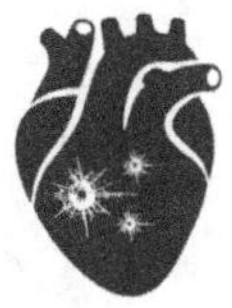

THE TRUTH AND LIES DUET:

The Harsher the Truth

The Sweeter the Lies

THE RENEGADES SERIES:

Skin

Lamb

Bells

STANDALONE NOVELS:

Half Cocked

Kill Joy

STANDALONE NOVELLAS:

The Sins of Our Fathers

V Card

I'll BE Seeing You

The More the Merrier

Eat Your Heart Out

Nutcracker

More titles to come...

ABOUT THE AUTHOR

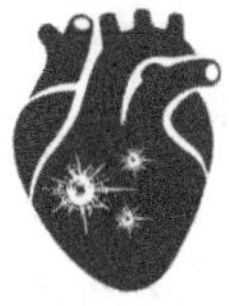

Sybil is a true east coaster with a love for true crime and caffeine. When she isn't working or writing, she is talking about working or writing.

Her stories range from gray to black, with darker themes throughout. She prefers heroines with a kick-ass mentality and the heroes who know how to rein them in. The mental and medical aspects of her books are well-researched, though they are given a humanistic approach and diagnoses aren't the focal points. She believes her characters don't need to wear labels in order to get their messages across.

Her books are mostly standalones, though her characters may interact and intersect worlds. Additionally, she works closely with and writes alongside author Dahlia Reign and some characters will appear in cameos in each of their publications.

Sybil welcomes emails from readers if there are concerns or questions regarding any of her publications.

Email: authorsybilknight@gmail.com